Shijak

To Begin: A Modern Martial Arts Story

By

Kathryn Yang

ISBN-13: 978-1-7356739-1-2

Olympic Dreams

As I exited the ring, I took off my helmet and sweat poured down my face and onto my already-soaked *dobok*. My *Sabumnim*, who was also my father and a Taekwondo Grandmaster with an 8th degree black belt, directed me toward the chair and then crouched in front of me and lifted my legs onto his thighs as he started to massage the lactic acid from my calves. I reached for my water bottle and took a quick drink before squirting the rest onto my head and down my neck as I re-centered myself and caught my breath.

I took a quick peek at the scoreboard to confirm what I already knew. I was ahead 8-7 going into the third and final round. I had defeated four of the best middleweight fighters in the country today, and if I could win the next three minutes against this opponent, I would secure my place on Team USA and earn a berth to the 2012 London Olympics. My body and legs were battered and beginning to tighten up after an entire day of fighting, but I willed myself into another adrenaline dump and silently roared from my lower belly until I could feel renewed energy suffusing every muscle and nerve fiber in my body.

Sabumnim watched as I gathered my strength. He nodded approvingly and whispered in Korean, "Last three minutes here and here..." as he jabbed a finger into the spot right above my eyebrows and then lightly punched my chest protector right above my heart. As the referee signaled for the fighters to return to the ring, I repositioned my helmet and stood facing him. I bowed deeply as always, expressing my love and respect, before striding back into the ring to make us both proud.

My opponent and I were both six feet five inches tall and weighed close to the 176-pound weight limit for our division. We were both long, lanky big men who moved with almost the same speed and agility as the lighter weights. The only difference was that we packed a much bigger wallop with our kicks and punches.

Through the first two rounds we had probed each other's defenses and laid elaborate traps with feints and counter-feints, occasionally capitalizing on an opening to score. With so much at stake, we had both fought cautiously, knowing that a single mistake or lapse in concentration could end the fight. I had expected the final round to flow the same way, but the instant the referee yelled '*Shijak!*' to start the round my opponent charged forward with a lightning-fast series of double kicks intended to drive me back on the defensive. His aggression caught me slightly flat-footed and I yielded two or three body shots as I mistakenly took a defensive step backward and tried to block the onslaught. Knowing I could not continue retreating, but still not quite balanced enough to launch a counter-attack, I had no choice but to absorb another hard body shot while stepping straight into his attacks in order to close the distance and neutralize his kicking offensive by clinching and blocking with my entire body. For several seconds we leaned hard into each other, frozen in the clinch while we jockeyed for positioning and leverage.

Then, just as the referee was about to break us out of the stalemate, I thought I felt a weakness in his stance and shoved hard into the opening to create just enough space to launch a short crescent kick at his head. But the instant my kick left the ground I realized too late that he had baited me with a deliberately weak stance. Time slowed as he took a balanced step backwards and let my crescent kick fly harmlessly by his face. As my foot swiped the air and was on the descent, he launched into another series of double kicks and scored hard on both sides of my chest guard. It was all I could do to finally re-clinch his upper body and stop the onslaught. A peek over his shoulder at the scoreboard showed that I was now behind 8-15 with only half of the round remaining.

Unfortunately, in the millisecond it took me to process the score and the clock, my opponent somehow sensed my lapse in concentration and further pushed his advantage by punching downward onto my collarbone from the clinch and pushing off to launch a back kick that landed right where the bottom of my chest guard ended. His foot drove through the oblique muscles right above my groin and felt like it could have come out the other side through my back if I had not immediately crumpled to the ground. No points were scored as his attacks all missed the electronic chest guard, but I had to concede a penalty point for falling.

As I lay on the ground, a merciful injury timeout was granted and the clock stopped while *Sabumnim* was allowed into the ring to check on his fighter. He slowly and superficially looked at and prodded my injury while speaking double-time in Korean about how to change my strategy and how to deal with my opponent's attacks. But with K-Pop music blaring at 120 decibels to compensate for the lack of action and with the crowd jeering the injury timeout, I wasn't able to concentrate on his words. Looking up at him, all I could comprehend was the urgent and angry lines deepening in the wrinkled expanse between his eyebrows, and my confidence was briefly eclipsed by the shadow of impending disappointment that seemed to darken behind his eyes. I looked away as he was talking and sought out the nonjudgmental scoreboard for guidance instead. How in the world did I give up nine points in just over two minutes?

After *Sabumnim* signaled that I was fit to continue and walked off the mat, the referee repositioned us in the middle of the ring for the final 50 seconds of the fight. It was 50 seconds to validate my 18 years of life and purpose; 50 seconds to determine the future of my dreams; 50 seconds to consecrate the faith that had been placed in me. Despite my mistakes earlier, I was well-trained enough to let my energy re-collect in my lower belly and to find the calmness I needed to block out everything that came before this moment. While waiting for the restart, I bounced lightly on my toes and wiped all thoughts and emotions from my mind. I deadened my five worldly senses and looked inward only to my sixth sense like *Sabumnim* had taught me. It was an instinct honed through 16 years of daily Taekwondo training, and in those last few seconds of the match I relaxed myself enough to find it and let it flow through my body and guide my movements.

Shijak! I could now sense my opponent's aggression and my foot found his face in a well-timed, but not perfectly executed lead-leg axe kick counterattack. 10-16. I transitioned that to a punch on the chest guard, a shove and another axe kick that just missed. 11-16. As he angled his head out of the way of my last kick, I double tapped a side kick and round kick into his chest protector. 15-16. We then exchanged scoring blows as I continued to pressure him toward the boundaries of the ring. 17-18. Sensing I was still behind and that only seconds remained in the match, I knew my best chance was to finish him with a series of power kicks that would send him out of bounds with no chance to counterattack.

With a confident war cry that bordered on the triumphant, I launched into my favorite attacking combination and executed it to perfection. The speed, timing, precision, everything was just as I imagined in all my Olympic daydreams; but unfortunately, my best met his better than day. I can remember feeling my foot connect with his chest guard, but what I have no memory of, even to this day, was his leg smashing the side of my head with a counter spin hook kick.

*   *   *

I eventually regained consciousness after my head bounced from the cradle of my father's hand onto the mat as I

4

recoiled and gagged from the smelling salts someone waved under my nose.

Like my head, the arena had erupted, and the fans were on their feet, stomping and cheering like maniacs. Everybody loves a knockout.

Working Hard

At least *Sabumnim* has been making it easy to keep up with my training log by writing out his daily instructions. As I slid my key into the *dojang's* front door at 8am my eyes were already searching out today's training regime written on the white board just inside the training hall's matted area. But first, I removed my snow-crusted shearling boots in the front entryway and stored them in one of the shoe cubbies lining the wall. I then brushed the frost off my light grey cashmere beanie and shed my matching gloves and long winter puffer coat to a bench in the waiting area. To save on expenses *Sabumnim* always lowered the thermostat overnight, and with a light snow shower outside, the temperature inside this morning probably hovered around 40 degrees. No matter though, I would be warm soon enough.

I flipped on the nearest set of overhead lights that illuminated a quarter of the dojang. I had been schooled by *Sabumnim* to conserve energy, so one set of lights was enough.

Sabumnim had written on the white board:

AM
3 miles at an eight-minute mile pace
5x400 meters
5x200 meters
5x100 meters
5x50 meters

5x20 meters
1 mile at 8-minute pace

PM
5 3-minute rounds footwork
5 3-minute rounds combinations
5 3-minute rounds targets
5 3-minute rounds shield
5 3-minute rounds bag
5 3-minute rounds sparring

EVENING
3x10 125lb back squats
3x10 95lb front squats
3x10 65lb overhead squats
3x6 200lb deadlift
2x50 25lb inclined sit-ups
2x50 10lb leg raises

It had been this way since I turned 18 and graduated from my online high school with a GED last spring. As a graduation present *Sabumnim* handed me a key to the *dojang* and told me that I was now in charge of my own morning and evening training. But in return for access to the *dojang,* I was also responsible for cleaning in the morning and occasionally closing up in the evening.

So, I started this morning like the previous 235 mornings since I was deputized… by pulling out the vacuum cleaner, cleaning rags and Windex from the supply closet. I started with the mats, first vacuuming and then disinfecting. I repeated the same process with the bathrooms, changing rooms and finally the waiting area. I finished by taking down all the pads, shields and other equipment and giving them a once over with a soapy, bleachy solution. Then, breathing in the deep Windex clean that temporarily masked the smell of sweat and exertion typical of the usual *dojang* funk, and seeing the morning sun finally rise enough to hit the practice area with a little warmth, I got ready to do some work.

I was already dressed in two pairs of compression leggings and a form-fitting neoprene sauna suit top, over which I layered a t-shirt and my mom's old Princeton sweatshirt. I pulled my long, straight blonde hair back into a ponytail and finished it with a loop to shorten the length by half. *Sabumnim* has been hinting about a more utilitarian and sportier haircut ever since I won my first junior national title and confessed my Olympic aspirations to him three years ago. But I was still several steps away from realizing that dream, so I continued to hold onto what I think is my best non-Taekwondo feature.

I walked over to the manual scale next to the weight area and exhaled as I gingerly stepped on. As I slid the bigger and then the smaller weights over to the right, the rod finally balanced around 117-ish pounds. I was 5 feet 7 inches tall and fighting in the 49 kilogram or 107.8-pound weight class, so 117-ish while wearing about three pounds of clothing in the off-season wasn't so bad. But it also wasn't so good that I could afford to relax. I entered my weight into the training log on my phone, snapped a picture of the white board and then grabbed a jump rope to start my warm-up.

After half an hour of skipping rope, I started on some dynamic stretching to waken my hamstrings and hips. I moved, lunging and twisting up and down the mats until I felt all of my muscles loosen and become more elastic. At the hour mark, I wiped my sweat off the mats and pulled on a pair of trail-running shoes to begin the day's first assignment.

I stepped outside into the light snowfall and started on the easy 12 laps around the suburban New Jersey shopping center that would make up my three-mile run. After that, the 400-meter sprints would be one lap around the shopping center and 200 meters was half a lap. Then, the shorter sprints were marked out by the storefronts, with the eastern edge of Ahn's Taekwondo as the starting line. From there to the deli was 100 meters, to Mrs. Kim's dry cleaners was 50 meters, and to the edge of the Domino's Pizza next door was 20 meters. The other tenants and patrons were used to *Sabumnim's* students running laps and sprints around the shopping center, but this morning in the slushy snow it was just me.

I recorded all my times on my watch and after the one-mile warm down jog I went back inside the *dojang* to download everything to my training log. I stepped out of my wet shoes at the entryway and casually shed my sweat-soaked top layers en route to the scale. Clad in just compression leggings and a dark purple sports bra, the sweat continued to bead and run off my face and down into my chest as I reweighed myself. 114-ish. I allowed myself a little satisfied smile before I sensed that I was not alone.

Adjusting my eyes toward the slightly darkened training area, I squinted and thought I imagined *Sabumnim's* youngest son, *Sabum* Dae Sung staring right back at me. Startled by what must have been an apparition, I hesitated and almost spoke out to the interloper before suddenly realizing that I was still only half-dressed. Mortified, I ran for cover under my puffer jacket just as the tall shadow started to laugh.

"You know you're at a disadvantage because of your breasts," he teased.

Sabum Dae Sung!

"That's an extra three, four pounds that flat Asian girls in your weight class don't carry." He laughed.

I zipped my coat all the way up, stuffed my hands deep into the pockets and scrunched my shoulders so I could hide my face in the collar, hoping to disappear completely. Oh. My. God.

Coming Home

That was not an unpleasant surprise, I thought, as the sweaty blonde girl ran for cover under her bulky winter coat. I don't remember the last time my father allowed half-clad beautiful blondes to parade around his *dojang* in nothing but spandex and a sports bra. The *Sabumnim* I knew had infused his *dojang* with a Korean special forces discipline that permeated every action and thought in his students. The Ahn's Taekwondo that I grew up in was in fact the opposite of the trendy, sexy Tae-kickboxing commercialism that is now all the rage in martial arts. But then again, I haven't been in the *dojang* since I failed to make the Olympics more than six years ago. Maybe things have changed. Maybe the old man finally made concessions to the modern way of running a business. Maybe after me, he finally gave up on the old ways.

I was the last of the three Ahn brothers that our father, our *Sabumnim*, had cultivated, trained and somehow, we think, warped and destroyed. Well, destroyed might be much too harsh when judging us on paper.

Tae Suk, the eldest, was a six-time national champion who qualified for the world championships once. In 2001 he was chosen to represent Team USA in Jeju, South Korea and *Sabumnim* was named the team's assistant head coach. Unfortunately, during a preliminary elimination stage a Moroccan fighter gapped him by 20 points and the match was called in the middle of the second round. Two years later, after a string of surprising defeats to lesser domestic opponents, he retired from Taekwondo and enrolled at Rutgers for college and then NYU for dental school. He is now a very successful and wealthy orthodontist in a New Jersey suburb with a beautiful Korean-American wife who gave up a promising legal career to raise his three kids and cook him two traditional Korean meals a day. His oldest boy just turned five, but instead of traveling 45 minutes to Ahn's Taekwondo, the little guy is learning Taekwondo in a Mighty Dragons program closer to home.

Eui Song, who had the misfortune of being born 11 months after Tae Suk and with the same physiology and bone structure as our older and more athletic brother, ceded the 176-pound weight class to Tae Suk and starved himself through his teenage years to fight at 68 kilograms, or 149.6 pounds. He is the brother with no national titles. After Tae Suk retired and left for college, Eui Song waffled between the two weight classes and was constantly adjusting his weight to try and capitalize on the perceived strengths or weaknesses of each weight class. He played that game for another four years before also retiring and following Tae Suk to Rutgers.

There, his body and mind finally surrendered its discipline and youthful elasticity to the excesses of late-night beers, pizza and *kimchi* fried rice. In the five years it took him to graduate and become a CPA he had filled out his six-feet three-inch frame with at least 240 pounds. He is now quickly climbing the corporate ladder at a consulting firm in New York City, but the long hours, incessant travel schedule and generous expense accounts have further transformed him to look more like a former college football lineman than a former elite middleweight Taekwondo athlete.

And then there is me. Right after getting knocked out at the Olympic Team Trials, I fought in a repechage (or loser's bracket) consolation match for a chance to make the team as an alternate. My brain was probably still concussed from the knockout and extremely foggy from trying to figure out why I was still fighting when my Olympic dreams had died a mere 30 minutes earlier. Halfway through the first round I actually felt myself give up. I wanted no more. And even though I

11

managed to finish the fight on my feet and drift to a 12-2 defeat, I remember the exact moment when the intensity of all of my Taekwondo aspirations just disappeared. I walked out of the ring feeling empty but relieved, and I think my father understood exactly what I lost that day and did not say a word. Right after we got home, I borrowed $3,000 from Tae Suk, packed a bag and left for South America. The final tally on my career was six national titles, one world championship title and no Olympics.

I spent a couple of months backpacking through South America, teaching English, living like a vagabond and rebelling against everything my father ever taught me. After I returned, I chose a college as far away from New Jersey as I could manage and spent four years at UCLA learning how to surf, let loose and enjoy life. I was tall with a swimmer's physique and had the unspoken, but universally appreciated, earning potential of being pre-med. Asian girls lined up to ask me out in hopes of dating and catching the perfect husband. And I guess all the other pretty girls must have seen something too. It was an amazingly educational four years. Then after graduating from the sun and the beach, Columbia accepted me into their medical school, and I've been back on the East Coast since.

The Ahn brothers by any measure are all athletically, professionally and socially very successful. But somehow there were always brief moments when each one of us suffered inexplicable paroxysms of inadequacy and feelings of guilt and shame that still leave us unable to stand being in our father's presence for very long.

For much of our lives our father and *Sabumnim* was our universe. After our mother passed away from cancer when I was three my father provided for our every need through the modest means he earned from running the *dojang*. He kept a very utilitarian household by preparing the same three meals every day, rationing each boy to two pairs of blue jeans and five button-down shirts each school year, and charting out homework, home chores and Taekwondo practice schedule down to the minute six days a week. Even though there never

12

seemed to be any extra money for vacations or for little luxuries like video games or name brand sneakers, he spared no expenses with our Taekwondo and academic educations. He sent us to compete at all the national and international competitions we needed to gain experience and ranking points and made sure all three of us finished our formal education without any student loans or financial burdens. In return, all that was expected of us was diligence and obedience, which was tantamount to loyalty and love in our filial relationship.

But his expectations weighed heavily on us. Like a master swordsmith who acquired the best ore and the best tools with the intention of crafting the world's most brilliant, lethal and dazzling weapon, my father pounded us, folded our imperfections back into ourselves over and over again before purifying us through fire. He invoked God and his ancestors to watch over us as he charted and planned the course of our development. And then, when the mature weapons started to take shape, he forced iron to sharpen iron until weakness broke. Growing up, it seemed like all we knew was the anvil and the blast of the inferno.

And in the end, he created a collection that was magnificent, but not transcendent. The swords were beautiful and of extraordinary quality, but not ethereal. Ultimately, there was something inherently brittle and imperfect in the soul of each sword that caused them to chip or waver during battle. The much-loved sons felt their imperfections deeply and helplessly. And those imperfections became an ever-greater distancing force between us and the grandmaster as we all eventually fled from Taekwondo and his universe of loyalty and love.

Sabum Dae Sung

My heart skipped a beat as I stole another peek at *Sabum* Dae Sung from over the collar of my puffy winter coat. I was instantly transported back to feeling like the pre-teen who was besotted by the tall, handsome champion who assisted *Sabumnim* with the children's classes when he was a high schooler. Every Taekwondo-obsessed girl at the *dojang* was star-struck by his Olympic-sized talent and K-Pop good looks. We spent the better part of our pre-teen years infatuated with *Sabunmin's* son, vying for his attention in class and gossiping, giggling and fantasizing about the day when he would finally acknowledge us as beautiful young women.

Even the boys in class were not immune to his superhero-like aura. Besides aspiring to become a champion like him, they all desperately wanted to be accepted as a little brother or maybe even as a friend. To all the kids at Ahn's Taekwondo *Sabum* Dae Sung was a god, a celebrity and royalty all combined into one perfect Taekwondo master. Our admiration of him knew no bounds. Even now, I felt such an unexpected but intense rush of giddiness and excitement rising from my chest and blossoming up through my neck and into my cheeks that I bashfully turtled my head back down into the collar of my jacket without being able to properly greet my former instructor and senior.

Just as I was working up the courage to look back up and say hello to *Sabum* Dae Sung, the *dojang* door slid open and a swirl of snow flurries ushered *Sabumnim* through the entrance.

14

I instinctively rose to my feet at attention and bowed deeply in his direction. I felt *Sabum* Dae Sung do the same from behind me as *Sabumnim* nodded in my direction and then peered at his son through the darkened *dojang*. He dismissed me with his customary instructions to go eat lunch and then return to the *dojang* by 2pm for my afternoon session. I bowed in acknowledgement and managed a half-bow toward *Sabum* Dae Sung before quickly gathering my workout gear, pulling on my Uggs and slipping out the front door.

Out in the parking lot, I piled my sweaty workout gear onto the beige leather passenger seat of my BMW M3 while I warmed up the engine and thought idly about *Sabum* Dae Sung. No one had seen him since the Olympic Trials six years ago, and we all eventually accepted the rumors of his burnout as true. Even though I was just 12 years old at the time, I had already heard stories of his two older brothers quitting Taekwondo years ago and then *Sabum* Dae Sung succumbing to the same unfathomable fate.

At the time, he was just 18 years old and trying to make his first Olympic team after winning a world championship the previous year. We assumed his loss at the Team Trials was just another step toward the next Olympiads in Rio, and the little set-back did not diminish our other-worldly estimation of him in the slightest. The kids at the *dojang* waited through the summer and then the fall and all through winter for his return. *Sabumnim* never mentioned *Sabum* Dae Sung in class and we never worked up the courage to ask. But by the following summer, even those of us who had the biggest crushes on him had given up hope of his return. Eventually, the rhythm of the *dojang* adjusted to the void he left and slowly re-energized itself with the talents and potential of the next generation of promising competitors. And over the years, thoughts of its past hero became increasingly muted by time and subsumed into lore. Besides walking past his plexiglass-encased world championship medal every day in the *dojang* and letting its brilliance reinforce my own goals, I had not thought of *Sabum* Dae Sung since I was a pre-teen.

Sitting there as the car started to warm, I realized that I am now about same age as *Sabum* Dae Sung was when he walked away from Taekwondo. To me the thought of ever abandoning my only love was insane. Almost every waking moment of my life since the second grade had been given to practicing Taekwondo or thinking about practicing Taekwondo.

I fell in love with Taekwondo after watching an elementary school talent show where some fifth grader dressed in a perfectly pressed *dobok* and a blue belt performed a pattern with all his heart and then jumped and spun around breaking boards held by his father and his Taekwondo teacher. I remember being awe-struck by that demonstration and pleading with my parents to let me go back stage after the talent show to find the blue belt and his teacher. And then in front of this teacher, who is now my *Sabumnim*, I begged and begged my parents for lessons. Little did my parents know then that their little girl and only child had found her destiny.

Warmed by the convictions of my former eight-year-old self and by the heated leather bucket seat, I put the car into gear and slowly eased across the unplowed parking lot onto the main street and towards the basement apartment in my parents' house. This little metallic blue sports car was a graduation gift from my dad. And the newly-renovated basement apartment was as much a gift from my mom as it was a gift for herself. My bachelorette pad had a separate entrance and thoroughly modern touches throughout that matched it to the rest of the house. But most importantly, it had enough space in the living area for me to lay down mats and hang a heavy bag in the corner.

Ever since I declared four years ago that I would not enroll in high school and wanted to home-school myself with online classes and spend six hours a day training Taekwondo, my parents have vacillated between apprehension and bewilderment. No one in their circle of friends had such a strong-willed and determined child. And while not entirely endorsing my crazy Taekwondo dreams, they nevertheless tried very hard to overcome their skepticism and provided me with as much love and support as they could muster for someone as alien as their own daughter.

Now, even after attending my Taekwondo competitions for over 10 years, my poor mom still wonders out loud about how a pretty young girl could enjoy something so uncivilized. When I was younger, she would sometimes come into my room and hold back tears while running her hands over the bumps and bruises on my skinny arms and legs. My dad was probably equally traumatized but more stoic. His doubts and misgivings about my Taekwondo dreams were conveyed more through the talks he would give me at our Sunday dinners... talks about college and a career, about my lack of a back-up plan in case I fail to win the Olympics, and about his absolute certainty that no man would ever be attracted to a young woman who did something so barbaric. But despite his deep misgivings, my dad allowed me to withdraw from my college fund to pursue my dreams and promised me an allowance just as if I had been a more obedient and college-bound daughter.

I parked my car near the basement entrance and walked into my apartment and added the mornings' workout gear to the rest of my dirty laundry before starting the washing machine. I then popped a cube of frozen rice and six of my mom's frozen meatballs onto a plate and into the microwave for five minutes on medium power. From the refrigerator I pulled out a plastic tub of salad greens, a handful of grape tomatoes, a handful of blueberries and a gallon-sized jar of *kimchi*. When the microwave beeped, I pulled out the hot food and added an unwieldy pile of *kimchi* to the top of the meatballs and sat down for lunch.

I have been adding *kimchi* to almost every meal since I was maybe 12 or 13 years old and overheard *Sabumnim* say to someone (I don't remember who or why) that eating *kimchi* and spicy foods is what made Koreans kick faster. It took about a week of me trying to convince my mom that I had found the secret to Taekwondo before she finally relented and took me shopping at a Korean grocery store the next town over. Ever since then, she and my dad have been pretty good sports about letting me add the red-hot, spicy, fishy, funky and fermented cabbage to everything from spaghetti to tuna casseroles to my ham and cheese sandwiches at school and even to my mom's specialty dish, borscht. Although I now know that *kimchi* and spicy foods probably do not make my kicks any speedier, the habit has become so ingrained that food just doesn't taste the same without it.

After lunch, I cleaned up the dishes, transferred my laundry into the dryer, packed another set of leggings and sauna suit along with two *doboks* and a black belt into my gym bag and headed back out. As I was getting into the car for the five-minute drive back to the *dojang* I found myself wondering again about *Sabum* Dae Sung.

Kimbap

I had never planned on returning to this *dojang* or any *dojang* for that matter. But during my obligatory visit home over Christmas last week, my father had beckoned me to follow him out to the patio after dinner, away from my brothers and their wives and away from the screaming grandchildren who were clamoring to open their presents early. There, while looking out into the darkness of the backyard and then up into the wintry, opaque New Jersey sky he went silent for a moment before quietly ordering me to report to the *dojang* when it reopened on January 2nd. I was to be present every day until my winter break ended in February.

Why me?! I was incensed.

But even before I had a chance to protest, my father implied that the request and my expected obedience was a matter of *Hyo*. In Korean culture, *Hyo* or filial piety is a virtue of paramount importance. It is as much ingrained in our values and identities as *kimchi* and rice are on our taste buds and palettes. It forms the basis of all our relationship expectations between parent and child and seniors and juniors, so much so that my place in the universe was mostly defined by my standing as my father's son and as the youngest of three brothers. This fundamental element of Korean culture had been inculcated in me since birth, and the hierarchical and quasi-military discipline and structure of a traditional Taekwondo education reinforced those constricts.

So, despite never wanting to think about Taekwondo ever again, that night the obedient Korean son and the dutiful student of the grandmaster in me answered, "Yes sir."

A week later, here I am, standing around in an empty *dojang* like a tall decorative plant that did not belong. My father had disappeared into his back office right after dismissing the blonde girl, leaving me to greet the handful of young housewives and teenagers on school holiday who started to trickle in for the noontime class. No one recognized me, though everyone greeted me politely enough in deference to the stripes on my black belt. My father always said that a *dojang* was like a stream. It was constantly flowing and the fishes never stayed the same. I think he meant that 99.9 percent of everyone who started martial arts practice eventually quit and move on… including me; except now he was demanding that I return upstream, back to the place of my birth.

As the clock inched toward 12 o'clock my father still had not emerged from his office. So, as the most senior black belt on the mat, I obligingly assumed the responsibility of calling the class to attention and started the warm-up, a duty that I had performed thousands of times in my previous life. Fifteen minutes later the office door finally slid open and my father strode out onto the mat and assumed his place as *Sabumnim*. As the students turned to greet him, I eagerly bowed myself off the mat and retreated to the waiting area.

From that vantage point, I watched my father call the class to order and then start the basics. Initially something struck me as odd about the way he stood and the way he strolled through the ranks of the students, correcting movements and lightly smacking legs and nudging arms and heads into the right positions. It was something I couldn't quite put my finger on until I realized that I had never seen my father wear a traditional Y-shaped, fold-over uniform. He had always favored the sporty, light-weight competition style V-neck uniforms made by Adidas and shipped to him directly from Korea twice a year. The top-of-the-line high-tech, high-performance Adidas uniforms were always seamed with a set of three black stripes across the shoulders and down the pant legs, a "grandmaster" detailing that emphasized his rank. And as an extra added vanity, his name and title were always embroidered in gold thread over his heart.

But today he was wearing a much heavier, old-fashioned canvas uniform with a small, but unmistakably Japanese *Tokaido* label on the bottom hem. The new look was starkly white with no trimmings or any markings. The more somber effect evoked tradition and austerity, but it also made him seem older and from an era whose time had passed. It might have been befitting a 72-year-old grandmaster, but I stood there slightly off-balanced by my father's recession in time.

The class moved on from basic kicks and punches to patterns practice, and I let my attention wander from the mat to the walls decorating the waiting area. I slowly examined the pictures from my era and from my older brothers' eras, and tried to put names to some of the faces I recognized. On the far wall hung a *dojang* directory of sorts, with all the students' names written in black permanent marker on little wooden slats that hung in rank order from 8th degree black belt down to the newest white belt. Below that, hanging in supposed perpetuity as a testament to the dojang's history and legacy, were hundreds of darker, sun-stained wooden slats representing the emeritus black belts who once upon a time trained at this *dojang* and earned their rank under my father. There I found Ahn Tae Suk, 5th dan; then further down on the same row Ahn Eui Song, 4th dan; and on the next row, Ahn Dae Sung, 3rd dan.

My eyes finally drifted toward the honors wall and settled onto my 2011 world championship medal. It had been preserved in a large plexiglass case along with a series of highlight photos and a bronze plate inscribed with my opponents' names, countries of origin and the winning scores from each round. I walked over for a closer look and silently mouthed the scores to myself as I tried to remember details of the fighters and the fights.

Ahn Dae Sung
v. Patrick Nngakou, Ethiopia 17-2
v. Daniel Chang, Canada 8-4
v. Mikheil Gelashvili, Republic of Georgia KO2
v. Tsai Ming Yu, People's Republic of China 12-4
v. Kim Byung Soo, South Korea 2-1

Seeing the highlight photos did nothing to jog my memory beyond the quarterfinal knockout of the Georgian. That I remember. Everything else was a blur.

For some reason, I can still torture myself with the pain of all my major losses and replay in my mind all the mistakes and lapses in concentration I committed. But with the victories, even the big ones, I remember very little and now feel almost nothing. I took one last indifferent look at the world championship medal that was not really a part of me and then returned my attention to the class.

My father now had the students padded up in their gear and lightly sparring in pairs. The students were gently tapping each other in a light game of foot tag, moving slower and with less conviction and grace than octogenarian sea turtles in order to minimize the chances of actually hitting anyone or getting hit. I got bored with the lack of action and picked up a children's book in the waiting area and started leafing through *Diaries of a Wimpy Teenage Ninja*. Fifteen, twenty minutes later my father assigned one of the senior students to lead the warm-down and walked over to motion for me to follow him to his office.

He then left me waiting outside for a brief second while he went in first to change out of his uniform and into track pants and an Ahn's Taekwondo T-shirt. As I entered, he pointed out two mugs and a tin of barley tea next to the tall cylindrical water heater on a side table and told me to make tea. With the *boricha* seeping and infusing the slightly chilly office with its warmth and grainy fragrance, he beckoned for me to bring the tea over and join him on a floor cushion at the low coffee table where he distributed our Tupperware lunches.

Before opening mine, I already knew what it contained. It was the same lunch he had been making himself for the last

23 years and for his boys up until we left the house. I peeled back the plastic lid to reveal 10 uniform pieces of *kimbap* (think a wide Korean sushi roll with rice, boiled and pickled vegetables, mushroom, ham and an omelet instead of raw fish), a small mound of *kimchi* in its own silicon cupcake mold so the juices remained isolated and three half-moon slices of bright yellow *danmuji* (pickled daikon radish). With two hands extended and my head slightly bowed in thanks, I accepted the disposable chopsticks he proffered and we both ate in silence.

After we finished, my father sent me to the side table to make more tea. While I waited for the water to come to a boil, he said softly in the direction of the seat cushion I had just vacated, "There are eight kinds of suffering in life. Birth, aging, illness and death. Separation from loved ones. Long term resentment."

And then he paused before looking at up me and whispering the final two, "Things you cannot have. And things you cannot let go."

I bristled but forced myself to remain calm while I poured the tea and walked over to set a fresh mug of *boricha* in front of him.

Why is he looking at me like that? He is the one who wants his sons around as part of his living legacy. And he's the one who's still chasing the dream of grooming an Olympian. Before lecturing me, maybe you should psycho-analyze yourself old man.

"I have let go," I said pointedly. "I've moved on. You're the one who hasn't let go. Dragging me back here. Hoping for things you cannot have."

He looked at me with bewildering eyes until I felt no purpose in continuing my rant and then he nodded, though I am not quite sure if it was a sign of acceptance, agreement or something else. "I have a small favor to ask you," he continued in the same whisper as before. "I need you to train Daria. She has national and international dreams that I think you can help with."

So, I was right.

"Why me?"

"Why not you?"

"I'm in medical school. I'm going to become a doctor, not an Olympian and not a Taekwondo teacher. That's why."

"But for the next five weeks you are a medical student on winter break. Your father is getting old and asking for help."

Again, I bristled and reminded him that I had board exams in the spring and then hospital rotations in the summer.

"But for now...."

He finalized his request by closing his eyes and telling me that he needed to lie down for 30 minutes. I nodded, seeing this new version of my father for the first time, and let myself out of the office.

A Lesson of Sorts

The clock on the *dojang* wall read 1:30 and the blonde girl was back, this time appropriately dressed in a clean *dobok* and a black belt with three gold stripes on one side and *Daria Kutznetsov* embroidered on the other side. She looked up from her stretching exercises and surprisingly gracefully and very seriously bowed in my direction, saying "*Sabum* Dae Sung." That was a form of address I had not heard in a long time. With dirty Tupperware and two mugs and a teapot balanced in my hands I extended her a half bow and half-questioning nod as I headed for the bathroom sink to clean the dishes.

She waited for me to reappear before squeaking and exclaiming, "You're back!" with a burst of enthusiasm that made me fear she was going to rush across the mat to hug me.

"I was a red belt in the advanced teens class when you started helping *Sabumnim* teach the kids classes," she said somewhat shyly, but excitedly. So, not all the fishes swim downstream. This one stuck around.

"I've watched and re-watched all your matches from the world championship! I'm working on a lead-leg axe kick just like yours. The one that sweeps across from the inside that you knocked out the Georgian with.

"Will you be teaching again? Are you thinking of making a come-back? There are some tall boys on the competition team now who are right on the verge of breaking through at nationals. They will be so excited to meet you!

"I'm Daria."

I sighed and nodded, suppressing a real urge to change out of my *dobok* and disappear before my father woke from his nap. And since there was no place to hide in a *dojang* except for the office where my father napped, I stood there politely making small talk and answering her questions about my Taekwondo past and what I was doing in my "retirement," as she called it. She droned on and on as I painfully relived and regretted my entire Taekwondo existence.

"Um, no, sorry, I don't remember you from the advanced teens class.

"No, I don't remember April Martinez or Brad Wales or the Korean kid who won Juniors five years in a row." Was that a trick question? Did some other Korean kid from this *dojang* also win the Junior National Championships five years in a row?

"No, no come back. No, not teaching here. Sorry, no, I'm not working with the competition team. No, I just go to school there. I'm not a part of the team."

As two o'clock approached and my father remained in his office, I finally confessed to this Daria that I had been instructed by my father to run her afternoon workout. Instead of asking how, why or what for or noticing my complete lack of enthusiasm for the task, she started beaming like she had just won the Olympics and was headed for Disney World. Girls.

I think I am going to burn her out and make it so she cannot walk straight tomorrow, let alone show up for another free private lesson.

Taking my cue from the workout my father had posted on the white board, I started with a series of footwork drills. In between the rounds, I laid out an agility ladder and some cones and timed her through a series of speed and plyometric footwork drills. Her athleticism and conditioning were not half bad.

We then moved onto combination drills. I called out a few of my favorite attacking and retreating combinations and had her kicking and punching and dodging and sliding up, back and across the matted area for 3-minute rounds. I then added a 30-second finisher to each round where she shadow-sparred using her own combinations.

She was surprisingly smooth and fluid, and after 10 rounds of work she was still not breathing particularly hard. Not bad, considering she wore a sauna suit under her uniform top and was now pouring sweat. A few strands of long blonde hair had escaped her ponytail and were now matted above her brow and around her face, but the steely blue-grey eyes betrayed nothing. Interesting.

I moved on to target drills, telling her that we would go freestyle for each of the 3-minute rounds. She was to respond to my movements and attack when I flashed the targets and defend or retreat when I swiped at her with the targets. The usual kick-rate for any round was about 10-15 attacks and counterattacks with a lot footwork, set-ups and feints to bridge and disguise the attacks. I decided to press her by doubling the kick rate and unnecessarily increasing the speed and frequency of the footwork.

I started the first round by swiping at the crown of her head with the kicking pad to check and see if she was awake. She was not. And the pad landed with a satisfying smack over her guard, leaving a broad red mark on the top part of her forehead. Besides taking a defensive step and switching her guard, there was no leaked emotional reaction. No anger, no frustration or indignation. Good. Instead, she refocused and finished the drill with much better awareness and attention to where her scoring opportunities presented themselves and where my attacks came from.

For the next five rounds I held a thick body shield and started incorporating clinches in a more physical fighting style. To add resistance and to challenge her balance and recovery I pushed the shield into all her attacks, forcing her to increase her power and control. I also incorporated body-checks with the shield to further upset her balance as well as to test her distance awareness and timing.

I felt no compunction over using my considerable size advantage to pressure her in the clinch or to knock her over with a body-check if she could not evade or deflect my movements. She ended up on her back several times and although she was bounding right back up to her feet without complaint, her movements slowed considerably. The level of her conditioning was obviously very high, but once tired, her physical strength faded quickly. At this point she could probably run a slow marathon but not a convincing 60-second sprint, and her decision-making became increasingly erratic. Were these the short-comings my father wanted me to work on?

The next five rounds were on the heavy bag but her kicks and punches barely moving the 70-pound weight. By this time her hair had turned from a sun-kissed blonde to a sweat-soaked amber and the sweat stain on her *dobok* extended all the way down to the knees of her pants. When she came in to clinch the heavy bag, she left almost a full-body sweat shadow as she pushed away. And although she persevered against the clock, her breathing became labored, then scattered and her *ki-aps* failed her completely. As she allowed her shoulders to slope and her chest to heave with short anxious breaths, she lost all the fluidity and athleticism she flashed earlier. There was plenty of energy remaining in her mind and body, but the two remained disconnected and neither could harness the power of the other to maximize her efforts. Her eyes lost focus and her brain stopped looking for solutions. Is this what my father thought I could help her with?

As if on cue, the office door slowly slid open and my father emerged once again in uniform. One glance across the *dojang* seemed to summarize the last hour and a half for him. He gathered a plastic folding chair from the wall and walked toward the head of the *dojang*. As he sat, folding his arms across his chest and extending his crossed ankles out in front of the chair, he told me to start the five rounds of sparring. No protective equipment for today, he said, just go light. He also grunted additional instructions to me in Korean that I was

28

limited to only throwing round kicks with my left, non-dominant leg and that I could only hit with the strength and power of a 107-pound fighter. To the girl he said nothing.

As my father growled *shijak* to start the first round, I charged forward with a series of sliding lead-leg round kicks to her torso, neck and head and used my length, speed and sheer aggression to pressure her straight off the mat. Unprepared for the intensity of my attacks, her defense devolved into an awkward retreat as she flew backward into the waiting area and on to her backside. Paying heed to my father's instructions I took care to barely touch her with the kicks and let the impact of her fall and the waiting area carpet burns make my point. It took a moment, but she eventually stepped back onto the mat rotating her injured right wrist while cradling her right elbow in her left hand. My father and I watched without words.

As she repositioned her left hand back into a fighting stance, I noticed a sizeable crimson, sweat-diluted stain blossoming on the right sleeve of her *dobok*. Looking to finish her quickly, I attacked again, this time mercilessly tapping her again and again on the injured right forearm. I was only allowed one variety of kick and attacked without variance or deception and yet she could not gather herself enough to think her way out of the predicament. Instead, she let herself get pushed back again by my attacks and instinctively prioritized her injured forearm over fighting her fight. Just as her eyes started to well with frustration, my father called for a 30-second break.

In the second round I directed my round kicks higher to the right side of her head, again barely touching her but forcing her to use her injured arm to block everything she could not evade. Whenever she slowed in her recognition of my attacks, I increased my speed to force her off balance and then finished her with gentle looping round kicks that would encircle her neck and nudge her head downward just enough to send her body stumbling to the ground. My father neither critiqued my exploitation of her defenses nor offered her any solutions.

I continued this tedious cat and mouse game into the third round until I felt a twinge in my lower back and then a slight pull in my right hamstring. I was not in Taekwondo shape. My three nights a week pushing vanity weights while socializing at the Columbia gym and my twice-weekly jogs around Morningside Park were not enough. The sudden volume of high kicks and the sharp cutting footwork required too much flexibility and pliability, and my study-carrel-bound body seized up with the exertion. I had to change my strategy.

In the next round I bounced around passively and defensively, inviting her to attack. But injured and weary as she was, she cautiously mirrored my motions in her own until my father bellowed at her to attack. And like a well-trained soldier, she immediately charged and nearly bayoneted me with a surprising back kick and spin hook kick combination that I was not aware she was capable of.

Amused by her amination and renewed fighting spirit, I slid past her blind side and smacked her hard with a short left round kick on her right butt cheek. The speed of my foot hitting the sweat-soaked seat of her pants produced a crisp smacking sound and a shock of pain and embarrassment on her face. I laughed. As her right hand instinctively flew to the insulted butt cheek, I stepped back into her defenseless right side and faked a kick to her head before angling another smack to the same spot on her butt. I felt another smirk cross my face as I entertained myself with this new game.

Low kicks or kicks below the belt are generally not allowed in Taekwondo, but like fouls in basketball or soccer or any other sport they are also quite common and often strategically deployed. Apparently, my bit of ungracious gamesmanship hit a nerve and what remained of her composure crumbled. For the final two rounds, she attacked with artless abandon and a complete disconnect between the actions of her body and any semblance of analysis from her mind. Her intuitions were terrible, so I continued to punish her lack of finesse by assaulting the same butt cheek. I interspersed light smacks with an occasional bone-deep

30

pounding into the soft flesh until my father finally called an end to the sparring.

We took a step backward and bowed first to each other and then to my father. My lower back tightened with the motion and sent a sobering shock of pain down my leg. As my father stepped off the mat, I looked over to the girl and saw that her head remained lowered as her body gently shook with silent sobs. In an instant all the childish fun that I just had at her expense filtered through my conscience and left me sifting uncomfortably through its guilty dregs. I might have even briefly considered apologizing.

Gut Check

What is wrong with me? Why couldn't I get a handle on myself during the sparring? Why can't I make myself stop crying right now?

After *Sabumnim* went back into to his office, *Sabum* Dae Sung walked over and wordlessly took my right arm and rolled up the sleeve to examine it. The rug burn had peeled off several layers of skin and was still bleeding freely near my elbow. Not unkindly, he shepherded me over to the bathroom like an older brother would do with a snot-nosed sister he just beat up and cleaned the wound before pulling out a first aid kit and dressing it with a light bandage. He then torqued my wrist and elbow in various directions and methodically applied pressure up and down my arm, nodding clinically to himself every time I winced or recoiled under his touch.

"You probably have a distal radius fracture. It doesn't seem displaced, but you should probably drive yourself to an urgent care center for a quick X-ray and maybe a soft cast," he diagnosed.

I tried my best to swallow my embarrassment and tears, but managed only to turn my sobs into hiccups, so I acknowledged his medical advice with nod and a half-choked hiccup.

But before I could start feeling too sorry for myself, I noticed that parents and nannies were starting to bring their kids in for the afternoon class. And in an instant my own problems faded and I quickly pulled my arm back before sprinting across the *dojang* into the women's changing room. I ignored the sharp stabs of pain radiating up my arm and into the base of my neck and hurriedly changed every stitch of my wet clothing for a clean and dry set. I held back tears while I tried to minimize the twisting of my right wrist as I brushed out my hair and re-styled it in a ballerina bun to hide the sweat. Thus refreshed, I forced myself to become *Sabum* Daria and stepped back onto the mat to greet my little students.

There is nothing like a roomful of kindergarteners, hyped up from the sugars of their afternoon snacks and the freedom from their school day, to 100% refocus my concentration and attention away from myself and onto them. Like any good teacher can tell you, kids know if you are not giving them 100% and will mercilessly rain chaos and mayhem into your universe if they sense that kind of weakness. So, I put all my efforts into playing the role of *Sabum* Daria for their sake and the kids responded like any other day. It was not until 45 minutes later when the last little kid bowed off the mat and back into the arms of his mom that the clouds began to regather in my head and my arm started throbbing again.

Sabumnim had returned to the mat and was now chatting with the parents of some of the older kids who were arriving for their practice. Since I was only assisting in the next three classes, I let myself slip out of my *Sabum* Daria persona a little and felt the self-pity party I had been suppressing start to rise up in the back of my throat, threatening the darker, weaker recesses of my confidence.

As I started to replay the humiliation of my afternoon practice back through my thoughts, *Sabum* Dae Sung approached me on his way out. He had changed from his *dobok* into a dark cashmere sweater and a pair of even darker distressed jeans. His shock of unruly wavy black hair had been partially tamed by a shower. A modern, black zipper-less backpack hung casually from one shoulder and balanced the effect of the thin overcoat and Columbia University gym bag he held in the opposite hand.

He paused momentarily on his way toward the exit and said without turning to look at me, "The composure and authority you just showed during the kids' class is the baseline amount of poise you have to have while fighting. Minimum. It's good that you seem capable of it or at least can do a good job of faking it."

He took another step toward the door before shaking his head and adding, "In addition to your lack of focus and mental fortitude, you are also way too slow. Your kicking, thinking, sensing, timing, everything. It's all too slow. How old are you? 16? 17? 18? You're not going to make it at this rate. It's too late."

Then he turned to fully face me and waited until my eyes rose to meet his before continuing, "When I turned 10 *Sabumnim* made my older brothers my sparring partners. Tae Suk was 18 and Eui Song was 17 and they beat the living shit out of me every day for five or six years until they couldn't any more. My brothers say I had the most success because I got pounded twice as hard and twice as often as they had been growing up. That's just the Korean way.

"My brothers and I were born into Taekwondo and never thought to question our destinies or the wisdom of our father. But it left scars that each of us is still discovering and trying to reconcile.

"Just so you know, when my father decides to invest his time and attention in you, the fun and games stop and what you got this afternoon is just a taste of what it's really like to be shaped and molded by his vision."

With that, the tall doctor strode toward *Sabumnim* to exchange a few words before bowing out of the *dojang*.

Regardless of the true intentions behind *Sabum* Dae Sung's words, the effect was that I stopped wallowing and started thinking. I did not question my love for Taekwondo or my goals of competing and winning at the highest levels, but I wondered if I had the mental strength and desire to endure this afternoon over and over again.

Hours later and after the last adult students left following the evening class, I dimmed the lights, collected the garbage and turned the heat back down to low before *Sabumnim* called me into his office. With me standing before his desk he started to repeat some of *Sabum* Dae Sung's words, "You are too slow, but Dae Sung can fix that. Your mind is too unsettled and wandering. Dae Sung can fix that. Question is, are you ready for this? Can you do this? Can you obey and give yourself over to this? No half answers. Only you can decide if you want this journey."

He then took a moment to study my face for a reaction to what he just said. I tried to maintain my equanimity but didn't have an answer and continued to gaze slightly downward at the scattered paperwork on his desk in order to hide my discomfort. Another silent moment passed, during which he checked his phone and then pulled out his wallet, watch and keys from the top desk drawer. He sighed.

"You have a broken arm, so no weights tonight. Do five miles at 7-minute pace to make sure your legs stay strong. Don't fall and break anything else," he said in dismissing me from the office. I guess no answers were required tonight. Thank goodness.

I had not packed another set of outdoor workout gear, so I took off my black belt and slipped on my winter hat and gloves and headed outside in my *dobok*. I set my pace much faster than 7 minutes so I wouldn't freeze. It was much colder than it was this morning and the frosty night air numbed both my arm and my mind, making the run a little easier.

On lap eight of 20 I saw the tail lights from *Sabumin's* Toyota Camry recede from the parking lot. By lap 12, all the lights in the shopping center had dimmed. By lap 15 I developed a stitch in my side and a cramp in my calf that told me I was probably dehydrated and overdoing it. As I pushed myself to finish, I suddenly realized that my nose was running and my eyes were watering. It took another half lap before I realized I was silently crying in little congested gasps. By the time I finished 20 laps I was sprinting and sobbing and had no idea why I was doing either.

Mom

I dragged my exhausted carcass back home and using just my left hand, started another load of laundry, microwaved and ate another rice, meatballs and *kimchi* meal and showered and changed into my pajamas before collapsing on the couch with ice packs on my shins and my wrist.

My mom probably timed all this from upstairs and just as I settled into a mountain of couch pillows with the television remote in my good hand, she presented herself at the French doors that led out into the back yard. Gently tapping the door frame with a chilled bottle of Sancerre in one hand while forking two wine glasses between the fingers of her other hand, she smiled an entreaty toward my warm basement.

Knowing it was impossible to leave my mom out in the snow flurries, I let the ice packs slip from my shins and while still cradling the ice pack on my right arm, padded over to unlock the French doors.

"I brought us a little something to unwind with," she said as she aimed an air kiss in my direction and pretended not to stare at my arm. She floated toward the couch and poured out half a glass for each of us before tuning the television to a kids' baking show on the Food Network.

"Mom, I'm training… no drinks," was my only protest to her intrusion as I resettled myself in the pillow mountain and rearranged the ice packs on my shins. "Besides, I'm only 18," I added.

"Don't worry. I take full responsibility for you," she answered before tapping my forehead with her glass and taking a sip. She pulled me into a half-hug and I eased into a curl beside her while we watched the baking show.

"Your Aunt Vivian and Uncle Morris and your cousins are staying with us Saturday on their way up to Montreal. The insurance company still hasn't paid out on the damage to their condo so they decided to vacation up north instead of south. Daddy offered up our cabin in the Outer Banks, but really, winter in the Carolinas is like a purgatory when you're used to the Florida sun," my mom said, breaking the silence during a commercial break.

"Oooh, I bet Noah and Emma will love the poutine and making their own maple syrup candies in the snow!" I said, remembering back to the wintry Canadian vacation we once took. "Are you recommending that same spa where we stayed at? It was so fun swimming and soaking in that huge thermal pool in the forest. And then at night we stayed in that igloo cabin and saw the most amazing sky ever. Remember?"

She snuggled me a little closer and reminisced, "That poutine was sooooo good."

We watched as a gangly 10-year-old boy won the episode with a sour gummy lemon cake. One judge's face puckered in feigned agony during the tasting and none of the judges took a second bite, but it was the only non-chocolate creation in the candy counter challenge so originality must have carried the day.

"I have to be in the city for a meeting tomorrow afternoon with the suits who decide our budget for the next round of testing on the drug. Half of them are from accounting and marketing and don't know the first thing about science," she said while stroking my hair.

"Mmm," I answered. My mom is a chemist at Pfizer. Her lab is two towns over, and she hates making trips into Manhattan to visit what she calls the corporate mothership.

"I'm trying to convince your dad to take me out on a lunch date since I'll be right by his office, but he's being kind of a grouch. You saw him over Christmas. Work, work, work. I hope he closes his deal soon."

I slept through the next kids' baking episode while my mom sipped from my untouched glass of wine and scrolled through the emails on her phone. I awoke when the garage door above the basement hummed open and announced my dad's return. My mom absent-mindedly started stroking my hair again saying, "I'm not a 'doctor' doctor, but I think your arm is broken."

I was too tired to refute or explain the now puffy and swollen arm situation.

"I'm fine, mom. I'll get it looked at tomorrow."

She narrowed her eyes and gave me an overly-dramatic 'I don't believe you' face before poking my wrist and causing me to yelp off the couch. "I love you, but what you do to your body is enough to drive any mother crazy," she sighed.

"No wine for you? I'm going to go see if your dad wants a nightcap. That wrist better have a cast on it tomorrow. Call me if you need anything. Good night, dear."

I let her kiss my forehead before she disappeared back upstairs. I then pulled another ice pack from the freezer and fell back asleep dreaming of thermal pools and igloos.

Abeoji and *Sabumnim*

The next couple of days continued in much the same way, except that the girl went to urgent care and had her wrist fracture treated with a soft cast and my lower back and hamstring got a little worse. Our sparring sessions became stale and uninspired as we each carefully nursed our injuries, but my father seemed unconcerned and let it slide.

As the weekend approached my father put the girl in charge of one of the Juniors classes he usually taught and summoned me into his office. It was already after 5 o'clock and I protested that I had to catch the express bus back into the city for a dinner thing. My father nodded understandingly and pointed with his chin to the one of the chairs in front of his desk.

"What do you think about Daria?" he asked without a preamble.

"She's not going to make it," I replied brusquely while slouching into the chair opposite my father and resigning myself to the 5:47 local bus.

"Not going to make it?" he echoed with a query.

"To the Olympics. No way."

"Who said anything about the Olympics?"

"Isn't that what she wants?" I asked, suddenly confused by his line of questioning. Was he asking me about the girl in some other context?

"Does it matter?"

"I don't get what you're talking about," I said, raising my voice in frustration.

"I am asking about Daria, the student, the martial artist, the human being you have been teaching this week," he said patiently. "Making it or not making it to the Olympics is not part of the question, and in fact is not all that important. The important thing is that you have become a small part of her journey and I was wondering about your thoughts."

I sighed, "She is an average athlete with average instincts and an average understanding of how to fight. She is diligent about her practice, but unexceptional about her approach. Average. She should stop dreaming and stop wasting her time."

"Hmmm," he considered. "Average. You're right. But still, there is something there, no? Perhaps the timing and the stimulus has not been right for her to evolve beyond average.

"That's why I asked you to come teach her," he continued, "Unfortunately, there have been aspects of her training that I have neglected these past years because I now lack the willpower and strength to push her further. It takes so much emotional energy from a teacher to force a student to break through her own barriers. The teacher must be merciless and risk everything at the right moment in order to create opportunities for the student to realize another evolution of her potential."

He then dropped his voice to a whisper. "But oftentimes when you push, things break, and that takes a heavy toll on both people. It's okay, just part of the process, but only if the teacher and the student have the strength to absorb the emotional turmoil caused by the damage and then the collective daily resolve to rebuild the martial artist back stronger and better. I might have had tens of thousands of students, but I only exerted that kind of all-consuming effort with you and your brothers, and now this girl. Because when I break you to force you higher... it breaks me too... and I cannot... anymore."

I sat there unsettled, emotionally unmoored as I heard only my father's confessions to his own mortality and decline.

My brain irrationally fast-forwarded and saw him as a frailer old man, and my heart unexpectedly ached at this lessened version of him.

"*Abeoji*, are you okay?" I asked. "You're fine, right? I saw you still doing 500 pushups and 500 squats a day over Christmas. There's no way you're sick or anything... no way you're hiding anything from me, right?" I inexplicably felt a need to confirm that he was still the same invincible grandmaster of my youth.

He blinked at me distractedly as if surprised by my reaction to his display of vulnerability. Then he waved his hand aggressively from side to side in front of his face and furrowed his brow as if his point was not getting across.

"I am explaining to you that from now on, I need you to push her like I used to push you and your brothers. I need you to force her through this muddled average-ness and pull her through the other side. Even if it breaks her. Even if it breaks you."

How long had he been rhythmically jabbing his finger into the desk like that? I don't know what stirred up my resentment more, his finger jabbing or his words. But just like that, the quiet confessions of an old man seismically shifted back to the demands of a tyrannical *Sabumnim* and swallowed my precarious empathy into the crevasse that always existed between us.

What is he asking of me? The more I thought about it, the more my bitterness resurfaced. Does he want me to become like him?

When my brothers first heard that I had agreed to help out at the *dojang*, they immediately expressed misgivings about our father's true intentions. Tae Suk and Eui Song warned me that our father always secretly desired for one of them to inherit his Taekwondo legacy and both fought long and hard against that fate. Logically speaking, they said I have already succeeded in avoiding that fate because there is no way the old man could expect me to abandon a medical career in favor of his Taekwondo school. But still, they warned me to be careful and not get sucked back in.

And yet, here I was, at the *dojang* on a Friday night, getting yelled at by the imperial grandmaster. I cursed him in my mind but remained outwardly calm and respectful. I would fulfill my promise to show up and assist in January, but once school restarts in February, I will become my own man again. I gently and politely told him as much, and he enigmatically nodded at my renewed concession.

"One last thing."

He then slowly and unexpectedly pressed his palms together in front of his lips as if in prayer and said, "Teach her and push her, but do so through your heart and with compassion."

What?

That little talk made me miss the last express bus. And as I settled onto a local that inched its way across the George Washington Bridge during rush hour, I let my indignation expand across my chest and explode into all of my stress points while I silently railed against the old man's machinations. How has he ever shown heart or compassion?!

Later that evening, I was in the arms of a petite and pretty undergrad from my *jiu jitsu* club who I took out to dinner and then back home to my apartment. The surprisingly strong and wiry black belt tied me up in knots and worked me from inside my own guard for hours. Afterwards while she slept, I laid there still seething and unable to take my mind off of how much I hated being back under my father's thumb.

Hill Repeats

It only took that first day for my crush on the old *Sabum* Dae Sung to fade. Out of propriety for his status as my senior I hesitated to label him as a jerk, even privately in my mind, but he obviously had no interest in teaching Taekwondo or helping at the *dojang* and barely tolerated the sessions with me because *Sabumnim* had forced the responsibility upon him. I mulled over what he said about the nature of the training he intended to mete out, and I tried to reconcile that with my goals.

Maybe sensing my hesitation, *Sabumnim* came up to me in between classes over the weekend and with students and parents still milling about and eavesdropping he said, "Your arm is sore and your butt is sore. But if your ego is sore then stay home. You can learn from anyone if your character is true and your temperament is unwavering. Dae Sung is being ungenerous right now, but you have not proven yourself a worthy student yet either."

Next to my parents, *Sabumnim* is the person I respected the most, but his tacit approval of *Sabum* Dae Sung's abusive and negative attitude toward me made me question if I was headed for my own #MeToo moment. I knew I had the strength to just suck it up and endure the insults and the rough treatment by *Sabum* Dae Sung. I could handle the pain and ignore the insensitivities, but the stories of abuse that are coming out from all across the sports world nagged at me, and I wondered if I was underestimating the egregiousness of his behavior and being complicit in my own abuse if I continued without complaint. How would my parents react if they knew of *Sabum* Dae Sung's condescension? Almost as confirmation of my own misgivings, I knew I could not tell them for fear of the truth.

These reservations loomed over me all through the weekend without resolution and for the first time I could remember, I dreaded going to the *dojang* on Monday. When I arrived, the white board was empty with no instructions from *Sabumnim*. Feeling slightly relieved, I leisurely went through my morning cleaning routine and imagined indulging in a couple hours of practice by myself afterwards. An hour later, however, as I was finishing with the mirrors and moving on to wiping down the equipment, *Sabum* Dae Sung appeared at the front entrance and greeted me with an angry stare before slyly saying, "I bet you're cleaning and teaching for free every day. In fact, you're probably even paying my father full tuition for that privilege, aren't you? Haven't you ever wondered if he isn't just taking advantage of you? Like it's indentured servitude?"

Stunned, I managed a slight bow and a "Good morning, Sir," as etiquette required before falling silent, struggling for an internal answer that would not sound trite or self-delusional. "I'm just helping out the *dojang*. It's like my second family," I thought to myself with my mouth slightly agape and about to defend myself and *Sabumnim*. But *Sabum* Dae Sung was already marching toward the office without letting me reply. That splash of cold water did have an effect though, as I paused and wondered why I was the only student who was ever asked to clean.

Sabum Dae Sung emerged a minute later and looked even more annoyed, as if his wisdom had fallen on deaf ears. "Let my father clean! He emailed me a list of other things you have to do. Get your running gear and meet me outside in 30 seconds."

I quickly abandoned the cleaning supplies and rushed to slip on my sauna suit top before jumping on the scale for a pre-run weigh-in. Damn. 119-ish, probably because my cousins were over this weekend and my parents took everyone

44

out to a steakhouse. I smiled ruefully. Porterhouse steaks and key lime pie with schlag were serious weaknesses of mine. I hurried outside to find *Sabum* Dae Sung stretching his legs. "Follow me," he said and took off at a moderate pace without looking back.

We slogged along the shoulder of several sloppily plowed streets before I realized we were headed for the local community college. Our brisk jog took us around the deserted campus and ended behind the athletic complex by a paved loading dock. *Sabum* Dae Sung pointed out the steep asphalt hill that led away from the area where we stopped. Looking up, I saw a slope that was lined with barren red oak trees on the wild side and bright yellow guard rails on the industrial side. At its terminus about 200 meters away was a secured yellow gate that probably led out to an access road when school was in session.

"You guys now run around that flat shopping center," he said with a little too much animus. "My brothers and I used to jog the two miles here and then run hill repeats and do all sorts of other crazy things until someone threw up or passed out."

And then he mumbled, almost to himself, "He used to carry a bamboo practice sword everywhere back then and the loser of each race had to jump up and hang from that tree for at least one whack on their backside depending on how slow he was and how close he was to giving up." He paused and pointed to a tree with a thick low-hanging branch near the base of the hill before continuing, "The loser was almost always me, but only because my brothers were so much older and stronger. Sometimes he would designate two losers when it seemed like I was the only one getting hit all the time.

"Lucky for you though… no races and no stick," he said. "In fact, not much at all today. Just sprints and one set of bunny hops. He probably doesn't want to scare you off because you're a girl and not bound by blood to him like us," he added matter-of-factly.

After leaving me a little confused and a lot apprehensive about what we were doing, *Sabum* Dae Sung described the morning workout and positioned me at the bottom of the hill to start. The first set of sprints was the full length of the hill to the yellow gate.

At about 80% up the hill that first time, it suddenly hit me how much pain I was going to be in for, and even that realization did no justice to how diabolical the workout actually ended up being. He was right; the hill sprints were about a million times harder than running circles around the shopping center.

On just my third trip up the hill something integral deep within in me unexpectedly cracked and I had to stop for a split second before reaching the top. As I approached *Sabum* Dae Sung on the descent he was livid, calling me a quitter and questioning my lack of fortitude and telling me I was not worthy of my black belt. He yelled that he wished he carried a bamboo sword like *Sabumnim* back in the old days. But since things like that were not allowed anymore, he offered me the option of hanging from the tree for 60 seconds or going home.

Damn, hanging from that fat branch with one arm in a cast was hard.

I finished the last two full-length sprints without stopping, but to call dragging my ass up that hill a sprint was a generous dispensation on *Sabum* Dae Sung's part. So generous in fact that he changed the rules for the next round. First, I got a little breather as he walked me a little more than half way up the hill and pointed out the lone black spruce that stood out raggedly among its oaken brethren. That was the marker I had to reach on the next set of sprints. Unlike the first set of sprints, I had to improve my time every time up the hill. The baseline he calculated was half the time it took me to reach the top on my fastest sprint during the first round, which turned out to be 30.5 seconds.

My second round started with 30.25, 30.18, 30.12 before I crashed with a 32.09 and then a 31.89 and suffered two more bouts of verbal assaults while hanging from the tree.

The third set of sprints was a quarter way up the hill and *Sabum* Dae Sung leaned against the guardrail to mark the distance. Again, I bested my times three times in a row before slowing for the fourth and fifth sprints. Perseverance, I know! Perseverance. But how do I get my mind and body to do that? I wondered as I hung from the tree again with a screaming maniac below.

The final set required bunny hops in place of the sprints, and my heart sank, knowing that my legs could not take much more. I pleaded ignorance with *Sabum* Dae Sung but he forced me into a butt to heel crouch with my hands on my head and ordered me to bounce up the hill on the balls of my feet. On the first trip up, I lost my balance twice and ripped through my leggings at the knees before making it up the hill. My hips and ankles and the arches of my feet burned as I gingerly walked down the hill. My second ascent was much slower as my right foot cramped up and I had to stop and take off my sneaker to massage it out. A blistering tirade on quitting and having no spirit rang in my ears as the blood pooled into my legs during another 60-second hang from the blasted tree.

On my third trip up, determined not to stop and pushing as hard as I could, my head started spinning with the strain and my stomach revolted as I lost my breakfast and all my fluids on the oaken side of the path. *Sabum* Dae Sung yelled at me not to come down until I finished, which I somehow managed to do. When I got back to the bottom of the hill, he pulled a bottle of water out of his parka and allowed me a break instead of forcing me to hang from the tree. On the fourth set of bunny hops I threw up the water all over myself and lost feeling in my right leg, but I did not stop. Again, silence and no tree. On the last trip I dry heaved repeatedly and fought the pain in my legs and a dizzying fear that I might lose control of my body and roll down the hill, but I did not stop. He held out the water bottle again and gave me 30 seconds before turning around to begin the jog back. Despite the much slower pace he set, I was not able to keep up and he was long gone by the time I managed to shuffle-jog back to the *dojang*.

When I got back, the *dojang* was dark and *Sabumnim* was vacuuming. He took one look at my dispirited self and stiffening gait and ordered me to shower and then present myself in his office. The hot water from the shower relaxed my muscles and soothed my joints but also sapped the remaining energy from my bones, and I stood like an unsteady zombie before his desk. He handed me two salt tablets and a 20-ounce bottle of water, which he made me take and drink while he watched. I was then directed to lie down on his office floor with my head on a floor cushion and nap while he taught the noon class. He turned the lights off as he left and I was asleep before the door closed.

The Definition of Training

I woke up when the fluorescent lights came back on a little over an hour later. My body felt like it had been hit by a truck and my head pounded as the lights seared into my eyes. *Sabumnim* walked over and felt my forehead with the back of his hand while he looked into my eyes. He then asked if I knew how to make tea.

"I could try, Sir," I answered, as I raised myself to a sitting position and then gingerly stood as the blood rushed from my head and left a constellation of stars before my eyes.

He walked me over to the side table and pointed out a metal container that I opened to reveal dusty green shards of tea mixed with what looked like toasted brown rice. He showed me the "Unlock" and the "Boil" and the "Dispense" buttons that were marked in Korean on the gallon-sized cylindrical water heater. I was instructed to put two spoonfuls of the tea and rice mixture into a sieve-like tea leaf holder that sat inside a heavy cast iron tea pot and to wait until the water reached 91 degrees Celsius before filling the tea pot to about 80 percent and letting the tea seep for five minutes. While I stared at the digital temperature reader and then the timer on the water heater, *Sabumnim* turned away and changed from his uniform top into a T-shirt. After seeping the tea for five minutes exactly I carefully poured the earthy, grainy brown liquid into an equally earthy, grainy brown and green mug that I found on the bottom shelf of the side table and brought it over to the low coffee table where he sat.

"You just brewed two cups of tea," he said. "Pour the other one for yourself."

49

After I poured myself a mug and took a seat on the only other cushion which laid 90 degrees from his side of the table, he handed me a Tupperware container identical to the one that sat in front of him. I took it with my good hand and instantly got smacked with a pair of disposable chopsticks before I was able to set it down on the table.

"When receiving something from your teacher or senior you must always use two hands and make a little bow with head and eyes and humbly receive," he corrected.

"Sorry, Sir." Damn, I knew that too! It was how we shook hands and passed equipment from one to another in class. I did better when he held out a pair of disposable chopsticks toward me.

"Dae Sung went back home today so you eat his lunch," *Sabumnim* explained as I opened the Tupperware to reveal two neat rows of unusually large sushi rolls, a cup of *kimchi* and three bright neon yellow half-moons of something. Famished, I separated my chopsticks and popped an entire piece of the giant sushi roll into my mouth before I got smacked again, this time on the head with his open palm. Trying not to spit out a big glob of vegetables and rice, I held my hand up to my mouth and looked at him in surprise. What?!

"Always wait for your teacher or senior to eat first," he sighed. "Eat first, drink first, walk first, sit first, stand first, talk first. Very bad manners for young impatient person. Do the same thing at home with your parents too." He calmly separated his chopsticks and starting eating, as I mumbled another "Sorry, Sir" through my mouthful. I waited until he started on a second bite before I resumed eating, and we ate in silence as I tried to match my pace to his. After he finished with one last bite of the crunchy yellow pickle, he asked for another mug of tea and I stood to brew more. When I returned to the low table with two full mugs, he motioned for me to sit again.

He let the tea cool for a minute before taking a sip and then waited while I did the same.

"There is a difference between working out and training," he started. "So far, you just work out. You sweat a little and get a good amount of exercise. Yes, you do get a little better, a little stronger and a little smarter, but mostly your skills are derived from your natural abilities. Training is very different. When you train, you have to push your body and your fighting spirit to the point of breaking every time. When you train, you have to go right up to the limits where your physical being and your spiritual self scream 'no more.' And at that barrier, which naturally evolved throughout your lifetime as protection against possible physical harm and mental anguish, you must force through or be forced through into a world of seemingly unreasonable pain in order to glimpse and then realize another level beyond your current abilities. This must happen over and over again in order to truly progress on this journey. And of course, the cruelty of all this is that the next level itself is illusory, as is the one after that, and the successive barriers you must force your way through will seem boundless."

"Even for the strongest person, training extracts a heavy and oftentimes damaging toll on your body and on your psychic health, which is why I rarely push my students that hard," he continued. "The harmful effects of such hard training is also why you need a trustworthy guide and teacher, someone who can catalyze your training but, more importantly, someone who can pull you from the abyss and show you that the white hot pressure to advance and constantly surpass your previous achievements is also an illusion in and of itself."

He then paused and sighed. "I am only warning you of the incongruence of the experience in case I do not have a chance to explain it to you again."

I was baffled.

"Truth be told, I am too old and fear that I do not have the strength to guide you safely through the entire journey, so I have to ask Dae Sung to teach you in my stead. But it is difficult for him as well. Right now, he resists because it inflames the scars and insecurities still etched into his own body and spirit from his younger training days."

He dropped his voice to a whisper and said, "The boys had no choice. When they were old enough, I only trained them through intense fire and pressure... at a time when I did not understand as much as I do now."

He stopped and then stood and walked over to his desk to pull on a sweater before sitting back down. "How much do you want to understand Taekwondo? How much do you want to really train Taekwondo? You say you want to become champion, and for this past year you worked hard and showed me something. But to really walk this path the risk is letting you get hurt too much... and perhaps Dae Sung again as well." His thoughts and voice trailed off, and he wove his fingers around his mug of tea and looked like an old man deliberating and conflicted. Sensing his questions were not for me to answer, I cupped my own tea and waited.

But I was wrong. A couple of steady, silent breaths later he demanded, "Well?"

Surprised that he was pressing for an answer this time, all I could manage was a 'Yes, Sir' to his obviously non-binary questions. "Uh, I love Taekwondo," I fumbled. "It's all I ever wanted to do. I can handle the training."

"What if you give everything, empty your whole self into trying to reach your full potential and never become champion?" he challenged.

"What if I never become champion?" I echoed to myself, pausing to seriously consider the possibility for the first time. "You mean if I'm just not good enough? Or something happens and the stars are completely misaligned and nothing breaks my way? Or I just can't find a way to win? And I eventually cannot continue pushing any longer?

"Well, my parents would probably be relieved. I don't know how much it will hurt to fail, but I think I would eventually like to find a job somewhere teaching Taekwondo for real. My dad would most likely start nagging me about college. And I will probably eat more ice cream, get a little fatter and maybe join my mom in a glass of wine once in a while," I spoke honestly in a stream of unfiltered thoughts.

When I looked to up to see his reaction, *Sabumnim* actually smiled with his eyes and patted me on the head before surprising me again. "Good. You'll start training tomorrow. Today, go home and register for Rutgers University online. Two classes. Introduction to Korean language and something else. Show me the receipt tomorrow."

He then laughed for real and said while waving an admonishing finger in my direction, "No ice cream, no wine," before sending me off to wash the Tupperware and the mugs while he closed his eyes and rested.

Wrestling

God, I hate the bus, I thought as I slowly walked through the slush toward the NJ Transit stop seven blocks from my father's *dojang*. While I waited for the express bus, I daydreamed about the motorcycle I always coveted but was too practical and safety-conscious to buy. Even in temperate, sunny California I had settled for a 125cc Vespa when what I truly wanted was a 400cc Kawasaki Ninja sport bike. Could 400cc's handle a New York City winter? I pulled out my cell phone to investigate.

About half an hour later, the bus pulled into the 179th Street stop in New York City and I headed down Broadway toward my apartment on West 170th Street. Along the way I stopped in my favorite Dominican restaurant that also doubled as a deli for a quick lunch of stewed oxtails, pigeon peas and yellow rice. From the deli in the back I grabbed a small container of *kimchi* and a bottle of raspberry soda. New York City is an amazing place if you know where to look. Actually, the best kept secret of the place was the sweet guava and cheese empanada and the cup of Dominican coffee I took to go. Enjoying my warm flaky desert as I continued my walk home, I reveled in the thought of the *kimbap* lunch that I avoided with my father. I could go a long time without eating that same lunch again.

Back home in my 300 square foot studio apartment I pried open my only window, which looked out into a government-mandated shaft of grime-filtered sunlight. I gently eased the tired and weather-beaten wooden window upward, taking care not to splinter the age old frame any further. A swirl of cold air came in to neutralize the stuffiness of the room and was a welcome offset to the oppressive heat generated by the ancient radiator that I could not control.

I changed into a pair of UCLA gym shorts and a tank top and dragged the low coffee table away from the wall into the middle of the room and sat cross-legged on a floor cushion. Leaning across to the opposite wall I grabbed my laptop and an organic chemistry textbook from the top of the textbook pile and rifled through the neighboring piles of notebooks and papers to gather my class and lab notes. While my laptop was loading, I stretched myself out like a starfish on the rug, trying to lengthen and then contract every muscle and sinew in my body in order to relax and clear my mind. Partially rejuvenated, I re-folded my legs under the tiny Ikea coffee table, propped open the textbook and started to study.

About four hours later, long after the winter sun had disappeared, I stretched my legs again and stood to take two long steps to reach the mini-fridge in my kitchenette. I pulled out a two-liter bottle of water and gave myself an ice cream headache as I drained half its contents in one swig. I recapped the bottle and dropped it with a slosh to the bottom of my gym bag as I removed my *dobok* and black belt and replaced it with a blue double weave *jiujitsu gi* and a relatively new purple belt. I carefully eased the window closed, changed back into my jeans and sweater and stashed a couple of bananas and energy bars in my coat pocket before heading out to practice.

I walked to the A train and managed to stuff big, efficient bites of banana and energy bar into my mouth while standing shoulder to shoulder in the crush of rush-hour commuters. Thirty minutes later I emerged from the subway near Penn Station with my stomach unsettled and slightly gurgling from the fiber and the highly processed food. Actually, my stomach always gurgled before class. Even though I was a fairly skilled martial artist and a good overall athlete, *jiujitsu* practice always jangled my nerves.

I originally let myself be dragged to a Columbia *jiujitsu* club practice by the pretty black belt I was seeing every once in a while. After just a few classes I was completely smitten by the world of ground fighting, if not so much by the girl. Despite all my Taekwondo training, I was almost completely helpless on the ground. Pinned on my back, I couldn't figure out how to use my arms and legs to find leverage and space. I would strain every muscle in my body to try and overpower this 130-pound girl who would spin and shift and move and pin and ultimately wait until I made a critical mistake, at which time she would casually isolate the misplaced arm, leg or neck and make me submit… over and over again until I was sure I was going to soil myself or pass out from the exertion. It was like nothing I had ever experienced before.

At first it might have been an attempt to salvage my male pride. But in any case, last year I decided that I needed to supplement the club practice to accelerate my progress so I signed up for the biggest and most well-known *dojo* in the city. Here, no one knows or cares about my Taekwondo background or medical school pedigree, and I get to spend 90 hard minutes going against other motivated athletes, grinding out our weaknesses and fighting our individual demons on the mat. Though the sparring is controlled and usually done without too much machismo or malice, there is no doubt that the immediacy of wrestling within a hair's breadth of your opponent's naked aggression and constantly trying to dominate or avoid being dominated by another human being activates all the antediluvian instincts of our most primal self. The desperate need for survival and the acceptance of pain and suffering mingled with temporary dominance, mercy and schizophrenic pride makes the workout exhausting and exhilarating. Thus, the somersaults in my stomach. Like always, I wondered a little about why I do this to myself, but I entered the *dojo* anyway.

Two hours later, I dragged my weary limbs back out onto the streets and into the subway with much more intimate knowledge about my vulnerabilities to the triangle choke. I was only accidentally choked out once tonight when I failed to realize how much danger I was in. I lost consciousness while thinking that I still had plenty of time to adjust my position to escape the choke, and I regained consciousness a minute later thinking the same thing but feeling a little light-headed and smelling vaguely like urine.

As the train now jerked from local stop to local stop, my neck and shoulders started stiffening and hinted at the discomfort I would be in tomorrow. At the 125th Street station the train slowed to a crawl before stopping with an announcement that there were track and signal problems ahead and that all train service above 125th Street had been temporarily suspended. Apparently shuttle bus service to all points north would be running soon.

Like the other disgruntled passengers, I emerged from underground and shivered toward the unruly line for the shuttle bus. As I neared, a fight appeared imminent between a group of loud and weary commuters and the clueless MTA officials trying to estimate the arrival of the shuttle buses, so I backed away and quickly translated blocks into miles in my head. Guessing that home was just over two miles away, I slipped my arms through my gym bag handles and carrying it like a rucksack, started a slow jog home.

Padding up the sidewalks of Broadway on a bitterly cold and empty night with silence as my only company, I thought back to the hill repeats my father used to make us run in the winter offseason. This morning I told the girl about our punishments for being slow, but what I didn't tell her was that we ran shirtless and in gym shorts during the winter. Not only were we mortified to be running in public like that, but obviously the impact of the bamboo sword stung that much more and left awful welts for the world to see... not that anyone ever did care or lift a finger to save us from our wretchedness.

In comparison, tonight's little jaunt felt like nothing under a warm winter coat and I got back a little after 10:30. Thankfully the enterprising street cart vendor was still parked around the corner and I was able to pick up a $5 dinner of chicken and rice with extra white dressing and red sauce. I took my meal and devoured it on the frozen steps outside my apartment so I could toss the Styrofoam container and utensils into a communal trashcan and not tempt any of the city's many critters by bringing too much food or garbage inside.

Once upstairs, I hung up the still damp and heavy *jiujitsu gi* on a cedar hanger from a hook I had pounded into the plaster wall above my demonic radiator and eased the window open again to air out both the room and the *gi*. I then showered my day away and attempted to continue studying but fell asleep in the starfish stretch while my laptop loaded and the radiator hissed.

A Different *Sabum Dae* Sung

Over dinner last night my dad insisted on Chekhov and my mom quietly appreciated his sentimentality with a smile. They had met their junior year at Princeton in a Chekhov seminar and now wished to pass a little of their history onto me, their legacy as my dad said. I explained this to *Sabumnim* when I showed him my enrollment in Online Elementary Korean I and Introduction to World Literature.

"Good list of writers here," he said while reading the course descriptions. "But, yes, read Chekhov for humanity."

I stared.

"Chekhov has been translated many times and in many ways in Korean," he smiled. "Wisdom is not from age, but from education and learning. Taekwondo teachers read too." With that, he dismissed me and stepped out of the office to teach the noontime class.

Sabum Dae Sung stirred from the chair beside me. "I don't want *kimbap* today," he said. "Let's go grab lunch. I hope you have a car."

I nodded.

"Go change and meet me outside."

I did as I was told and bowed to *Sabumnim* on my way out. *Sabum* Dae Sung had a quick word with his father and then followed me out.

I silently led the way to my car and as the key fob unlocked the doors with a beep and a blink of the headlights, *Sabum* Dae Sung huffed, "Nice ride. Rich family?" I got in without answering and started the engine. As he lowered and then folded his lanky frame into the bucket seat beside me, he asked, "What do you usually do for lunch?"

Without admitting to the details of microwaving leftovers and consuming piles of *kimchi*, I muttered something about going home and fixing meals for myself. He answered with a casual laugh, "Well, I guess I can't go inviting myself over to your home just quite yet." Instead, he gave me instructions to get on Route 4 and head east.

I followed his directions into a small township that I didn't recognize, past streets lined with neat, economical, single-family homes dating to the middle of the last century and before. From there we wound our way past a quaint Main Street America neighborhood before turning onto the township's more utilitarian stretch of road that included a senior assisted-living facility, an Ultimate Champions Taekwondo center, a Dunkin' Donuts, a Holy Trinity Church, an Islamic Center, a police station and a medical plaza. Once we passed the medical plaza he told me to slow and park in front of Gabriella's, a turquoise blue two-story clapboard siding establishment that refused to blend with the mud and brick-colored buildings surrounding it.

Once we were seated inside a dining room comprised of mismatched chairs and wobbly Formica table tops amongst a lunchtime crowd of construction workers, cops and medical workers, *Sabum* Dae Sung proceeded to order without consulting me or the menu. Ten minutes later our table was covered with small, well-worn china plates filled with hummus, olives, a charred tomato salad, some sort of thick yogurt with cucumbers, dark and oily rolls of mysterious green leaves, and a basket of fresh pita bread that bore char marks and smelled faintly like a summertime campfire.

He looked excitedly at the spread and then at me before asking, "Why aren't you eating?"

I hesitated and then told him that *Sabumnim* had just scolded me yesterday about waiting for my seniors to start first. He paused and stared blankly at me before laughing so hard that he tilted his weight back and almost toppled himself from

60

the rickety second-hand chair that barely bore his weight on four legs, let alone two. It took a second, but he forced himself back upright and leaned forward to fork a tomato, which he popped into his mouth before saying, "There, eat." His eyes were still laughing at me as he chewed and I reached for the bread.

A large platter of grilled chicken and grilled vegetables crowned our feast and we slowly worked our way through some of the most delicious food I had ever tasted. I told him as much when the empty plates were cleared and the waiter returned to pour Turkish coffee from an ornate little metal pot. Finishing his coffee in two large swigs, he intercepted the check and stood with one arm already through his jacket sleeve before turning and saying in all seriousness, "The food here is great, but everything can be improved with a little *kimchi* on the side." I nodded and suppressed an unexpected urge to smile.

As I retraced the slow meandering local streets back, I played some Muddy Waters at a low volume to reflect my Mediterranean luncheon mood on a cold winter day with hours of work ahead. *Sabum* Dae Sung closed his eyes when the music started and didn't open them again until I pulled into the parking lot of Ahn's Taekwondo.

Fighting

Like I was warned, training in Taekwondo was completely different than the Taekwondo practice I was used to. The sparring sessions with *Sabum* Dae Sung lasted 90 minutes at a time and consisted of a seemingly endless stream of 30-second, 20-second and 10-second rounds that started with my back to a corner trying to fight my way out against a bigger, stronger, nastier opponent. He pressured me with his physical advantages and mentally caged me with his unrelenting attacks. No matter how hard I fought, he would not let me out of the corner except when time ran out or I crumpled to the ground out of bounds. I considered it a small victory just to survive the beatings on my feet, because falling to the mat or stepping completely out of bounds earned me a hundred squat jumps per offense. That first day, I lost my entire lunch within 30 minutes, and shortly thereafter, I started mentally negotiating with myself about quitting Taekwondo.

Neither *Sabumnim* nor *Sabum* Dae Sung said a word as I struggled against my own body and mind. Whenever I felt like I couldn't continue for a second longer and shamefully petitioned *Sabumnim* for a reprieve through my eyes, I received only a stern, challenging gaze in return and the slow burn of unremitting pressure continued unpityingly. I was still not so spiritually marooned and bereft of propriety that I would dare to open my mouth and plead the same, so I endured without complaint.

Although every round seemed to bring some part of me closer to the rage and the despair that must precede quitting, I somehow managed to continue with the practice. I kept on going because when I did pause and process the pain and anguish during the mini-breaks between each round, I felt nothing and emotionally accepted that the fire was necessary.

Sabum Dae Sung put me through two more hill sessions that week, each more insidious than the previous. The surprising part however was that he voluntarily suffered alongside me both times. The sprints up the hill were ever-present, but by Wednesday the bunny hops had transformed to broad jumps and by Friday the broad jumps had evolved into single-leg broad jumps. I almost always trailed him to the finish line and as a result ended up hanging from the blasted tree while he rested in between the rounds.

The first time I outlasted him was when he was felled by a calf cramp. He slowly limped down behind me and then silently jumped up to the tree and performed piked toe touches to the branch for a minute. I tried to emulate the same on my next hang, but my abdominal muscles were at a lost. He laughed as I cheated by tucking and then attempting to straighten my legs skyward. On his next turn on the branch, he upped the ante and showed off with a minute's worth of windshield wipers, silently challenging me with an easy smile. I wondered if he purposefully lost that race in order to taunt me and fumed a little while vowing to YouTube those exercises and start practicing immediately.

By Friday afternoon I could barely move my legs, and my forearms and shins felt dented and bruised beyond anything I had ever experienced. I had abandoned the bulky soft cast in favor of a couple of pieces of athletic tape for my still-injured wrist, but I couldn't help obsessively Googling 'edema' and 'hematoma' with 'blood clot,' 'stroke' and 'permanent damage' whenever the swelling in my legs became too unsightly or painful.

That afternoon *Sabumnim* took an extra-long post-lunch nap, and since he did not give me or *Sabum* Dae Sung any specific instructions I tried to loosen up my body by slowly walking through some higher-level patterns. *Sabum* Dae Sung lounged across the room on the mat with a pile of index cards on his chest and his head propped up on a kicking shield while silently reciting formulas and quizzing himself.

I didn't realize he was watching or even cared until after I finished walking through *Moon Moo* for a fifth time and he said, "Do it again, but this time for real." I nodded, then turned and faced away from him toward the front of the *dojang* and started *Moon Moo* again as if I was performing in front of a panel of judges and against actual opponents.

When I finished with a sharp bow toward the imaginary judges and refocused on the present, I turned to hear him say, "We don't even do those patterns you were practicing. And even if we did, that is way above your rank. Who taught you that?"

He was right. *Moon Moo* is from an older, more traditional school of Taekwondo and not used in the Olympic-style *Sabumnim* taught. And, yes, it was intended for master-level practitioners, which was far beyond my rank. However, among all the patterns I know it was my favorite because it demanded martial severity, intensity, beauty, showmanship and sheer athleticism if it was to be performed well. When I practiced on my own, I always include parts of *Moon Moo*. When I think of Taekwondo, I think of the martial as fighting and the art as embodied by *Moon Moo*.

"*Sabumnim*," I answered, as a matter of course. "He taught me all the patterns from our style and all the patterns from ITF Taekwondo, the *Palgwe* patterns and the *Bassai* patterns. He also gave me a textbook on Shotokan karate and told me to learn those patterns on my own."

"Why?" he wondered, incredulous.

"Probably because I asked whether our patterns were the best," I answered. "And *Sabumnim* told me he would teach me all the patterns he knew so I could decide for myself."

"When did this happen? Like in the middle of a regular class?" he asked.

I said no and told him that I dropped out of high school to home-school myself with online courses and spent six to eight hours a day practicing and assisting at the *dojang*. "There's so much down time between the noon class and the afternoon kids' classes. And then during the summer and all the holidays the dojang is pretty much empty. So, whenever I had a chance, I would just ask *Sabumnim* to teach me more."

"Wait, you dropped out of high school to hang out at my father's Taekwondo school?!" He was now sitting upright and dramatically shaking his hyperbolically slackened jaw in disbelief. "That is insane! Your parents let you do that?"

I shrugged... as if I really needed to explain myself to him. "How do you know what pattern I just did?" I re-directed. "It's above your rank and not your style either."

"Guess...," he snarled as he laid his head back down to rest on the kicking shield again. "Not because I asked though and not because I was a big fan of patterns or Taekwondo," he added before turning his attention back to the index cards.

I pretended to ignore him as well and walked through a few more patterns and continued my work on a particularly difficult jump split kick sequence of moves that ended in an awkward diagonal stance. By the time *Sabumnim* emerged from his office, I was feeling limber and light and *Sabum* Dae Sung was snoring softly.

"Dae Sung-a," *Sabumnim* said in an almost lyrical good-morning-sleepy-head tone of voice. "Time to practice."

Sabum Dae Sung opened his eyes and did a languid isometric full-body animal stretch while still lying on his back. It took a minute, but he eventually roused himself, straightened his dobok and stood before me sleepy-faced and with his wavy hair asymmetrically flattened.

Sabumnim looked at his tired, disinterested son and announced that today we would only do 10 three-minute rounds without sparring equipment. Furthermore, he limited *Sabum* Dae Sung to only using his hands at 50% power. He was allowed no kicks.

In Olympic-style Taekwondo, offensive hand techniques are limited to just straight punches that land on the torso. Unlike other martial arts styles, hand strikes to the face and head are not allowed. Also, round strikes (like a hook punch or uppercut), back fists, elbows, and knife-hand, palm or finger strikes are forbidden. In addition to those limitations, a punch powerful enough to register on an electronic chest guard scored only one point while kicks generally scored two, three, four and sometimes even five points depending on type, style of entry (spinning and/or jumping kicks are awarded more points) and location of the kicks (head shots scored higher). All told, punching was a very limited and not so popular technique in Olympic-style Taekwondo and was therefore rarely practiced.

Nevertheless, with just the undervalued middle punch in his arsenal, *Sabum* Dae Sung managed to drill me over and over again with impeccable timing and distance control. I was able to get more shots in than usual because my legs were longer than his arms, but he strategically attacked only my left collar bone and my leg bicep and kept out of range of my stronger right kicks. After just four rounds I was unable to use to my left arm to defend myself anymore, and the pain shooting from my left shoulder up through my neck and back into my shoulder blade made me fear having to explain another broken bone to my mom that night. My movements became slower and less confident as I tried to protect my left side from any further damage. But when exposing my right side, I stood and moved awkwardly to shield my fractured right wrist from any further damage.

By the middle of the fifth round, I was forced to retreat far out of kicking range to regather myself, but as I attempted to re-enter the kicking range with a feint, *Sabum* Dae Sung quickly lowered his stance and shot straight in with a lunging reverse punch to the center of my sternum. It felt like my heart and lungs exploded with the blow, and as I fought for my breath, I failed to notice his other hand shoot in at the same time to undo the first knot of my belt. He then pushed off before immediately shooting back in with another punch aimed at my left collar bone, which at this point felt like it was already broken. Still trying to recover my air, I recoiled and tried to retreat. Without actually landing the blow on my collar bone he instead reached down and undid the second knot on my belt and whisked it away from my waist.

Before I could register what happened, he halved the belt by holding both ends in his hand and snapped it at my butt. He then whipped it at the same spot again three times in rapid succession before I could retreat. Thoroughly flustered and embarrassed but determined to fight, I tried to counter his lashings with all varieties of kicks, but his longer weapon always found my backside first. A thick cotton/poly blend belt doesn't really hurt and I doubt he was all that good with weapons, but the laughter in his eyes brought out a viscous conceit in my resolve that I had not known existed.

I flew at him with a left side kick, which he easily evaded before snapping my belt into my butt again. I then lunged forward as if to grab at the retreating belt and forced him to stand flat-footed for an instant as he snapped the belt up and out of my reach. That diversion gave me enough time to press my attack with another penetrating left side kick. This time I aimed below his waist and missed behind his legs on purpose in order to jump into a right back kick that was also low and missed in front of his legs. With his lower body caught between my legs, I scissored hard and could feel his lower body fly out from under him as he landed violently on his back.

Ending up on my back as well, I quickly posted on my right arm, pivoted my top right leg on top of his body and dug that knee deep into his abdomen while spinning my way to his right side. With my right shin wedged into his ribcage I grabbed at the sleeve of his right arm, threw my left leg over his face and squeezed his trapped arm tight between my thighs. I fully intended to break his arm and had arched my hips upward to apply the extra leverage needed to snap his elbow joint when *Sabumnim*'s voice thundered into my consciousness.

"Idiots!" he roared. "Both of you! Enough! *Charyot! Kyuneyt!* Get changed and get out of my *dojang!*"

Barely able to contain the adrenaline that for a moment had sharpened all my instincts to a level I had never before experienced, I reluctantly released *Sabum* Dae Sung's arm and slowly untangled myself from the hold. We stood and then warily facing each other, slouched into half-hearted mutual bows and then turned to repeat the same toward *Sabumnim* before heading to the locker rooms.

Flying Tigers

My father called the girl into his office first so I pulled out my organic chemistry cards and studied while I waited. Fifteen minutes later the office door slid open. She quietly came out with her eyes cast downward and walked past me across the *dojang* without a word. In the waiting area she greeted a little kid with her teacher face and shook hands with a lawerly-looking parent before slipping on her snow boots and bowing her way out without even a look in my direction. That was rude.

I stuck my head into the office and saw my father staring back at me and motioning me toward the chair opposite his desk. He had pulled a bulky-looking sweater on over his thick canvas uniform, and I found myself suddenly and irrationally annoyed, thinking that he should just stop being a cheapskate and turn up the heat if he was cold. I walked in and sat.

"What did you think?" he asked as he casually propped his elbows on the desk and leaned towards me.

What do you mean, 'what do I think?' I tried hard to maintain my composure.

"That's not Taekwondo! Did you teach her that throw and the armbar? Is it the Flying Tiger stuff that you never showed us?" I couldn't help blurting out and thereby crossing a line with my surprisingly hurt-filled accusations.

My father had served in the Korean Army 3rd Special Forces Brigade and deployed to Vietnam for three years in support of the United States 101st Airborne Division.

Knowing this as boys, my brothers and I researched and read everything we could find about the Korean Special Forces divisions that fought alongside the Americans during that war. But even though the deployment was 50,000 strong at the height of the war, not much has been written about it in English. What we did find out was that the Flying Tigers unit specialized in Taekwondo, and the hand-picked warriors were often deployed behind enemy lines with no reinforcements and very light artillery and air support. Several of the books we found alluded to the unit's ferocity and gave estimates of their extremely high kill rate, but the details were scarce.

Not sure whether to be in awe of him or to fear him even more than we already did, we were always judicious in questioning him about details of the mysterious Taekwondo division. And it was only when he was drinking *soju* or celebrating a championship or relaxing during the holidays, did we ever press him for actual war stories and ask about the killings. Sometimes he would let little vignettes slip, but more often than not, he was quick to squelch our curiosity by threatening us with the brutal training methods that he had undergone to join the unit. Once he said, "You want to know about the Flying Tigers? Let's go march 20 miles into the mountains, then live no food, no water and no shelter for 10 days. Then you fight two-on-one, three-on-one, five-on-one with just Taekwondo against sticks, knives and other weapons until you can't fight anymore. If you finish in good enough shape, they send you to Vietnam." Convinced that he would really march us into the mountains right then and there and have us fight each other to the death, we immediately shut our mouths.

Today the old man just sighed and answered his own question. "Dumb girl. Stupid move. A scissor sweep and armbar is too dangerous. It would have been better to go level change, groin attack, ankle pick and then maybe knee bar against a bigger opponent."

Then as if losing his enthusiasm for our conversation, he reversed positions and slumped back indifferently into his chair. "Yes, I taught her some things. There is no one else to teach these days," he sniffed.

Ignoring the shock that must have shown on my face and speaking again before I could make any more childish protests, he continued, "She was finally smooth today. There wasn't any hesitation when she decided to fight. Instead, there was a synthesis of her instincts. Her movement and execution flowed from a source and an understanding that existed antecedent to the fight, before any external stimulus forced her into action. Not everything was perfect, of course, but finally she was able to let go of the narrowness in her mind and fight with her entirety." He smiled.

"But that isn't even the kind of Taekwondo she's training for," I insisted. "That's not Olympic Taekwondo! What good is that for?"

"First of all, you started the mess with that stupid belt thing," my father answered pointedly. "But that wasn't all bad. She has to learn that Taekwondo is a fighting art. And when you really train in the fighting arts, you have to confront the fact that it is a world full of bullies and inequities. And rules and referees are often luxuries that cannot be depended upon. Today you pushed her mind and her resolve as a fighter. My hope is that little steps like this will eventually expand her awareness beyond just scoring points in a sport for competition. There is so much more to Taekwondo than just that, as I think you know."

Then, getting up and starting a light stretch of his lower back and legs, he continued, "Ultimately, it is a mindset. A state of commitment in which you must be willing to sacrifice an arm, a leg, and maybe even your life in order to fight. When you can accept that, then you can begin to understand the fighting art. That is maybe your answer to the Flying Tigers. There are no special techniques, Dae Sung."

He moved onto a set of light leg raises and changed the subject, "Daria will drive you home tonight."

"What?! No, that's fine. I don't need a ride."

"It's starting to blizzard outside. You will freeze waiting for a bus that might not come."

I looked out the small office window and saw the white-out conditions of an oncoming Nor'easter and sighed, "She already left."

"No, she's waiting outside for you. Here. Take the lunch you didn't eat; have it for dinner tonight or breakfast tomorrow." He walked over to the coffee table and handed me the familiar Tupperware box.

"No thanks," I said, leaving it in his hand. "Why don't you eat it for dinner. You'll be here late tonight with classes."

"I'm having dinner with Master Pak," he said. "Don't waste the food I made for you."

I grudgingly took the Tupperware with both hands and stood to leave. "Don't drink too much with Master Pak and then drive in this weather."

"He'll call his wife or his daughter to pick us up," my father answered, waving me away as he turned his back and continued his pre-class warm up.

I bowed to the old man who was slowly exhaling into a deep horse stance as I let myself out of the office.

More *Kimbap*

He was right about the weather. And also true to his word, the girl was waiting curbside in front of the *dojang* in her little BMW. I knocked on the passenger-side window to give her a heads-up before opening the door and letting myself in along with a violent gust of snow and wind.

"Thanks for the ride," I mumbled as I buckled up and guiltily swiped a little snow from my jacket onto the floor mat.

"Thanks for coming in every day to work with me," she answered rather bashfully.

That surprised me. I had expected her to be more belligerent about my bullying or still chafing against all the little indignities I had made her suffer. At the very least, I imagined her querulous about having to chauffeur her tormentor home in rush hour traffic on a Friday evening. Instead, I was confounded by the shy little morsel of gratitude she proffered.

"Um," I hesitated, trying to moderate my own residual annoyance in response to her graciousness. "No problem."

"How's your collarbone?" I asked, feeling more secure in the role of doctor. "Can you move your elbow above your shoulder?"

She chicken-winged her left elbow skyward into the seat belt. Paying close attention to the noticeable wince on her face I asked, "How is the pain on a scale of 1 to 10?"

"About a three," she replied and gave her left shoulder a few rotations forward and back. "It's not too bad. I'm okay."

"Good, good," I said, relieved, as I offered my diagnosis. "With that kind of mobility your collarbone is probably okay."

We then drove in silence, which didn't feel that awkward considering the severity of the snow storm the little car was trying to power through. As we neared the George Washington Bridge toll booths, the traffic started grinding to a halt and the BMW sat with hundreds of other cars in a sea of red tail lights trying to funnel their way into the city and beyond.

"Here's money for the toll," I said, reaching into my wallet for a twenty.

"That's okay," she said. "I have an E-Z Pass. There's a discount."

I pressed the twenty-dollar bill toward her again, and she refused, "No thanks."

Returning the bill to the wallet in my pocket, I fingered my flash cards for a second and considered pulling them out in order to survive the silence.

"I don't mind if you study," she said. "Or nap. Either is fine."

Disliking, but not entirely fighting my recent contrarian disposition, I attempted to make small talk instead. "Nice scissor sweep and arm bar transition," I said. "Did my father teach you that?"

"Yes, but apparently I did it all wrong," she sighed. "He said because you're so much taller and bigger I should have leveraged lower and then transitioned to a groin strike or a leg lock. Traveling so far up for an arm bar was stupid and gave you too many chances to escape or sit up and trap me in your guard."

"Did you ask to learn all this *jiujitsu* stuff?" I baited. "How did you even know he could teach that too?"

"Actually, I just wanted to learn how to do a sweep," she answered. "You know, the one that looks like a spin hook kick on the ground. I wanted to work on a board-breaking demonstration of a jump spin hook kick, regular spin hook kick

74

and then finishing with that sweep. I saw it on YouTube and asked *Sabumnim* to teach it to me."

She stopped and looked over to see if I was truly interested in her answer before continuing, "After teaching me the spin hook kick sweep, *Sabumnim* asked what I was going to do to an opponent once I swept him off his feet. I told him nothing because that technique was only for demonstration and can't be used in competitions. He then smacked me on the head and told me I had no idea what Taekwondo is. And then a split second later, he dropped down and swept me hard. After I hit the ground, he held me down and showed me a bunch of things you can do to someone on their back. I think he started with an arc-hand to my throat, then a palm strike into the sternum right below the heart and then the straight arm bar. I didn't even know techniques like that were a part of Taekwondo!"

"No face strikes?" I asked, testing her even though I knew my father's philosophies on attacking.

"I asked him that, but he said without a weapon in your hand you risk cutting yourself on someone's teeth or breaking your hand on their skull. Plus, the face bleeds a lot and there's a lot of other bodily fluids that might give you an infection if you're unlucky. He said the throat was the safest deadly strike if you have your opponent pinned to the ground, and the sternum and heart strikes work if you're accurate and strong enough. And, of course, the joint locks can immobilize your opponent if you're looking to not cause too much damage."

Those were the old man's thoughts exactly. I then pressed, "Did you ask to learn weapons too?"

"Um, yeah, how did you know?" she mused. "But *Sabumnim* said anything can be used as a weapon if I kept my mind open enough to the objects around me. Instead, he said it was more important to learn empty-hand techniques like sweeps and locks and vital point attacks. He also showed me a bunch of chokes... and even how to twist someone's neck... you know... like to... kill them," she rambled with her voice trailing off, as if she was suddenly unsure how much she should reveal to me.

I paused, "You do know where he learned all that, right?"

"Umm, I don't know. His teacher? Some grandmaster in Korea?" she quietly guessed.

"He never told you that he was in the Flying Tigers?" I awkwardly turned in the bucket seat to semi-face her in order to see her reaction.

No reaction. "Is that a demo group in Korea?" she asked, slightly confused. "The guys who jump and break 10 balloons while flying through the air? I've always wondered whether they have pins stuck between their toes." She then looked at me staring at her.

"No. It's a special forces division in the Korean army that deployed a bunch of Taekwondo experts to fight the Vietcong during the Vietnam war," I corrected. Ah ha, now she looked appropriately stunned and maybe a little frightened. "Google it." I said triumphantly as I turned back in my seat.

"Oh my God," she whispered. "How old is he? When was Vietnam? 1960s?"

"The Flying Tigers were sent in 1968."

"That makes so much sense," she thought out loud. "All the times he talked about fighting and the test of character required in a fight and being willing to give your life to the fight... and dying... and killing." Again, her voice trailed off, as if unsure whether to acknowledge what she might have already implicitly known.

We continued to inch across the bridge.

"You're pretty violent too if all this stuff excites you," I said, not knowing exactly why I continued along this vein.

She seemed nonplussed but lamely joked, "Not any more violent than someone performing open-heart surgery or hunting or doing mergers and acquisitions."

She then paused and weighed the truth in my assumption with what she knew about herself and was willing to acknowledge before saying, "But, you might be right though.

76

There is something about it that fits my personality. I like the violence and the fight. I always felt like I could understand myself better in a physical battle... like everything was sharper and the universe made more sense... like I fit."

"Mergers and acquisitions?"

"Oh, yeah, that's my dad. It's a joke. The way he describes conquering and taking over companies sounds like a war too. And it seems like you need a different kind of aggressive personality and capacity to inflict damage to love doing that kind of thing."

"Right here, take the 178th Street exit and turn down Broadway," I said just in time as the traffic started to flow faster coming off of the bridge. "You can drop me off at that first corner so it's easier for you to get back onto the bridge. Just turn right, circle back around the block and follow the signs."

"*Sabumnim* told me to take you home, not just deliver you into the city," she said adamantly.

"There's a Nor'easter out there," she said, echoing my father.

Half-relived at her insistence, I relented and gave her direction to my apartment. The snow plows had not yet reached this part of Manhattan, so the little car valiantly spun its wheels and tried to gain enough traction. We reverted back to silence as the BMW slipped and crawled its way over a thick crust of matted, sugary snow and ice before reaching my building.

"Thanks again," I said as she double-parked out front.

"Here," I added, reaching into my gym bag and handing her the Tupperware containing the uneaten *kimbap* lunch. "Eat it for dinner, and don't waste the food. You can wash and return the Tupperware to the Flying Tiger grandmaster tomorrow or Monday." I stepped out of the car and smiled into the blizzard, feeling lighter than before.

Snow Day

Sabumnim called at 6am the next morning to tell me that the blizzard had caused a countywide blackout with downed utility poles, felled trees and cut power lines all over northern New Jersey. He also asked if my family was safe and whether his son got home last night. I told him that I drove *Sabum* Dae Sung to his doorstep, and that everyone in my family was okay. He then explained that he had already canceled classes and the *dojang* will be closed until power was restored. He ended the short conversation by telling me not to be lazy while the *dojang* was closed.

Freed from my regular Saturday obligations and curious about the enormity of the blizzard, I layered some sweats over my fleecy pajamas, grabbed a jacket and slipped on snow boots before pushing through almost a foot of snow to arc open the French doors leading to the backyard. I always loved snowy days, and I headed across the backyard toward the tree line at the far edge of the property just so I could savor the crunchy stomping steps I made through the blanket of wet sugary whiteness. Looking back at the house, I saw a tiny version of my mom wrapped tight in a terry-cloth robe and waving at me from the master bedroom balcony. I gave a little wave back and forged another virgin trail through the snow as I headed back toward the house.

At the back door I keyed in the security code and let myself into the kitchen-side mud room. My parents were still upstairs, so I padded into my dad's coffee nook. I pulled one of his medium four-cup Chemexes off the shelf and examined the beans my dad had stocked and displayed in a row of 12 stainless-steel vacuum-sealed containers. I skipped over the Ethiopian Geshas because I knew he was always scouring the City and the Internet for that variety and would want the pleasure of brewing and experimenting with that bean himself. Instead, I chose a more common Brazilian single origin from a cooperative he subscribed to, knowing that he could always easily restock this bean.

I filled his new matte black Scandinavian electronic water kettle and waved my finger over the sensor. A pale blue light came on, and the button-less panel indicted that the water was starting to warm to 95 degrees Celsius. I then reached up and pulled out a decidedly low-tech coffee grinder from one of the cabinets. In addition to collecting beans and various brewing methods, my dad also collected manual coffee grinders. He insisted on hand grinding all his beans and experimented with grinders from all over the coffee-drinking world. Most times, he thought a region's beans worked best with indigenous grinders and brewing methods, but he also has a serious affinity for Japanese grinders and brewing equipment, despite the fact that that country produced no beans.

The grinder I pulled out was Japanese. It was my favorite because it was crafted from a beautiful combination of warm dark wood and cold matte metal. With a large dark metal bowl sitting atop a hand-carved wooden box and a handle in the middle of the bowl controlling the ceramic burr grinder within, the contraption looked more like an antique Victrola than a kitchen appliance. Besides the beauty of the simple mechanical grinder, I also loved watching the beans disappear in a slow, bumpy whirlpool from the bowl as I turned the handle, only to reappear as grounds when I slid open the wooden drawer.

After finishing the grind, I set a cloth filter over the Chemex and started the slow pour-over coffee-making process. I first wet the filter with a 100-milliliter pour and then swirled the hot water around to warm the walls of the Chemex. After discarding that initial pour, I emptied the fresh grounds into the filter and performed a slow circular 45-second pour to wet and bloom the coffee. Then I let the dampened grounds breathe and rest for 30 seconds before I started another in a series of five more slow circular pours. About four minutes later, the entire kitchen smelled of chocolate, almonds and tropical flowers. My dad had come into the coffee nook and quietly watched the last pour before gathering and setting three demitasses in front of me. Once I finished the pour, he greeted me with a kiss on the head and a 'that's my girl' under his breath.

He was a stickler for four-ounce cups of coffee, so we always ended up consuming at least three to four of these tiny cups over a meal. I decanted the first cup for him from the Chemex and waited.

He tasted and let his senses deliberate before saying, "Perfect temperature, good timing on the pour and beautiful expression of the bean. But why did you use something so ordinary on such a beautiful snow day? Didn't you see the new ones I just got?"

"Those are your treasures, Dad," I said. "I wanted to save the fun of those for you."

"Everything of mine is also yours," he answered while carrying his coffee into the kitchen, toward the refrigerator. "Are you staying for breakfast? Your mother tricked me into making her pancakes and eggs, and I can probably manage something for you too if you promise to do the dishes."

"Yeah, the power is out all over the county so the *dojang* is closed today," I answered. "Are you making cinnamon and pumpkin pancakes?"

"Halloween is over, D," he said while depositing an armful of eggs, butter, milk, sugar, and flour onto the prep counter. "But I can make out-of-season pancakes just for you if I can find some pumpkin."

He disappeared into the pantry and re-emerged triumphant with an orange-colored can held high in one hand and a fistful of spice bottles and vanilla in the other.

"Go take a cup of coffee up to your mom. I also promised her coffee."

After a long and languid breakfast of cinnamon and pumpkin pancakes covered with stewed maple, cinnamon apples and a buttery French omelet on the side, and after my dad brewed two more rounds of coffee with his prized Gesha beans (one of which magically tasted like a field of sun-ripened strawberries), I started on the dishes.

"Wow, honey, thanks!" my mom said.

"Dad negotiated this into the pancake making," I confessed, and she turned her thanks toward my dad by running her hand through the back of his hair and letting it land lightly across his shoulder.

"How long do you think the generators will be able to run for?" my mom asked, sitting back down and pouring herself another coffee.

"The main generator runs on natural gas and that supply seems to be okay. The back-up generator is on propane and we have enough in the tank for three-ish days," my dad answered. "I'll call Mike and ask about adding to or changing the cooling oil though."

"Hmmm, what about all this snow?" my mom continued.

"We can call the kid who usually clears it," my dad patiently replied while passing the rest of the breakfast dishes to me. "But I'm guessing he probably has his hands full today. Do you need to go somewhere? Just take my car, it'll crush through enough snow to get you out."

My dad then briefly reached across me and ran his hands under the water before wiping them dry on the kitchen towel folded over my shoulder. He took his coffee and the half-full Chemex and headed toward his home office with my mom trailing after him and asking about whether they should stop the charge on the Tesla to save power and other such things.

They will probably spend the rest of the morning in the study. My dad will be working from his desk, sometimes silently on his laptop and sometimes loudly over the phone. And my mom will probably be draped over the chaise across from his desk, alternating between cat-napping and reading from their collective library.

I finished tidying up the kitchen and headed back to my basement apartment. I was not really in the mood for a workout, but I forced myself to change into the hated sauna suit and a ratty set of sweats. Resisting the temptation to play music or turn on the television for background noise, I started a light warm-up by shuffling in and out around the heavy bag that always hung from the corner of the basement. I knew that if I touched the television remote or flipped open my laptop, I would fall down a rabbit hole of playlist selection or channel surfing and probably not emerge for hours. That is the problem with working out in a warm, comfortable and homey environment. I had succumbed so many times to hours wasted 'preparing' for what eventually amounted to a half-hearted, distracted workout that I now knew that only a silent workout could prevent procrastination and eliminate excuses.

My body ached from *Sabum* Dae Sung's beatings and the unfamiliar hill workouts of the past week, so I purposefully moved slow and kept my mind empty. As I started to sweat a little with the circling and the footwork, I added some light punches and then kicks to the bag. Unfortunately, when I was not motivated to practice, not only would my mind be empty, but it would also be bored and wandering. It was then just a matter of time before I took a break on the couch or headed to the refrigerator for a snack or outdoors for a breath of fresh air. Understanding my weaknesses and all the temptations that surrounded me in the basement *dojang*, I knew that the only way I could solidify my resolve and create the right mindset for a worthwhile workout was to give myself an almost impossible assignment. Sometimes I would set a target of 1,000 back kicks on the heavy bag or 100 sets of 25 fast round kicks interspersed with burpees in between rounds. It was only with such a concrete goal to aim for that I would be able to motivate myself, crank my obstinacy into overdrive and put my head down to do the work of Sisyphus.

Today I decided to focus on speed and power because *Sabum* Dae Sung had said both were so lacking. Positioning a 24-inch-high wooden plyometric box 25 feet away from the heavy bag, I would kneel behind the box, spring from there into a squat position, jump onto the box and then step forward off the box into a depth drop straight into a tuck jump before galloping two steps toward the heavy bag for a skipping side kick. My goal was to hit the bag so hard that it swings horizontal at its highest point. *Sabumnim* showed me this exercise last year and told me that plyometric work was essential for developing speed and power. In fact, he said the best Taekwondo athletes were built like racehorses with skinny ankles and legs but explosively muscular thighs and butts. My goal was 100 kicks on each side, which doesn't sound like much until you add in all the jumps.

An hour later, I took a short break to mop my sweat off the floor and to change into a new sweatshirt. Not even stopping for water, I pressed on with hand techniques, another weakness of mine. With an injured wrist and a bruised collarbone, I decided against using the heavy bag and aimed instead for circling and punching the air with a simple jab-cross combination. I aimed for 500 clockwise and 500 counter-clockwise circles, each time keeping my hands chin-high and trying to punch fast enough so my knuckles were a blur. Halfway through, my arms felt like lead and my legs lost their bounce. A few hundred circles after that my punches were barely recognizable as such and the circles had shrunk because my feet now dragged across the mat. I finished the punching sets on fumes and in slow motion, relying solely on my obsessive nature to push me toward reaching a random, predetermined number.

It was almost one o'clock before I gave myself a water break and started a warm-down. For that, I stood on the plyometric box and took the heavy bag down from its hook. With the heavy bag lying on the ground, I practiced spinning from side to side with one knee anchored in the bag's midsection for the swivel. From there I would transition to an imaginary arm-bar by wedging a shin into the bag's 'ribcage', crossing my opposite leg over the bag's 'head' area and leaning back with a fake arm for the submission. For most of the reps I was mentally recreating the arm bar that I almost successfully put on *Sabum* Dae Sung yesterday. The memory of feeling the technique flow and hit for the first time easily powered me through the set of two hundred. Finally, I finished the workout with a half hour of core work and then a half hour of hydrating and stretching, all daily mandates from *Sabumnim* to injury-proof my muscles, joints and lower back as much as possible.

Afterwards, while still in my sauna suit and pouring sweat from the workout, I stood in the kitchenette and bolted down a peanut butter jelly sandwich with a side of *kimchi* and a carton of blueberries before chasing everything with a 16-ounce mug of coffee made with Dunkin' Donuts grounds in my Mr. Coffee brewer. I then headed for the shower and a glorious weekend nap.

Bitter and Sweet

I only had two weeks remaining on my promise. And even though working out and sparring with the girl turned out to be not so bad, I found myself increasingly irritable and annoyed at having to play the role of the good son and obedient student in the house built by the imperious grandmaster. For no reason at all or for reasons that can only be ascribed to self-preservation (or selfishness, depending on your point of view), I could not wait to escape from him and his Taekwondo universe. The Taekwondo brought me no joy. And the worn-out, provincial shopping center *dojang* setting of my misery only haunted me with memories of the smaller and drearier life that I had once known.

I watched as the girl methodically ran the industrial vacuum cleaner up and down the mats, and I wanted desperately to shout my hard-earned wisdom to her over the noise. "Olympic dreams are a colossal waste of time! The path of pain and more pain is not worth those few minutes in the ring. And it's definitely not worth the impermanence of a chunk of metal on a ribbon or the vanity of the record books.... let alone the agony of obscurity if you fail!"

Tormenting myself further with the fury that was building in my chest, I telepathically continued my lecture in her direction, "And what are you to the *dojang* and to the *Sabumnim* once you become a loser? No doubt about it, everyone will lose eventually and sometimes lose spectacularly. But to lose and then to come back here where the shame will be on display every day in the eyes of the students and be reflected in the pain that you will have etched on the old man's soul… can you handle that?"

Then more practically, as if I had reached the bargaining stage of acceptance, I continued my internal reproach, "You better be diversified. Olympic dreams are like putting all your money in a start-up company. Everyone dreams of finding Google, but most of them end up going to zero. Better have a Plan B, because living life like a has-been is brutal."

The vacuum cleaner suddenly switched off as she overextended the cord and accidentally dislodged the plug from the outlet. The silence short-circuited my thoughts. "Could you please, Sir?" she enquired sweetly from across the room. I obligingly plugged the cord back in and then took out my organic chemistry flash cards to ambush my brain before it could launch another psych offensive.

An hour later the *dojang* smelled like Windex and the girl had changed into a *dobok* and was practicing her patterns when my father walked through the front door and furiously demanded, "What are you two doing here?" We turned and bowed toward him, she in deference and me with barely-concealed irritation.

"What do you mean?" I asked. "If I'm not supposed to be here, I'll go back to New York."

"No, why aren't you on the hill?!" he yelled, not used to his assignments being ignored.

"After all that snow, it's probably still unplowed and iced over," I answered. "I thought it would be safer to skip the morning workout." The girl stood silent, but looked away from us.

"Then… go… de-ice… it!" he commanded. "Take a shovel and a bag of salt and go de-ice it. Then do your work on the hill!"

"Cars aren't even allowed onto that campus right now because school's out," I protested while simultaneously getting a sick feeling over where this conversation was headed.

"Run it over!" he steamed while heading into his office and sliding the door shut.

"Shit…" the girl murmured before heading to the locker room, not doubt to change into her running gear.

I wanted to continue venting by shouting something incendiary at the old man hiding behind his office door, but seeing the girl's instant compliance I instead moped over to the storage room and resignedly dragged out two snow shovels and a bag of rock salt. Thank goodness the bags I found were 25-pounders and not double that. I lugged everything to the front entryway where the girl was already waiting, and we laced our shoes in an uncomfortable silence. I mumbled that I would carry the salt first, but that it was only fair to trade halfway through. She silently indicated her agreement and we headed out.

There is nothing like slowly shuffle-jogging along the dirty snowbanks of a sidewalk-less New Jersey country road with a concrete-hard 25-pound bag of rock salt digging into your shoulder on your way to shovel and clear someone else's hill so you can kill yourself with hill repeats to make you fully appreciate the absurdities of being born into my father's world. I knew I was cursed, but the question was why was this girl here? I asked her as much at about the one-mile mark when we stopped to swap our burdens.

"At first, I was just too afraid of *Sabumnim* to say no to anything," she said, a little out of breath and happy to be taking a break on the side of the road. "But then I guess I went through a teenage questioning and super-cynical stage and started rebelling against all the training I thought was nonsense… like stuff like this. But that was when he sat me down and started explaining to me that he was just throwing up mental roadblocks to teach me about the nature of obstacles. He said everything we encounter are illusions, and it's only our minds that color the experience as oppressive or unfair or bitter or worse. I'm supposed to try and learn how to break free of those negative emotions and use my mind to create positive solutions."

"And he wasn't pissed that you challenged him?"

"He said it was important that I dared to challenge him… because he is also an illusion. That part I haven't figured out."

She then paused before quietly continuing, "If you don't want to play along, I don't think he'd force you. But if you do play along, you just have to see the kindness in him in order not to flip out at some of the insanity."

"You're a weirdo," I lamely countered before shouldering the shovels and restarting the trek without bothering to look back to see how she managed with the rock salt. "The kindness in him…," I half-grumbled and half-contemplated under my frosty breath.

When we left the *dojang* I had decided to make her clear the hill and do the sprints all by herself, but thinking over her little comment during that last mile changed my mind. When we arrived at the snow-frosted area behind the athletic center I pitched in as we got to work on the six or so inches of snow and ice that remained on the hill. Shoveling and salting in chain gang silence, I contemplated her lack of bitterness and complete acceptance of my father as an all-knowing and ultimately benevolent teacher. What a strange girl.

When we had cleared enough room for two lanes up the hill, I pulled out my cell phone to double check the assignment my father emailed me last night. Shit, I thought. I forgot to bring weight vests from the *dojang*. I told her that the sprints and the lunges and the bounding skips she was supposed to do today required weight vests. Instead of celebrating my oversight, she asked me how heavy, and I showed her the email that said 20 pounds.

"Too bad we just used most of the rock salt on the hill," she said, genuinely disappointed.

Wow… you are a crazy little lady!

"How about taking a shovel across our shoulders?" she suggested. "It's real metal and wood and probably close to 10 pounds each."

Maybe there is no bitterness toward my father for his cruelties because she was just as looney and masochistic as the old man! I was tempted to ask her what she meant by 'our shoulders' and then just ordering her up the hill alone with both shovels for her insubordination… but I didn't. Instead, I took one for myself, toed the starting line and waited for her to do the same before calling the first race.

An hour and a half later, the girl looked like a mangled alley kitten with scraped up palms, a bruised cheek and torn up knees after a series of falls and slips on the still-icy hill. Her arms shook on the tree hangs and wobbled precariously every time she unevenly pressed the shovel up over her head and onto her shoulders. She lost every race, but never stopped. On the tree hangs, she even attempted to show off her much improved but still terrible toes-to-branch move. I golf clapped at her mockingly in my mind.

After she finished the last tree hang, she stumbled over to the empty parking lot rimmed with freshly-piled snow banks and tossed herself on top of a crusty hill of still-newish snow. I anticipated a childish snow angel or maybe the start of a snowball fight, but instead, she remained deathly still, somehow ethereal, enshrouded in white and with her eyes closed. After a half minute, I walked over to check on her. As I neared with wet, crunching steps she suddenly opened her eyes skyward and smiled.

"What are you doing?" I asked.

"Giving myself a reward," she answered. She remained so still that I found myself wondering if she even moved her lips, or was that just her mind replying.

I stared up into the cloudy but UV-light drenched sky and felt a similar urge to lie down. Climbing up into the neighboring snow bank, I let my body sink into the days-old but still-untouched snow and gifted myself with a minute-long pause. In my snow mausoleum it was quiet, and I rested.

When I opened my eyes and broke free from the snow walls around me, she was standing nearby to hand me a shovel, and together we started the slow, stiff jog back to the shopping center *dojang*.

Choked Out and Up

This week passed in much the same way as the last two. Conditioning work on the hill, lots of agility and footwork drills, a little plyometric work and lots of sparring. There were only two little incidents the whole week and neither really involved me.

The first started with a mistakenly low back kick that caught *Sabum* Dae Sung half in the balls and half in his groin. I knew something was wrong the second my foot dug into the unfamiliar target, and I was horrified when he groaned and dropped to his knees. Apologizing profusely, I was instantly by his side and starting to crouch over him to offer him assistance. What I didn't expect was for *Sabum* Dae Sung to wait until I fully dropped my center of balance before shooting his hand out behind my planted foot and cupping the ankle and heel to scoop my leg out from under me.

The startling fall onto my back knocked the wind out of me, and he immediately repositioned himself on my right side for an arm bar. In a matter of seconds, he had my upper body trapped and my right arm isolated. But instead of applying the arm bar, he somehow transitioned his legs to encircle both my neck and my arm and started to slowly squeeze. My head felt like it was about to explode between his vice-like legs, and I started to struggle by hammering indiscriminately at whatever I could reach with my left hand while desperately bucking my lower half like a dying fish trying to escape.

As I frantically fought against the armbar and the choke, I saw *Sabumnim* calmly hovering over us at various angles just inside the periphery of my quickly narrowing vision. He seemed not to notice me at all as he finally leaned over and guided *Sabum* Dae Sung's hand to the side of my head. Together they made a little motion and my world went dark.

When I came to, I found myself in a little heap on the mat, slightly confused and awfully tired. Both *Sabumnim* and *Sabum* Dae Sung peered over me and asked if I was okay. I slowly sat up and nodded a tentative yes as I reached up to fix my disheveled hair. They left me alone as *Sabumnim* laid down and had *Sabum* Dae Sung practice that same chokehold on him. *Sabumnim* issued short staccato corrections in Korean as *Sabum* Dae Sung shifted his crossed legs to find the precise position for the triangle choke. Then *Sabumnim* showed him how to tilt his victim's head toward himself to further expose the carotid artery and finish the choke. After another animated stream of explanations in Korean, *Sabumnim* motioned for him to practice on me. I was instructed to lay down and sacrifice my arm as *Sabum* Dae Sung transitioned over and over again from the armbar to the triangle choke until he could instantly find the sweet spot and apply the choke without giving me any chance to attempt a defense. Another one-sided dialogue in Korean and they both nodded and stood. I followed their example and we bowed to finish the session. Before stepping back into his office *Sabumnim* turned to me and said, "Better study more Korean."

The second little incident involved lunch. By this point I had become a repository for all of *Sabum* Dae Sung's unwanted *kimbap* lunches. Of course, the easiest solution to not wasting food might have been to stop making two lunches, but it seemed to me that *Sabumnim* persisted out of sentiment and maybe a little bit of longing.

Another Nor'easter swept through the region that Friday, adding to the towering snowbanks and the winter misery that had not yet dissipated from the previous storm. Not unexpectedly, zero students showed up for the noontime class and with the forecast calling for worsening conditions in the afternoon *Sabumnim* decided to cancel the remaining classes for the day, leaving the three of us unaccustomedly idle.

Most likely feeling unsettled about the weather and chafing at the prospect of another long, dreary afternoon as my sparring partner, *Sabum* Dae Sung announced in a loud voice to me across the room and to his father in his office that he was done for the day and heading home. I was secretly relieved and started toward the locker room when *Sabumnim* came out of his office to declare that we were all eating lunch together first before I drove his son home. I had no objections to that plan and redirected myself toward the office, but *Sabum* Dae Sung reached *Sabumnim* first and speaking in Korean, started to protest about something in a restrained but obstinately headstrong manner.

Seething in a deliberately low and calm voice that was probably meant to maintain a modicum of propriety (possibly because an outsider like me was already a part of the crossfire), *Sabum* Dae Sung gutturally voiced his displeasures while intentionally towering over *Sabumnim* with his fists clenched and an apoplectic look in his eyes that threatened violence and fury. I hurriedly turned away and pretended to head elsewhere, away from the conflict, but *Sabumnim* merely retreated into his office and declared that one of us should make the tea.

I looked at *Sabum* Dae Sung, who continued to emanate loathing and open resentment as he glowered into the office at *Sabumnim's* receding form. As I tried to edge past him to make the tea, he viscously barked, "Don't be his pawn!" before turning and storming toward the locker room.

Unsure what to do, I froze.

From within his office *Sabumnim* sighed and said, "Just make two cups of tea."

With the tea brewed, we sat as usual at the low table. Staring straight forward into our Tupperware containers, we mechanically chewed and swallowed in silence, deliberately ignoring the crashing of the front sliding door as *Sabum* Dae Sung stormed out of the *dojang*. After lunch, I washed the dishes and was replacing the teapot and the mugs to the side table when *Sabumnim* said, "Please go drive my son home."

I looked over at *Sabumnim*, who had remained seated at the low table, and answered, "Yes, Sir."

I didn't need any further explanation but he continued quietly in a confessional tone, "He won't take a ride from me, so you have to go. It's too cold to be waiting for a bus today."

I bowed toward him on my way out and asked if he will be okay getting home in this weather. "Just make sure Dae Sung gets back safe," he answered while staring at his hands on the table. "Thank you for being such a good kid."

I Googled the nearest New Jersey Transit bus stop, which turned out to be seven blocks from the *dojang*, and drove there slowly, scanning the streets for a tall Korean guy in case he was still en route. I found him hatless and head down, sitting on a metal bench at the uncovered bus stop with 30 miles per hour winds whipping up ice and snow around him. I pulled up and instead of rolling down the passenger side window or honking, I engaged the parking brake and got out of the car. He kept his head down and his body hunched over as I neared, which made me hesitate and shout, "Don't ankle pick me... Sir." It was 90 percent a joke and 10 percent precautionary.

I crouched next to his folded form and looked into his frozen, distraught face and told him *Sabumnim* sent me to take him home. Without a word, he reached out to take my elbow and together we stood and walked toward the car.

Pneumonia

arly Monday morning my father emailed to say that he caught a little cold over the weekend and was not feeling well. He sent detailed instructions for the girl's training and cautioned me against overworking her since she would be teaching a lot of classes in his absence and competing in a local tournament on Sunday. All weekend long I had considered skipping this last week of practice, but seeing as the old man was taking at least Monday off I reconsidered and took the bus in.

As usual, the girl was cleaning when I arrived. She quickly switched off the vacuum and bowed to me in greeting as I was letting myself into the *dojang*.

"Did you hear that *Sabumnim* is sick?" she asked. "He sounded okay over the phone, but I'll check in again with him later."

"Hmmm…. Let's skip the morning run then. You can work out on your own. I'll be in the office."

I didn't give her a chance to answer before heading into my father's office and sliding the door closed. I dropped my gym bag at the entrance and then settled into the well-worn faux-leather chair behind his desk. The place smelled faintly of barley tea and laundry detergent. I scanned the office and saw six white canvas *doboks* on sturdy wooden hangers suspended from an industrial metal towel bar that my father installed for the sole purpose of drying his laundry.

There was a small washing machine in the storage room because my father insisted on neatness and cleanliness. I am sure the girl used it most of the time to launder all the cleaning rags. But twice a week, always on Wednesdays and Saturdays, my father would wash his own *doboks*. Afterwards, he would hang them to dry about 90% on that rack before fastidiously ironing them and folding them back into his closet. Looking over at the slightly wrinkled white soldiers, each hanging at exactly the same angle away from the wall, I idly wondered how tired or sick he must have been on Saturday to have skipped the last step of such a long-standing ritual. But just as quickly, I reconsidered and thought that maybe he should just save himself the trouble and drop his uniforms off at Mrs. Kim's a few doors down. Bulk laundry was cheap, and Mrs. Kim liked him so much that she would probably even offer to do it for free.

Distracted and amused at the thought of the colorfully-aged and meddlesome Mrs. Kim with my Spartan father as a couple, I roused myself to my feet and ambled over to the side table to brew some tea. Really in need of coffee, but willing to settle for tea in this perpetually chilly office, I made myself a pot and brought it over to the desk along with my most current set of flash cards.

In addition to the coursework that will start up again next week, second-year medical students had to pass the Boards in the spring. The Boards were not only a crucial first step in eventually obtaining a medical license, but they were also the most important factor in matching medical students with a top residency and specialty program upon graduation. Because our professional futures relied so much on this one series of tests, most second-year medical students studied as if their lives depended upon it. My weakness was organic chemistry, so those flash cards followed me everywhere. I cleared a space on my father's desk, pulled out some blank paper from his printer drawer, uncapped his heavy fountain pen and started to work. As I concentrated, the noise of the vacuum cleaner eventually gave way to silence, and hours later the shouts and *kiaps* of the noon class gave way to a small knock on the office door.

"I'm going home for a quick lunch," said she with her coat on and keys in hand. "Do you want anything?"

"What's for lunch?"

"Leftover pot roast, rice and some salad."

"Do you have enough for two?"

"Yeah, my mom made a lot of food yesterday. I'll bring you some…. Hmmm…. Do you want *kimchi* too?"

"You have? What kind?"

"Something from HMart."

"Like from a big plastic bag with a red label?"

"More like from a glass jar with a white lid."

"Hmmm…. I guess I'll try some. Thanks."

"I'll be back in forty-five to an hour."

"Okay."

Ten minutes after she left, I got up to use the restroom. My father must have successfully passed his penny-pinching ways on to her I thought as I squinted and moved through the dark and slightly chilly *dojang*. On my way back to the office I detoured across the matted area to check and see if she locked the front door. Yup. Back on the mat and just for fun, I did a few forward rolls and breakfalls toward the office. Liking how my body felt, I went back the other way with another set. Then I added in some other *jujitsu* warmups. I shrimped on my back toward the front of the *dojang* and then made a return trip the other way with a reverse shrimping move.

Now really enjoying my body's freedom from the stillness of studying I did a set of 20 clapping pushups, 20 Hindu pushups, 20 diamond pushups, 20 fingertip pushups and 20 regular pushups. I then turned over and did a set of 100 V-ups and 100 tuck-ups. Again, another bunch of random rolls and some breakfalls. Then, really feeling my oats, I kicked up to a handstand and tried to walk across the mat on my hands like I used to do when I was a kid in this *dojang*. After falling a few times, I gave up and settled for another set of pushups and some ab work.

After 15 minutes my body was feeling loose and limber and for some reason, I felt the urge to try *Moon Moo*, the master-level pattern I saw the girl do. Since it had been almost 10 years since I learned the pattern, I first jogged to the office and took out my phone to consult a YouTube video. Then I stepped back onto the mat, faced the front of the *dojang* and started to walk through the steps. My movements were hesitant and often out of order or just plain wrong as I repeatedly checked my steps against the video I kept palmed in one hand. After a few repetitions though, all 61 moves came back to me and I tried to piece the entire pattern together.

The simple techniques flowed, but I couldn't find my balance and focus on the harder ones. Every few steps required a balance check and my feet shuffled inelegantly in transition. I pressed and tried it a few more times with equally fitful results. Looking up at the clock and knowing the girl would be back soon, I gave myself an ultimatum to perform the pattern perfectly on this one last try... but I still couldn't do it. The techniques were terrible and nothing flowed. I wanted to run through it again and again until I could recapture what I know the pattern should feel like, but instead I took my phone and retreated back into the office.

"Hi," she said popping her head in a few minutes later. "I couldn't keep it hot, but it's still pretty warm." She set a round Pyrex bowl of pot roast over rice on the desk alongside a boxy Tupperware that contained salad greens and a mound of *kimchi*.

"Wow, thanks."

"I also made some coffee, if you want. It's just pre-ground Dunkin' from the supermarket. Nothing fancy."

I drained the lukewarm tea from my mug and lifted it up for a pour. "Amazing, just what I needed."

"Bon appétit!" she said. "I'm going to stretch a little."

The food didn't come with any utensils, so I scoured my father's desk for his stash of chopsticks and found some in the bottom drawer. Pot roast is such an American family-style dish that I don't recall ever having it. Have I ever been invited over to a friend's home for a pot roast dinner? Not that I could remember. Is it usually eaten with rice? Potatoes? Bread? I had no idea. I pulled off the red Pyrex lid in anticipation.

Her mom's version turned out to be amazingly rich and flavorful and reminded me of my father's *galbijjim*, which is a moist, tender and unctuous version of Korean beef stew made by braising large sections of short ribs with vegetables. I mixed big bites of the melty, fatty pot roast with the *kimchi* and the rice and made a mental note to tell my father about this revelation. Left with just the undressed green salad at the end, I opened my chopsticks wide to grab as many of the bitter leaves as I could and stuffed them in my mouth all at once. I chewed and swallowed without inhaling in order to minimize the taste. Too bad the supermarket-quality black coffee brought out the bitterness of the greens anyway, but all in all the meal was pretty good.

I told the girl as much when I got up to wash the dishes.

She smiled as she gave half the credit to her mom and half the credit to the store-bought *kimchi*.

"Yeah, by the way, why did you randomly offer me *kimchi* with the pot roast?"

She looked a little embarrassed, but answered, "*Sabumnim* once said eating it makes you kick faster. And you told me that *kimchi* makes everything taste better."

"Well, it's true," I groused, as if she was wasting my time by stating the obvious. "Both are true," I laughed to myself and then immediately scowled in her direction in order to hide any hint of amusement.

Simultaneous Counterattacks

After lunch we sat cross-legged facing each other in the middle of the *dojang*. *Sabum* Dae Sung explained that *Sabumnim* wanted me to take it easy this week in order to be fresh for the first competition of the year on Sunday. He then sidetracked and added that back when he was competing, *Sabumnim* insisted on wearing him and his brothers out completely before these minor local competitions so they learned how to fight with tired legs and beaten-up and worn-out bodies. I looked straight at him as he shared his bitter memories and just let him talk. We then both endured a little bit of silence and eventually he let his mind slip away from his past to refocus on the present.

In a pretty pedantic tone, he started to lecture me about the importance of counter techniques. "There are three general levels of movement and execution in Taekwondo. First are the straight-forward, boldly aggressive movements we teach the lower belts. In fact, I can teach a big, strong, athletic white belt, say like a young football player, a few simple kicks and punches, and chances are he could win a lot of fights just by charging forward and relying on his natural abilities. If two fighters used this method exclusively, the bigger, stronger, faster, more athletic guy will almost always win.

"Second are evasive counters that require understanding just enough timing and distance control to make opponents miss before exploiting the holes in their techniques and their defense. The way to counter that big, strong, athletic white belt is to bait him into moving first and then changing the distance and angle between you and him to counter attack where and when he is most vulnerable and off-balanced. No matter how big and strong you are, every action exposes at least one weak spot, and this second set of movements focuses on exploiting those weaknesses.

"The third level of movement is the simultaneous counter. It is the most difficult to master because it requires almost a sixth sense in order to feel your opponent's intentions and launch the appropriate counterattack at almost the same instant as or even before he starts his offensive attack. You have to learn how to read your opponent's mind and how to hone your instincts to intuit his attacks. When you get in a zone with this level of movement, the entire game slows down and the targets come at you with such clarity that it feels almost impossible to miss. Unfortunately, this kind of grace is elusive and usually runs both ways between high level competitors."

He paused and then briefly slipped back into the past. "I know because that was how I got clocked at the Olympic Trials." Then looking at me suspiciously he asked, "Why are you smiling? Are you laughing at me?!"

"No, no, no," I insisted, a little embarrassed by how transparent my thoughts were. "I was just thinking that you sound exactly like *Sabumnim*. You know I get this same lecture from him at least once a week, right? It's almost verbatim." I let myself relax into a little smile as I teased him.

"Well, that's probably because you're not doing a good job of learning this lesson," he harrumphed. "Get off your lazy ass and let's start practicing!"

For the next two hours *Sabum* Dae Sung patiently held the pads and shields and attacked me slowly so I could understand the timing of the counters. We started with simple counters like the punch and the front kick, before moving onto the side kick and eventually the axe kick, back kick and spin hook kick. He then increased the speed of the attacks, and my anticipation and reaction times sharpened to the point where I could almost feel his attacking intentions. Then, during the last half hour he started to mix in feints and direction changes before the attacks and my rhythm and timing were so thrown off that I failed to connect on even one counter in fifty tries. It felt like I had regressed straight back to the beginning.

"That is the difference between a major league baseball player and someone who is merely good," he explained, adding to my confusion and growing frustration.

"Did my father use baseball analogies too?" he smirked while putting the equipment away.

"Uh, no," I said. "I don't get it."

"In baseball, it's not hard for a good player to hit a fastball that comes straight down the middle. You just have to go to the batting cages and practice first with slower pitches and just increase the speed a little bit at a time until you can time a fastball. The difference between a major leaguer and a really good player who never makes it is the ability to hit a change-up, which is an off-speed pitch that looks just like a fastball, and a breaking pitch like a curveball, which is an off-speed pitch that will also move and not travel in a straight line. So, unless you learn how to adapt to deceptions in rhythm, timing, angles and speed you will always strike out against high level competition.

"A player eventually learns how to adapt to those deceptions and to correctly intuit the pitch coming at him based on his opponent's tendencies, movements, the pitches he's already thrown and all the circumstances of where they are in the game. Then he has to make a split-second decision on how to react. That is like counterattacking in Taekwondo. Easier said than done though. Counterattacking is incredibly difficult, but crucial if you're going to play at an elite level.

"Of course," he continued. "Fighting is way more complicated than baseball because you get to play pitcher and batter at the same time. That's where the analogy falls apart. But that's also where this game becomes infinitely more elegant."

Sahum Dae Sung then looked straight at me and gave me his brutally honest assessment. "Realistically though right now you can only handle the first and second levels of

Taekwondo. If I can trick you fifty times in a row, your simultaneous counters won't hold up in real competition."

"How do I get better?"

He looked at me incredulously. "Practice. And then try it out against live bullets until you can get it to work."

"And what if I never learn how to hit a curveball?"

"Then no major leagues for you."

With that, he directed my attention to the first kids coming in for the afternoon classes and slipped away to the shower before I could turn back and begin to process what he just said. After his shower, *Sabum* Dae Sung retreated to the office instead of disappearing back to New York like usual and I spent the next few hours teaching four back-to-back classes in *Sabumnim's* absence.

A little after seven o'clock *Sabum* Dae Sung re-emerged and stood with his hands on his hips in a manner not unlike his father and surveyed the class. In keeping with protocol, I made the students pause their drills, pivot to attention and bow toward him. The students followed my instructions without knowing exactly who the tall young man in black skinny jeans was.

Sabum Dae Sung ignored the bows and did not introduce himself or interrupt the class beyond calling me over. "The class schedule says this is the Competition Class," he stated, apparently looking for confirmation as he surveyed the twelve older teens and young adults on the mat.

"Yes, sir," I answered.

"Good," he continued. "I want you to spar every one of them in turn and show me you can knock out every one with a simultaneous counter. Don't actually knock them out, you know. I think my father would say that's not good for business. But show me enough timing, technique and precision to convince me that if you went 100% the technique would knock them out. Two-minute rounds. You have twelve chances. You owe me one hundred pushups for each person you don't knock out. Have them all put on sparring gear."

"What?!" I thought. But I obeyed, stopping the drills and ordering everyone to put on their gear. Then I lined up the four most senior black belts on one side of the room, myself included, and called up the four lowest ranking students to stand in front of one black belt each. I assigned a student to monitor the clock and we started the first round.

I figured I might as well warm up with the green belts and blue belts. The first person I faced was a tall, awkward 17-year-old and I easily pegged him with a spin hook kick to the head as he came charging in. But because I held the kick and just tapped his temple, he remained undeterred and charged over and over again during the round. Finally understanding what *Sabum* Dae Sung wanted me to practice, I worked on an assortment of simultaneous counters with the slow, lumbering and infinitely predictable kid.

After the first round, I had the four lower belts rotate and face another black belt. We did this for four rounds total, and in each of the rounds I realized how easy it was to control these less experienced but very aggressive opponents by relying on the simultaneous counter. Before tonight, I always sparred the lower belts by either moving around and playing defense, making them miss but encouraging their attacking spirit, or picking my spots and connecting with light attacks when I could expose holes in their defense. The simultaneous counter, I discovered, was a far more elegant tool.

After the first four students finished their rounds, I called up the next group of slightly more experience students. This group of young and fast red belts and first-degree black belts was much more difficult to counter. My strategy was to blend in offense and footwork to try and induce a specific attack that I knew I could successfully counter. By this time, I had discovered that my most reliable counter was a right leg back kick or spin hook kick from a left foot forward fighting stance against an opponent who also stood left foot forward and attacked with the lead leg.

Once I had whittled the game down to just a few options, I played defense against all their other attacks and waited until I could sense a left leg attack before pulling the trigger. Sometimes I was forced to retreat and gave up free points to try and induce the ideal attack that I could then counter. But for the first time ever, I felt like a hunter setting up traps and the resultant feeling of catching them with a premeditated counterattack as they unwittingly flew into my strike zone was exhilarating and empowering.

With just four of the most senior students left in the last group, *Sabum* Dae Sung yelled from the sidelines for everyone to clear the mats and for me to face each black belt in turn. The first student was a little older, a little shorter and a little slower than me, and I had no problems timing a lead leg axe kick that caught her straight in the face as she rushed forward with a double kick. Even though hardly a minute had passed in the round, *Sabum* Dae Sung called a stop to the match and ordered the next student up.

The second black belt was a tall and supremely athletic and fearless fighter who started just five years ago. I have had epic battles in competition class with him and this evening was no different. We both began with a game plan, but the match quickly devolved into a street fight with stray techniques landing hard all over the place. Wanting to neutralize his superior length and speed, I stayed close and concentrated on in-fighting. Unfortunately, that meant I had to sacrifice some of the distance I needed to successfully maneuver a counterattack, and as a result we both went at each other sloppily and clinched mightily for the entire two minutes before the round was called. I was easily fifty pounds lighter than this guy and came out of the match bruised, battered and exhausted.

The next guy was a savvier defensive opponent who played with feints and set-ups to try and off-balance or flat-foot me before coming in for his attacks. Since we were both playing a sort of cat and mouse game, the action was slower and more subtle. Concentrating on just his left leg movements and knowing I had very little margin for error, my nerves were on a hair-trigger and when I finally kicked, I exploded at him with a kind of speed and timing that I didn't realize that I possessed.

Unfortunately, my timing and placement were a little too perfect and I knocked the poor guy out with a back kick to the sternum. It was like a head-on collision between two fast moving vehicles and the driver who didn't see the crash coming got the worse of it. Knockouts were extremely rare in practice, and the other students quickly came rushing toward us, rubbernecking and whispering nervously and excitedly about what they just witnessed. Ah crap, I thought, as I knelt next to the student I just felled. *Sabumnim* is going to kill me.

Thankfully *Sabum* Dae Sung was able to somewhat salvage the situation by stepping onto the mat and calmly ordering me to bow everyone out to end the class. As I did that, he untied the guy's chest protector and seated him upright in order to revive him. Dazed and a little embarrassed but ultimately unhurt, the guy let *Sabum* Dae Sung check out his ribs and his breathing while the other students filed by and offered their good wishes before quickly heading to the locker rooms and then out the door.

Much later, in a dark and emptied *dojang* I was gathering my things to leave when *Sabum* Dae Sung came out of the office with his overcoat on and his gym bag slung over his shoulder.

"You owe me 300 pushups," he said as he turned the main lights back on.

Huh?! You've got to be kidding me!

"Three hundred pushups or no more Taekwondo lessons," he said without emotion.

I reluctantly dropped my things and stepped back onto the mat. As I started the pushups, he moved to stand over me and started counting.

"*Hana, dul, set…*"

I am terrible at pushups and had to stop after thirty-five sloppy ones

"Why three hundred?" I groaned. "I only messed up that one fight with the really tall guy."

"One hundred for him. That was a terrible fight by the way. One hundred for losing control and knocking the next guy out. And one hundred for the last round that we didn't get to. *Sasib hana, sasib dul...*"

Oh God. I made it to eighty before flopping to the mat again.

"Why are you stopping? *Yeodeun hana, yeodeun dul...* Your timing on the back kick was pretty incredible though. Go home tonight and take a cold shower. Stand with your eyes closed under the water and try to figure out exactly how it felt and what your body understood right before and right as you did that counter. Do that kick again one hundred times in your mind and feel it every time. Study it. The cold water will help focus your attention and not let your concentration wander. Uh, how many pushups is this?"

"One twenty," I muttered.

"Keep going, it's getting late."

I could barely bend my arms for any of the last hundred-plus pushups, and *Sabum* Dae Sung's count eventually went silent as he stood impassively over my pathetic form and let the sloppiness slide. Quite a while later, I declared my three hundredth pushup with a whimper and *Sabum* Dae Sung finally sighed to let me off the hook.

Then, with the lights off, the heat off and the *dojang* locked up for the night, we shuffled out together across the icy, forlorn shopping center parking lot. It was bitterly cold and I was half-debating whether to offer him a ride to the bus stop when he quietly asked me for a favor. "Can you please take me to my father's place? I just want to pop in and see if he needs anything."

"Of course," I said, choking down my indecision and exhaling a little puff of frozen breath.

Following his directions, I wound through a maze of sleepy, darkened streets and ended up in front of a 1970s ranch-style house one town over. The lights were off, but I saw *Sabumnim*'s Toyota in the driveway. "Do you want me to wait?" I offered.

"Go home and meditate on that back kick," he said while stepping out of the car.

As his darken silhouette slowly glided away and up toward the house, he raised his right arm in a wave just before he reached the porch.

I smiled and offered a similarly silent goodnight as I watched him disappear into the house.

Sick Day

It turned out to be a touch of pneumonia that probably started out as a cold and then worsened when he refused to rest until it finally knocked him off his feet. He was slouched in his favorite recliner and huddled under an electric blanket, reading a dense-looking Korean paperback book when I let myself into the chilly house.

"You should turn the thermostat up," I said in greeting. "Maybe that way you'll get over your cold sooner."

"I didn't know you still had a key," he answered. "Did you eat? There's *miyeok guk* and *jook* on the stove you can heat up."

"Let me listen to your lungs and see if you're running a fever first."

With my ear up against his chest I heard faint rattles and slightly mucous-laced inhalations that indicated the onset of pneumonia. The age-old mercury thermometer that I recognized from when I was a child registered a slight fever. "It doesn't seem that bad, but I'm taking you to urgent care tomorrow for a chest X-ray and maybe some antibiotics if the doctor thinks it's necessary," I said as he pulled down his over-sized Rutgers sweatshirt and repositioned himself under the blanket. I headed to the kitchen to reheat the convalescent meal of seaweed soup and rice porridge.

"You're not that young anymore," I shouted from the kitchen. "Working six days a week is probably taking a toll on your body!"

I cracked two eggs into a bowl and whisked them with a pair of chopsticks. Once the seaweed soup reached a gentle boil, I swirled the eggs onto the surface of the soup to make the soft ribbons of a classic egg drop soup. Into the pot of eggy rice porridge, I piled a small mountain of *kimchi* and emptied a plate of leftover *myulchi bokkeum* (small fried anchovies). I then loaded everything onto a tray and took a seat at the coffee table next to my father.

"Sorry, I'm starving. I'll get more food for you tomorrow."

"Don't worry about me, eat all you want. How was Daria today?"

We spent the rest of the evening talking about her progress, the accidental knockout and theories of counterattacking.

"Where are you learning *jiujitsu,* or is it *judo*?" he asked at some point.

I told him where and he smiled and said, "It is in your blood."

Then he continued, "Enjoy the feeling of being a beginner and learning all over again. It's a precious experience and can add so much perspective to what you already know. But don't forget that even though *jiujitsu* and Taekwondo are very different technique-wise, the underlying principles of fighting are the same. Rhythm, timing, distance, flow, energy, counterattacking, strategy and mastery are all very similar experiences. Have fun."

I grunted half in acknowledgement and half in exasperation at his single-track mind. Thus silenced, he watched me eat. Right before I finished, he eased himself out of the recliner and produced two crisp Asian pears from the refrigerator and expertly removed their translucent peels with a paring knife. He carefully arranged the cut wedges on a dish and presented the fruit to me. As I looked up to say thanks, he gently rested his hand on my head and then silently padded off to bed.

I relaxed and slowly savored the sweet, crunchy fruit. After I finished, I washed the dishes and tidied up the kitchen before settling into the familiar deep grooves of his recliner. I absent-mindedly flipped through my flash cards while trying to reorganize my thoughts in the disorienting environment of the house where I was raised. Eventually I gave up on the studying and slipped into one of the deepest, most dreamless sleeps I have ever had. I awoke at dawn, still seated in the chair and hugging a light down comforter, feeling surprisingly refreshed and whole.

After taking my father to urgent care in the morning, we shopped for his antibiotics and loaded up on pre-made food from his favorite Korean restaurant. I resettled him back into bed around noon and through a worsening cough he rasped as I was leaving, "You have to coach Daria on Sunday. Make sure she fights aggressively. She has a tendency to hold back." Since it was impossible to argue with a sick old man, I nodded my head vaguely in agreement.

Queens College Tournament

He walked into the Queens College gymnasium on Sunday morning wearing a dark grey European-cut, single-button sports jacket that hung perfectly over a darker grey cashmere sweater and long tapered trousers that ended right at his ankles, exposing a sliver of his dark maroon socks which disappeared into a pair of soft-looking chocolate brown loafers. Crowned with his floppy head of curls, *Sabum* Dae Sung looked impossibly tall, debonair and completely out of place at the N.Y. Open Taekwondo Championships. However, as if to offset his international pop star appearance, he strode toward the Ahn's Taekwondo team that morning with an uncharacteristically open and friendly smile while juggling three large boxes of donuts and a bulging bagful of drinks.

The rest of the team, myself included, were decked out in our over-sized black and red satin Ahn's Taekwondo warm-up jackets worn over our *doboks*. It was the first competition of the season and everyone was anxiously milling about, tinkering with their equipment and trying to stretch and loosen up while internally wrestling with their nerves. The competitors' parents were getting reacquainted with one another after the long off-season and stood off to one side exchanging their own scouting reports and eyeing the other teams scattered around the gym. As I gathered our students to stand and greet *Sabum* Dae Sung, he approached with the donuts held high and said, "Breakfast of champions! Who wants a turbo boost?"

The kids quickly surrounded him and groped skyward toward the donuts like a litter of underfed puppies. Knowing it was my job to teach the kids courtesy and discipline in addition to kicking and punching, I raised my voice and reproachfully dropped them all for pushups on the spot. While the stunned adults looked on as their kids started to count out the pushups in unison, I sternly lectured the students on their manners and then ordered them to line up at attention to first greet *Sabum* Dae Sung with a bow and then to thank him after receiving their donut. He smiled enigmatically at the lecture and knelt down on one knee to help the kids pick out their donuts and their milk or juice boxes in turn. After the kids were done, he stood and offered the remaining donuts and the cans of coffee to the parents, who reflexively bowed their awkward thanks toward the unknown gentleman. At last, he consolidated the remaining donuts into a single box and fished out an unwanted and slightly misshapen old-fashioned glazed donut which he held in front of me and said with mock seriousness, "You'll need this to survive the day, *Sabumnim*."

For a moment everyone relaxed as they munched on their greasy, sugary treats. After we polished off all the donuts, I regathered the kids and their parents and introduced *Sabum* Dae Sung, telling them that he would be helping me coach that day. The parents gushed in awe and excitement as I announced the presence of a former world champion, and they quickly crowded around *Sabumnim's* illustrious son to shake his hand, make his acquaintance and point out their own young aspiring athlete. The kids though were mostly unimpressed and started horsing around as the rush of sugar mixed with the excitement and nervousness of the tournament spurred them into hyperactivity. Once again, I lowered the tenor and raised the volume of my voice to call everyone to attention.

Once settled, I gave everyone the warm-up and competition schedules for the rest of the morning and into the early afternoon. The kids would be competing based on age and experience level, and I divided everyone by rank in order to start the warm-ups. The first group to compete was the five-

and six-year-olds, and I sent them and their parents into the holding area mats with *Sabum* Dae Sung. I positioned everyone else in a circle and assigned a pair of senior students to start the warm-ups.

For the next seven hours, *Sabum* Dae Sung and I held pads for the kids, gave them pep talks, helped them put on and take off their fighting gear, searched high and low for lost belts and mouthpieces and other unmarked gear, answered anxious questions from their parents, protested scoring inequities, rushed frantically to coach simultaneous matches, posed for pictures with the winners, wiped away tears from both winners and losers, hugged away hurt feelings, found ice packs for bumps and bruises, explained the vagaries of judging and scoring to the parents, pleaded for replacement medals when the kids broke or lost theirs and gratefully bid goodbye to the last student competitors around four o'clock.

By the late afternoon the gymnasium and everyone in it began to smell like the hundreds of pairs of bare feet and sweaty bodies that had tromped through it all day. Combined with the stale fast-food musk of concession stand pizza, popcorn and hot dogs and the thousands of people's worth of garbage now overflowing from the 25-gallon trash cans from all corners of the overheated gym, it was no wonder that most of the spectators and their kids cleared out as quickly as they could.

After the most lucrative part of their day was complete, volunteers from the tournament director's *dojang* started dissembling the mats and electronic scoring equipment from four of the six rings. They also took down all of the advertising and merchandising stands from around the periphery of the gym, leaving just two rings and twenty or so adult competitors in the dirty, putrid-smelling and now mostly-empty gym. It was in inglorious settings like this all around the country where aspirational Taekwondo players on the cusp of gaining regional or national team standing cut their teeth and gained experience.

My parents arrived around 5pm to find me warming up with *Sabum* Dae Sung, who was holding pads and calling out kicking combinations. As they approached, *Sabum* Dae Sung stopped the drills and watched my mom envelope me in the depths of her unbelievably soft, voluminous and politically incorrect fur coat while my dad leaned over and completed the emperor penguin-like tableau by giving me a kiss on the head.

"You need a shower, D," he declared before turning his attention ever so slightly toward *Sabum* Dae Sung.

"Mom, Dad," I said eagerly in introduction. "This is *Sabum* Dae Sung, *Sabumnim's* son who I've been telling you about. He's been training me and giving me sparring lessons."

My mom smiled and warmly shook his hand. My dad did the same while adding a thank you before encircling my mom's waist to guide her toward a seat in the stands. "Good luck D. Listen to your coach," he said while walking away.

"Yeah, listen to your coach," *Sabum* Dae Sung teased, or so I thought, before he continued in all seriousness. "You only have two fights today, and I've been watching both girls warm up. I want you to gap both of them."

Huh?! Under the rules of this competition, a fight was automatically ended if a competitor opened up a 12-point gap in the score any time after the first round. Such a large margin theoretically indicated a severe mismatch and the gap rule was meant to keep the overwhelmed fighter safe. This type of mercy rule was often used in the little kids matches and I saw it several times that day, but I had never seen it in a senior level competition.

I stood there confused and silent for a minute while *Sabum* Dae Sung explained, "My father used to order us to do the same thing at tournaments like this. Basically, he was saying that if you can't fight with the mindset of dominating lower-level competition, then there's no way you'll make it through the bigger and deeper tournaments."

I was still incredulous when he continued, "If any one of us couldn't manage to gap all of our matches, then all three of us would be running endless sprints in the parking lot afterwards. I've puked and cried so many times on this stupid campus over just a couple of points, and I'll make you do the same even with your parents looking on." He then looked me in the eye and dared me to fail.

The one positive effect of his little speech was that I was oddly no longer afraid of losing. Instead, I was now terrified that I could not sufficiently cream my opponents, which was a feeling I had never experienced. I excused myself to rush to the restroom, suddenly worried that I was about to lose the last remnants of my lunch and the energy drinks I had been sipping all afternoon long. I stood over the sink shaking a little and trying not to hyperventilate, but nothing happened. Then, like the hundreds of times since I was 11 years old and was first taught this technique, I looked dispassionately at myself in the mirror and consciously removed all traces of myself, my ego, my thoughts, my fears and my identity, and everything Daria from the face staring back at me. I emptied my person and entrusted the match to my body and my fighting spirit.

Thus transformed, I walked back to the gymnasium and waited in the quiet emptiness of my mind until my match was called. Stepping into the ring for the first round, I tried to stand straighter, taller and bolder, knowing that I had to physically intimidate and dominate. Just as the referee started the match, I aggressively charged forward, covering half the length of the matted area with a long, loping rear leg axe kick right down Broadway and clocked the girl flush in her face with the entire bottom of my foot. As she stumbled, I used both hands to clinch and hold her upright as I slapped a crescent kick across her face. Still clinching and not letting her regain any sense of balance, I pushed for space and pummeled her low with a series of short round kicks to the lower belly. Then, I forcibly shoved her off of me and chased her with a series of double kicks before finishing with a back kick that knocked her off the mat and into the judges' table. The referee quickly threw himself between us and moved to restrain me, taking me by the shoulders and roughly redirecting me toward the center of the ring. Having extinguished most of the fight in my opponent with that initial onslaught, I continued to pile on the points during that first round while the referee tried his best to keep her safe and run out the clock. The match was called a few seconds into the second round and I won by a final score of 23-1.

Feeling like an apex predator, and having shocked the other competitors with that almost reckless and ruthless display of violence, I stalked the edge of the mat, eager to face my next opponent and doing nothing to staunch the savageness coursing through my blood. My next opponent turned out to be a recreational player and quite possibly a brand-new black belt. The problem with these local tournaments is that it is an open competition and anyone can sign up to participate. One-day-old black belts with no experience are thrown into the same ring as black belts like myself who practically live in the *dojang* and have legitimate dreams of competing nationally and internationally.

I could feel her give up immediately after I finished my first combination with a resounding round kick across her face. But since I desperately needed to gap her by at least 12 points I kept pressing until she started crying, first softly and then uncontrollably, before she crumbled to the mat at the 27-second mark. This time her coach ran onto the mat and jumped in between us. He frantically threw down a water bottle in lieu of a towel and used his body to shield his fallen student from my attacks. I was declared the winner at 10-0 and with intoxicating waves of dominance still pulsing through my system, I approached *Sabum* Dae Sung's coach's chair after the match and snarled, "Don't you dare."

He laughed, stood up and spun me around to help me out of the chest guard. "That was amazing. Maybe there is some bite to you after all."

My parents rushed down from the stands and crowded around us a little dazed and astonished at my vicious performance.

"Wow D, that was frightening," my mom said while seemingly trying to squeeze me back into being the sweet, angelic little kid she thought she had raised. "That was just...," she stopped, and I looked up to see tears of sadness and bewilderment in her eyes.

My dad saved me from having to see her cry by taking my mom into his arms and telling me to go get changed. "We'll wait for you here," he added as he turned to engage *Sabum* Dae Sung in conversation.

When I got back, my mom, dad and *Sabum* Dae Sung were smiling and chatting as if they had met at a cocktail party instead of at the increasingly foul-smelling Queens College gym where the surprise Dr. Jekyll in me just made a poor girl and my poor mother cry. As I approached, my dad spoke first and said, "I'm taking you two kids out to celebrate. Where do you want to go D?"

Famished, but exhausted and slightly embarrassed by my sweats and fuzzy shearling boots, I mumbled something about maybe next time. Undeterred, he turned to *Sabum* Dae Sung and pressed, "I have to thank you for all the work you've done with D. I have never seen that kind of... fire in her. You choose a place for dinner."

Sabum Dae Sung glanced over at me and then pulled out his phone. "Okay. What's your number Mr. Kutznetsov? I'll text you a place I know. When you get there, just circle around for street parking. The meters are off on Sundays."

I offered *Sabum* Dae Sung a ride on the way out, and we walked with my parents to the parking lot. He insisted that we escort my parents to their car first and see them off before heading to my car. When we finally got to the BMW, he held out a red Gatorade in exchange for my key.

"I'll drive," he said. "Drink this and take a nap." I was so tired that I headed to the passenger side without protest and snuggled into the bucket seat with my knees pulled into the fetal position. As soon as the engine started to hum, my exhausted form retreated into oblivion.

Comida Típica Dominicana

I awoke to a series of gentle nudges against my shoulder. When I finally opened my eyes and remembered where I was, I saw his hand extending a red Gatorade in front of me and heard him softly chiding, "Drink this. We're almost there so you might want to rub out your eyes and wipe the drool from your face."

Five minutes later we were parked and waiting outside a garishly bright yellow and orange dinette with no visible signage. We stood shivering on a sidewalk half-piled with thick black trash bags in the shape of body bags and stacks of deconstructed cardboard boxes bound in twine. The chatter on the surprisingly busy thoroughfare was primarily in Spanish, and while *Sabum* Dae Sung scanned the street for my parents' car, I stared into the men's barbershop next door that was packed and overflowing into a sidewalk barbeque centered around a homemade oil barrel smoker. The music was loud and the smell of grilled chicken and charcoal intermingled with intoxicating clouds of pot and spicy cigarillo smoke. It was a curbside party in the dead of winter. Why were so many people crowded into a barbershop on a Sunday evening? And are sidewalk cookouts allowed in New York City? Before I could ask *Sabum* Dae Sung, my parents appeared before us from the other direction and he turned to greet them before pulling the door to the dinette open and ushering us inside.

We entered with our heads on a swivel and took in the sights and smells of the mounds of food on the steam tables, the piles of fried patties and plantains, the fully bronzed face of a piglet with its roasted flesh spilling from its sides into a basin of meat and juices, and the open kitchen with meats and vegetables sizzling on the flattops and mysterious vats of soups and stews on boil beside it. Up front, all the tables were filled and the staff was in full catering or delivery mode and occupied the tables in the middle with an assembly line of Styrofoam boxes, plastic soup containers and an assortment of plastic utensils and bags.

Sabum Dae Sung led us toward the back and seated us at a cracked yellow vinyl table for six and asked about allergies and dislikes before politely requesting my parents' permission to order family style for everyone. He then excused himself to shake hands with the cook behind the counter and placed our order in rapid fire Spanish. He came back to ask my parents if they wanted a drink and disappeared again briefly into the kitchen before re-emerging with a half-bottle of dark rum and a label-less bottle of what looked like sticks and leaves and bark immersed in some dark liquid. The cook followed behind him with a pitcher of coconut juice and a fruit smoothie, which he placed in front of me.

"Welcome to my little restaurant! Dae Sung's friends are my friends, and you will eat well tonight!"

Sabum Dae Sung grabbed three clear plastic cups from the stack in the middle of the table and poured a wrist flick's worth of both rum and the other dark liquid into each cup before distributing them to my parents and holding up his own for a toast.

"This is Manuel's homemade Mamajuana mixed with a little Añejo," he announced with his cup in the air. "It's an old Dominican medicinal drink that is supposed to make you strong. Since Daria here is already ridiculously strong, she gets a passion fruit smoothie. Here's to Olympic dreams and the love that supports them."

Not sure whether to sip or shoot, my parents hesitated until *Sabum* Dae Sung made the universal bottom's up motion with his opposite hand. After my parents drank, he shot his and I tasted my smoothie. Wow, it was good.

120

My dad, who was usually a red wine or single malt whiskey kind of guy, must have approved of the homemade cocktail, because he held out both his and my mom's cup for another round.

My mom asked, "What is in that other bottle? I see bark, roots, and herbs maybe?"

This time pouring more liberally to create a sipping-sized drink, *Sabum* Dae Sung answered, "That's as far as I can tell too. Bark, roots and herbs of unknown and inexact origins, and maybe some dirt and definitely some kind of sugar."

He explained that this place had no liquor license, but after eating most of his meals here over the past year he became friends with the cook and owner Manuel and started getting Mamajuana privileges. "I live a few blocks from here and would wander in for late-night meals around 1:30 after the med school library closed. I was the out-of-place Asian guy who had no idea about Dominican food but I methodically ate my way through the entire menu until Manuel ran out of things to cook for me and started offering me nightcaps. This stuff is good, isn't it?" He clinked plastic cups with my parents again just as the food began to flow.

It seemed like he had ordered the entire menu all over again as Manuel started stacking little plastic plates of fried empanada-type pastries, croquettes, salads, sliced avocados, fried fish, fried plantains, mashed plantains, plantains mashed with a whole bunch of other things, beans, different beans, more beans, stewed peas, stewed chicken, stewed goat, oxtail stew, a yellowish stew with all sorts of meats, small bits of something wrapped in banana leaves, rice, squash, pork cracklings, shredded pork, cubed pork and something *Sabum* Dae Sung later identified as a tripe stew.

The genius of his ordering was that he asked for little portions of everything so each plate only held a bite or two for everyone. Since it was difficult to divide, we were soon double dipping our spoons and ladling for each other and holding out halves of the fried morsels for each other to taste. We ate slowly and savored the new experiences. After they finished the Mamajuana and the rum, bottles of slushy-cold Presidente appeared and *Sabum* Dae Sung and my dad became fast drinking buddies while my mom wistfully begged off with the promise to drive.

Finally, a creamy bean pudding, two more empanadas and four small paper cups of coffee arrived to round out our meal. I cradled the coffee and inhaled appreciatively before looking at my dad as he brought it up for a taste. A smile that he usually reserves for his Gesha beans broke out across his face. Good Dominican roasts were also high on his list of coffee pleasures. We each took a spoonful of the sweet kidney bean desert and finished with a perfect bite of the warm guava and cheese pastry. Manuel came by with two more shots of rum from his private stash before we called it a night and piled back out onto the sidewalk.

"That was one of the best meals I have ever had," my dad said while moving in to shake *Sabum* Dae Sung's hand before changing his mind and giving him a full man hug with a clap on the shoulder. He then turned to embrace me and emphatically told me how proud he was of my wins today with a series of rhythmic pats on my back and head. My mom eventually pulled him away and blew me and *Sabum* Dae Sung air kisses before leading my dad down the sidewalk and back toward their car.

"I live pretty close to here, but do you mind driving me back?"

"No problem."

He handed me my key from his front pocket and we made the two-minute drive over one block and down five more.

"Thanks for everything today, *Sabum* Dae Sung," I said while bowing as much as I could while remaining seat-belted in the car.

"Actually, this is it for me," he answered while unbuckling his seat belt and reaching for the door handle. "I told my father I could only help out until school started up again."

He was almost out the door, but something in my silence must have made him look back. I am not sure what he saw, but I was fighting hard not to show my devastation. He coldly stuck out his hand, which I limply took in mine, and offered an indifferent 'good luck' before climbing out of the car and heading up the stairs to his apartment without another backward glance.

Without *Sabum* Dae Sung

I couldn't believe the sudden goodbye, but I was also so tired that all I could manage that evening was to navigate myself safely home and collapse into bed without unpacking my smelly gym bag or even taking a shower. The next day I awoke dehydrated and feeling like I had been buried by a sand storm. I had to force my leaden limbs into action and roll my heavy head sideways off the pillow. While still moving in a haze, I stood over the kitchen sink and drained several cups of water before shuffling into the shower for an epically long scrub down. Enervated by the steamy waters, I sleepwalked out of the bathroom and plopped onto the couch before closing my eyes again. For the first time ever, I was seriously contemplating skipping morning practice.

I'm not sure what roused me from the stupor but I was soon up again and operating on autopilot to throw my dirty *doboks* and workout gear into the washer and to fry up two eggs, *kimchi* and ham with two slices of American cheese for my version of a breakfast sandwich. Wishing that I could go upstairs for a cup of my dad's coffee but knowing it was getting late, I ran my Mr. Coffee straight into a 20-ounce thermos and took it to go along with the sandwich.

I got to the *dojang* five minutes before 8 o'clock and finished my breakfast in the car. While I ate, I scanned the parking lot, glumly hoping to see a tall figure with a shock of wavy hair stroll toward the shopping center from the direction of the bus stop. My hopes faded as my coffee cooled to an undrinkable lukewarm, and then I allowed myself to wallow for an additional five minutes with my forehead on the steering wheel before I abandoned the parking lot vigil and dragged myself into the *dojang*. My eyes immediately wandered over to the white board, which was again filled with *Sabumnim's* handwriting. I sighed as I shed my winter layers and stowed my gym bag. While I cleaned the *dojang*, I was still half hoping that *Sabum* Dae Sung would walk through the front door with his familiar scowl and cloud of petulance. Every time the morning light shifted and created a new shadow, my head popped up and swiveled toward the front door. It was not until I laced up my running shoes and started to head out for the hill that I finally accepted that perhaps he really did mean goodbye.

The jog was numbingly cold, but it was not until I reached the hill that my spirits really sank. All of a sudden, the pain of the goodbye overwhelmed me and I slumped disconsolately against the trunk of the hanging tree as waves of unfamiliar sadness threatened to drown me. This might have been how I felt when *Sabum* Dae Sung disappeared from the *dojang* that first time when I was 12, but today it seemed a million times worse and hurt in places in my mind and heart that had not yet been fully formed back then. I hugged my knees to my head and for a foolish instant wished that the world would end with me frozen in that spot. But as the cold eventually pierced my sauna suit and started to induce a shiver, I slowly stood and started half-trudging and half-running up the hill.

As I worked out, my thoughts drifted to the empty lane beside me and I let my melancholy weigh down my legs and my spirit. I jogged with my eyes cast downward, never leaving my shoes tops, up and down the hill, and called that effort sprints. I also dispensed with recording my times because I just didn't care. Following the sprints, the assignment was hopping in a fighting stance on one leg up the hill while jabbing and cut kicking with the lead leg for several rounds. This new torture caused my legs to cramp in all sorts of unpleasant ways, but with no one screaming invectives in my face or challenging my courage from the other lane, I went easy on myself and put my leg down as many times as I needed in order to complete the assignment.

I finished in a desolate mood made even more hollow by my embarrassingly lackluster effort. For some reason I just wasn't able to snap myself out of the funk, and I slowly let my despondency spiral downward into truculence on the slow jog back to the *dojang*. A few blocks into the jog, I started hating the conditioning, hating the training, hating the long and difficult path I chose, but most of all I hated the anguish brought about by *Sabum* Dae Sung's abandonment.

That vertiginous descent into anger brought out the distraught four-year-old in me who wanted to explode into a temper tantrum just so the world could acknowledge how hurt and upset I was. Like an irrational child, I tested my simmering rage with a few kicks and strikes against a snow bank only to realize that my misery needed a bigger outlet. Feeling malicious, I climbed the softened snow bank and started flinging dirty wet snow in all directions hoping to destroy the mountain and maybe even hit some sentient being who could then react and share in my pain. Wildly yelling, kicking and scooping the snow off the banks and onto the streets, I expressed my frustrations with the universe by creating as much havoc and chaos as my insignificant personage could manage.

I was finally snapped out of my madness when a car skidded to a stop after a spray from my snow tantrum splattered his windshield. That near-accident quickly sobered me into a state of teenage cowardliness and panic. Fearing reproach or worse from a deservedly angry motorist, I slid down the snow bank and took off in a dead sprint before the driver could clear his windshield and identify the culprit.

Running for my life, I arrived back at the *dojang* looking like the dervish that was spinning crazily in my mind. *Sabumnim* took one look at my eyes and instead of sending me home for lunch as usual, he pointed toward the heavy bag and gave a vague order for back kicks. What?! I chafed, but inured to a lifetime's worth of seemingly unreasonable demands, I obeyed.

Without changing out of my running gear, I thwacked the bag relentlessly all throughout the noontime class. *Sabumnim* issued no further instructions and the students pretended not to notice the noise or the tension.

I tried to destroy the bag with my first couple of hundred kicks, as if the 70-pound lump of leather and sand had somehow also wronged me. But by kick 300 or so my power decreased significantly and my shoulders began to sag. Around 500 my mind turned to jello and started to melt. As 700, 800 and 900 rolled by with a whimper, I had to marshal all my strength and discipline just to go through the motions and perform one more kick. The *dojang* had long emptied of the noontime students and the lights were dimmed and the heat turned off by the time I finally rediscovered my equilibrium.

I was at the point of barely being able to move the bag with my kicks when *Sabumnim* finally called out for me to join him in his office. He was seated at the low table with two mugs of cooling tea, two pairs of chopsticks and one Tupperware box laid out in the middle. He motioned for me to sit and leaned forward to open the Tupperware as I made my way over to him. Seeing only lunch for one person in the box, I politely told him that I could not eat his lunch. He answered, *"Meogeo."* Then, seeing the confusion in my eyes he translated 'eat' before growling, "study harder."

I followed his lead and we ate in silence. After lunch he made a motion that I interpreted as asking for more tea, and I brewed another pot and brought it back to the table.

"No more Dae Sung," he started. "Now that you know the difference between working out and training, you have to push yourself, punish yourself with impossible high standards, and polish your own weaknesses. Everything you need is already within you. Be guided by that."

I nodded diffidently and mouthed a barely audible "Yes, Sir" before he moved on.

"Your hill repeats were slow and lazy today, no? I can tell. You are sitting here like a sad, lost, panicky little puppy without Dae Sung. Those kicks were to calm your crazy mood today and to make up for the morning sloppiness."

I remained silent and tried not to blush.

Sabumnim then sighed and let the sternness slip from his demeanor for a minute. "Good job yesterday. But don't get too big of a head. If Dae Sung was here today, I would have him beat you silly so you don't get a big head. Too bad your teacher is an old man though, and I cannot do that myself. Instead, listen to my words. It is not very often you can just walk all over your opponent. It's good to find that aggression and power and to learn how to intimidate. But it is more important to be able to control it. While it could be effective sometimes, it is rarely advisable to fight like a crazy lunatic. You must be smarter aggressive and not suicidally charging forward aggressive, because even a lesser fighter has a chance to knock you out with a lucky, desperate shot."

Looking at my gloomy, unfocused eyes and seeing that his lecture found no purchase, *Sabumnim* gently repeated, "He's not coming back. For now, you must learn how to move forward without someone pushing you from behind."

I sighed and nodded again.

Sabumnim seemed to echo my sigh and reflect my lingering melancholy with a slight slumping of his own shoulders before sending me away with the dishes and closing his office door for an hour respite.

An Education

Despite *Sabumnim's* warning against being recklessly aggressive, the experience of fighting like I owned the ring and everyone in it stayed with my imagination and transformed my approach to sparring. Sensing the change in my attitude, *Sabumnim* started treating me more like he did *Sabum* Dae Sung and purposely limited my arsenal when I sparred the lower ranks in competition class. Even against bigger and stronger male black belts he would restrict me to only doing a certain attack or a certain counterattack and force me to problem solve in order to survive the fight. And at the end of some very long days, I was almost always grinding out laps around the shopping center parking lot as penance for the number of sparring rounds I lost. But for the rest of that winter and into the spring, sparring with those restrictions taught me how to strategize, how to manipulate distance and disrupt timing when I lacked attacking options, and how to recognize and exploit the multitude of empty spaces during a match.

I sparred mostly at night with the young competition team members. During the day *Sabumnim* concentrated on teaching me the other side of Taekwondo. With him as my partner, I learned how to grab and sweep out kicks from all angles and how to move obliquely and attack pressure points and more vulnerable parts of the body with elbow strikes, knee strikes and a variety of hand techniques that I thought belonged to the province of other martial arts. Once overwhelmed with strikes or swept to ground, he continued my education in pins, holds, joint locks, chokes and other quick finishing techniques. And almost every day for 30 minutes to an hour he would fight me on the ground, pinning me, choking me and joint locking me with no concept of tapping or surrendering allowed.

Unlike fighting on one's feet, once isolated on the ground distance is mostly eliminated and the unremitting pressure increases manifold with the mat acting as a second opponent restricting motion and escape options. In this claustrophobic crucible I learned how to focus my fighting even as darkness and pain threatened my consciousness. It was under these circumstances that I learned that when you are drowning and getting crushed by forces beyond your control, sometimes all that is left to define you is the fight. But most of all, I learned that even when you fight with spirit beyond what you thought was humanly possible you can sometimes still lose everything. Repeatedly blacking out on the mat or getting my joints stretched to the point of snapping, I continued to sacrifice in order to gain an education in an entirely different arena of pain, struggle and the violence of the fight.

During this time, I also easily won all the local tournaments our *dojang* entered. *Sabumnim* now regularly commanded that I win the matches by gapping my opponents, and I learned how to do that with more calculating and clinical game plans. Post-match he always quizzed me on every technique I threw and every strategy I employed, forcing me to correctly justify every motion and decision I made. He would then point out holes in my judgment and all the opportunities missed, both by myself and my opponent.

It was also around this time that he taught me how to meditate. But instead of sitting and trying to empty my mind, he gave me the nightly assignment of sitting for an hour and fighting against the world number one in my weight class. I was to watch the YouTube videos on my own and then visual the same girl and the same fight with me as the opponent. When I tired of 'fighting' her for days and weeks on end, I eventually expanded this practice to international players beyond my weight class and thoroughly enjoyed this method of meditation.

As spring approached, the second Tupperware box reappeared. Those lunches started out relatively silent like the ones before but slowly *Sabumnim* started to open up and tell stories of the *dojang* and his own Taekwondo journey with his sons. He described the *dojang* in its infancy when he and his wife first arrived in New Jersey with no English language skills and no friends or family to rely on. Those days they trained on industrial carpet tiles laid over a concrete floor, and he taught with a bamboo sword, apparently using it liberally in place of the communication skills he lacked.

He reminisced openly about the lean years when he and his wife lived off of homemade *kimchi* and instant noodles and slept on the office floor. Apparently, it was not until after their first son was born that *Sabumnim* took a second job washing dishes and scrubbing down the kitchen at a Korean restaurant from eight o'clock at night until two o'clock in the morning in order to move the family into a rented house. After their second son was born, he added a morning shift at the restaurant cleaning fish, cutting vegetables and peeling frozen shrimp. And it was not until *Sabum* Dae Sung was born several years later that the *dojang* finally found its footing and was able to support his family.

When his sons were young, *Sabumnim* told me he emphasized strength and flexibility in their development. He told stories of stretching his sons into full splits and back bridges right after they could walk. He also told of the contests he devised where the boys would compete with each other, holding their front splits over two chairs or holding their side splits vertically straight up a wall, holding through barely-stifled tears and not-so-silent protests in order to avoid his bamboo sword. In the early mornings before school or late at night after his workday was finished, he taught his sons gymnastics and wrestling on the hard-packed ground of his backyard. He described middle school years when he made his sons wear five-pound ankle weights all day at school and then all afternoon on the hill and finally all evening through their Taekwondo practice. For weight training, the boys spent

131

countless hours shouldering heavy, awkward objects like patio furniture, canvas bags filled with bricks and rocks or rolls of garden hoses in races across their backyard, before they finally graduated to the free weights in the *dojang*. The tales were non-linear and sometimes mere interjections into other stories or examples of Taekwondo training, but each vignette left a vivid, slashing brushstroke in the picture he was painting.

"I'm a little smarter now because of the many mistakes I made," he said as a preamble one day. "However, even if I show you everything, you will still make many mistakes of your own. But hopefully different mistakes. Better, less stupid mistakes."

Once, he softly and discursively hinted at regret for not fulfilling his duties as a teacher to wholly understand his sons and to guide them individually, to give each son what he needed the most, and to, above all else, give selflessly. "It took me years to realize that potential was ultimately meaningless without the corresponding self-motivation to fully actualize it. And I struggled and struggled mightily with trusting them to guide their own selves in ways counter to the potential I saw in them, especially when I knew their paths would ultimately stray from what I thought was best. I didn't understand that there was timing involved in holding on... and in letting go."

He lectured me on *Hyo*, the Korean concept of obligation and duty... that of a son to a father, a student to a teacher, a junior to a senior, and also the reverse. There were rhetorical afternoons filled with thoughts on how *Hyo* contrasted with the American concepts of liberty and freedom and self-determination. He asked, "Could there be freedom without structure and responsibility? Could there be a future without preserving and caring for the past? What can we reasonably expect from others if we ourselves answer to no one?" After a lifetime of study and no satisfactory universal truth that could succinctly bridge the ethos of both cultures, he essentially passed those questions on to me.

That spring I continued to fight well and solidify my regional standing. With *Sabumnim* in my corner, I easily won the New York, New Jersey, Massachusetts and Pennsylvania state championships and the Northeast regional championship that qualified me for the national championships over the summer.

I was undefeated on the season when *Sabumnim* started registering me for the heavier weight classes. When that happened, I was no longer in a position to physically dominate the bigger and stronger opponents. Instead, I had to learn how to play defense and how to fight a little ugly and a little dirty. Those matches were often determined by less than a few points, so I also had to learn the difference between winning 2-1 and losing 1-2. Understanding how to navigate that razor's edge required another level of focus and determination that could only be gained through experience and more experience. *Sabumnim* made me compete almost every weekend, and eventually after a multitude of very close fights I started to discover a comfort level and awareness of how to shift the balance and momentum in those types of matches. Neither one of us could verbalize the intuition I slowly developed, except to say that I now understood *Sabumnim* better when he places his finger between my brows and then punches me lightly on the chest guard over my heart to tell me that close fights are won when those two things are harmonized.

Over our daily *kimbap* lunch one afternoon in May *Sabumnim* told me it was time to start preparing for the national championship and then the U.S. National Team Trials. He handed me a training schedule for the next couple of months and reviewed the areas of my game that he thought needed the most improvement. Then he paused before saying, "You are 19 now. This time in your life is your best chance to make the jump to national and maybe international level player. If you cannot make the jump this year, it will become harder next year because of the world championships and even harder the following year because of the Olympics. The time has to be now."

After letting his words sink in, he continued, "There is an old saying that when a student is ready, the teacher appears.

But I think that is quite a stupid saying. Leaving your education and future to the vagaries of someone else's timing is not always very wise. I think life, like fighting, can be gamed with smart planning and aggressive action. Timing is important, but sometimes you can make your own timing. Moving forward with purpose and direction will bring you much more luck and opportunity than just waiting about. In any case, it's worth a try.

"I think it's time for you to go to him and ask for his help again along the rest of the way. The young doctor just earned almost perfect marks on his medical boards and has a light academic schedule this term. So maybe the timing is right."

After lecturing directly into his teacup this whole time, he concluded by slowly looking in my direction to make sure I understood. The surprise on my face and the sudden jolt in my chest must have been answer enough. I bowed my head and thanked him, ostensibly for lunch as I started to gather up the dishes, but in actuality for everything.

Waiting at the Gate

I arrived around seven o'clock on Sunday morning hoping that guava and cheese empanadas were a breakfast food. As luck would have it, they are not but the lady behind the counter said she could make me some if I had time. I sat down with a cup of coffee and a fresh cinnamon and sugar donut and read *Kashtanka* while I waited. The warm donut was so perfectly crispy on the outside and cakey on the inside that I took two more to go along with two empanadas and two cups of coffee. By 7:30 I was on the steps leading to *Sabum* Dae Sung's apartment, eating a second donut and re-immersing myself in the tale of the circus dog.

Around ten o'clock *Sabum* Dae Sung finally emerged from the building two steps behind a beautiful Asian girl with glossy, ebony hair flowing most of the way down her back. She was dressed in a man's oxford shirt and a slightly wrinkled skirt showing off impossibly long legs that ended in a pair of designer Jimmy Choos. She paused on the steps and slid her sunglasses down over her nose to glare suspiciously at me after I jumped to my feet and greeted *Sabum* Dae Sung with a cheerful good morning and a bow.

"Um, sorry to bother you, Sir," I said, stumbling away from my prepared script in the presence of his stunning girlfriend. "I was wondering if I could talk to you for a second."

His girlfriend shifted her attention upward towards him as we both awaited his response.

"Sure, what's up?"

Abandoning the speech that I had prepared for days I decided to cut right to the heart of the matter before I lost my nerve completely. I bowed exaggeratingly from the waist until my own long hair covered my entire face and asked, "Please can you coach me for the nationals and the team trials?" I stayed with my head bowed hoping he would respond favorably to my humility and sincerity. No answer. And nothing from the girlfriend. Nervous, I slowly raised my head from the bow to see that neither had moved, but *Sabum* Dae Sung's face was slowly contorting and on the verge of exploding into laughter.

"I got you these," I continued hopefully, holding out the pastries and coffee.

He walked down five steps towards me and took the brown paper bags to investigate. His girlfriend eyed him with a touch of animosity as he opened the bags and then joyously rolled them back shut after seeing the contents. "Thanks kid, but the answer is no," he said as he kept the bags in one hand and offered his other to his girlfriend before walking past me and off together down the block and around the corner.

I had expected this to be difficult but assumed that I would at least be able to fully present my case. I had planned on telling him that all my recent success and improvement had been because of his efforts with my training in January. I was going to congratulate him on crushing the Boards and relay to him *Sabumnim's* pride and approval. I was definitely going to offer to pay him for the coaching at any private lesson rate he thought was reasonable. And if all that failed, I was going to pathetically beg and beg and beg, telling him that my life dreams depended upon his help. But because his summary rejection was so shocking and unexpected, my only instinct at that point was to shake it off in disbelief and wait to fully present my appeal. After all, it couldn't get any worse than that first try. I settled in with the circus dog story and whiled away the morning and early afternoon on his doorsteps.

Around three o'clock I was wilting and regretted my lack of preparation. I had already spent the last few hours in indecision over whether to risk a bathroom run to the Irish bar down the street. But now it was urgent. I could clearly see the bright green awnings in front of Coogan's and assumed that the interior offered at least an oblique view of *Sabum* Dae Sung's building. If I hurried and the bar was empty, I would only be out of sight of the apartment steps for a few minutes. Desperate, I sprinted down the block and across the street and rushed past the bartender with an order for honey mustard chicken fingers and a plea to use his facilities. A couple of minutes later, I was back at the bar downing a pint of ice water while ignoring a group of old men offering to buy me drinks. After paying for the chicken fingers, I stood with one foot out the door and peered anxiously down the street while I waited for my food. In no time, I was able to resettle myself back onto the steps with only a slightly uneasy feeling about briefly abandoning my vigil.

The day dragged on and I was still reading in the after-seven o'clock gloaming, now completely absorbed by and a little distraught over the story of Vanka's lost letter when *Sabum* Dae Sung finally returned home to tower over the hunkered-down figure of me still sitting on his steps. I initially assumed the worst about the shadow standing over me and jumped up and out of my skin in fear, tripping backwards on a step and landing on my side while trying to right myself and scurry away. As the shadow started to laugh, I scampered to my feet and looked up. Feeling like a moron and sensing that I was now a completely lost cause, I bowed unsteadily toward the now familiar tall figure and was just about to relaunch into my entreaty with a silent stutter when he spoke first.

"You've been here the whole day?! That's like stalking, you know. You really are some kind of nut job."

Expecting anger and an angry girlfriend beside him, I looked more closely and was surprised to see him standing all alone and smirking. I opened my mouth to explain, but he cut me off again.

"I can only do Sunday mornings. Maybe nine to noon-ish. It'll cost you though. Bring me a breakfast of champions every week. Use your imagination."

He then brushed past me up the stairs. As I turned to try and thank him, he offered a no-look and completely indecipherable wave before quickly disappearing through the front door.

The Fight

I had heard all about her progress from my father, who invariably included a line or two about the girl in every email he sent. Since she was headed to nationals and then the team trials in about two months, I knew exactly what the next evolution of her training should entail. I said yes to coaching her again because once upon a time this was the part of my own training that I enjoyed the most.

The following Sunday she showed up bearing an açai bowl with granola and a crunchy coconut chip topping presented in a green half coconut with a biodegradable wooden spoon and a bamboo straw. Very yuppie, but also quite delicious. She also brought a Thermos filled with the most amazing coffee I have ever tasted. When sipped with the tropical breakfast, the coffee tasted like sweet summer strawberries... the delicate, perishable kind you get at a farmers' markets, not the industrial tasteless variety you get at grocery stores.

Sitting on the steps of my apartment, I shared my bounty with Naomi while explaining to Daria the next step of her training.

"All fighters love the fight," I started. "And it's more than just about winning. If it's about winning every fight, you might as well just bring a serious weapon. But for guys... and girls, I guess... who train to fight, who train their whole lives to fight, it's also about testing yourself and your skills and your courage against other martial artists.

"The most famous example of this is maybe the ronin or masterless Samurai from a bygone era in Japan. Of course, most were dirty, filthy mercenaries, but some lived for the purpose of perfecting their fighting craft and would spend years traveling to seek out worthy opponents. There are similar stories of fighters from ancient China who roamed across the empires and lived by the codes of *jianghu*. They were also mercenaries and bandits and the like, but some were drawn to that marginal world of violence because it was the martial and the allure of the fight that defined them.

"And then in modern times, there's the concept of *dojang* storming where people or even entire schools would challenge other organizations or teachers in order to humiliate and assert dominance. Some of these were turf wars over students and recruitment. But a lot of these were just plain tribal battles over reputation or some other such nonsense because humans are really not all that evolved, and humans who really like to fight are probably even less so, I think."

I smiled at Naomi, and when she scowled back, I laughed.

"There are also illegal underground fights in New York City and all over the world. These are usually dark and seedy events where desperate men fight for pocket change or for sport or because they got mixed up with the wrong people. But lots of totally legitimate martial artists also use these fights to test their skills and to find an outlet for their true natures."

I paused when I started to sense Naomi's scowl deepen into a grimace as uncertainty and unease stiffened her posture. This time I didn't smile or even look up. Instead, I decided to skip over street fights and bar fights and changed my approach.

"Really though, all that stuff is pretty rare. It exists, but come on, we live in a world of lawsuits, cell phone videos and the internet. You do underground shit like that or storm a *dojang* and it's a trip to central booking and a criminal record that'll stick to your name and identity forever."

She relaxed a bit.

"Instead, what we have now are the UFC and stuff like Taekwondo and karate and BJJ tournaments with medical staffs, licensing, sponsors, rules, liability waivers, merchandising and it's slowly becoming a sport that's packaged and branded as consumer-friendly media. Everything is out in the open and on the up and up, but everything is also about the money and the fame and the politics of belonging to a certain organization or getting picked for a certain team or making a name for yourself and then exploiting that for some other business venture. And that goes for the Olympics too. Win a medal for Team USA and you get some local fame and glory and self-satisfaction for the rest of your life, but NBC makes millions broadcasting your image and your story. Fighting has become like a classic game of pimps and hos; and guess who gets the short end of that stick."

I said all this for Naomi's sake as much as for Daria's. She might as well know a little about where my mind wanders to when I'm not studying my ass off trying to catch her in our class rankings. She knew about my Olympic Trials experience, but I figured that if we were ever going to get more serious, it might be best if she also knew how totally warped my Taekwondo training has made me. As of now, I was just laying down some bread crumbs, half hoping that she would eventually be interested enough to follow.

I continued, "Good fights still exist though. Fights for the sake of learning. Fights for the sake of getting better at fighting. Fights that test whether you have what it takes to get to the next level. Most of these fights are far away from the spotlight of the arena and there is no real glory in winning. But these fights are what makes the martial artist, and the only combatants come out of them knowing the true value of the experience…"

This time I looked at Daria. "That's what we'll be doing for the next few weeks. *Sabumnim* and I have set up a few opponents to fine-tune and polish your skills. Get through these guys and the nationals and team trials will feel like a cakewalk." She stared back breathlessly, but I could sense her excitement.

I got up and tossed the coconut shell in the trash and told Naomi I would swing by her place with groceries to make dinner later that evening. I figured that was the least I could do to make up for the insane way I was going to spend the other half of my day. As Naomi nodded and walked away, I followed Daria to her car.

Even on a Sunday morning there was still quite a bit of traffic between Washington Heights and the heart of Queens. It took us about 45 minutes to get from the Cross Bronx, to I-678, across the Whitestone Bridge and down into the heart of Flushing. Once we reached the neighborhood where first-generation Koreans, Chinese and Mexicans intersected in a uniquely dense, determined and talented couple of square miles of immigrant Americana we left the BMW in a municipal lot far from our destination and walked toward Main Street. Along the way I detoured her into a Citibank and asked that she take out $300 in fresh bills and seal it in a bank envelop. That was the agreed-upon tuition for today's lesson.

Our destination was a tiny *dojang* in the basement of a five-story walk-up that housed a traditional Chinese medicine and herb dispensary on the ground floor, a shady $25 an hour foot massage parlor on the second floor, and a host of other legitimate and not-so-legitimate enterprises on the third through fifth floors. We took the rounded concrete steps down below street level and greeted my father's friend Grandmaster Kim Won Suk as he unlocked the door upon our arrival.

"So, this is Ahn Jae Hun's student," Grandmaster Kim said, unimpressed with Daria after looking her up and down.

We exchanged formalities in Korean. I played my part as the young beseeching student, and he assumed the role of supreme grandmaster. My father was his junior from their days back in Korea, and although I was unclear whether their ties were military or just through Taekwondo, as the son of his junior my status clearly required subservience. I lowered my eyes and bowed from the waist, carefully holding out the envelop of cash as a token of good faith. Without a word, he smoothly disappeared the envelop by reaching out with a hand the size and shape of a bear claw with darkened knobby scar tissue on the knuckles and thickened sinew and callouses reinforcing the weapon all over. As the envelop slipped out of my hands, I looked up to see a set of cold, penetrating onyx eyes that reflected almost 80 years of survival.

"We humbly request a lesson, Sir," I said.

He swept us inside and pointed out a small wash closet for Daria. While she changed, I looked over at the three students he called in for today's lesson. They were all teenage boys about Daria's weight, but shorter, stronger and meaner-looking. With similarly sun-darkened skin, hungry eyes and spikey black hair I couldn't tell for sure what nationality any of the boys were. They were all dressed in dirty, greyish Taekwondo pants and three different soccer jerseys... Mexico, ManU and Barça. The boys leaned impatiently against the grime-streaked far wall with just a hint of practiced defiance and toughness, character traits undoubtedly inherited from their teacher. I decided against introducing myself and instead waited in silence from across the room. When she finally emerged from the wash closet, I noticed that she took her cue from the boys and wore just a plain black T-shirt and no belt with her Taekwondo pants.

Grandmaster Kim came over and said the lesson would last one hour and the boys would rotate through two-minute rounds with Daria. Then addressing me in Korean with a level of condescension usually reserved for disparaging young boys, he half-goaded that I could rotate in too if I was up for the challenge. Remembering my own visit to this Flushing dungeon with my father when I was about the same age as those teenagers put a defiant smile on my face.

"Maybe next time, Sir," I answered, declining with half-bow of apology.

"Whatever you say, fancy doctor," he mocked while looking me in the eye and play-punching me hard enough in the ribs to probably produce a bruise tomorrow.

"Tony, you first!" was the order and the middle boy straightened and bowed to Grandmaster Kim before running to stand at attention in the middle of the mat with his fists thrust in front of his waist and his eyes directed straight forward.

"No fighting gear, Sir?" Daria asked.

"Whatever you like, little lady," Grandmaster Kim taunted as his boys laughed.

Daria then made a smart decision by slipping on her shin guards, but a certain amount of needless pride made her forego the arm guards, chest protector and helmet. Not wanting to embarrass her by nagging, I stayed silent but was secretly relieved when she also produced a mouthpiece and popped it in. She then bowed to me and made her way to the center of the mat to face Tony.

The entire *dojang* was maybe one-fifth of the size of my father's *dojang* and in far worse condition. The thin blue puzzle mats in the practice area were so worn that splotches of underlying white foam were exposed in several of the high-use areas. Strips of mismatched blue duct tape ran up and down the length of the practice area, no doubt to reinforce the seams where the mats should have been securely interlocked. The practice area itself was so narrow that when standing in the center, someone Daria's height could do a skipping side kick to either side and touch the walls with her foot. For someone my size, a skipping side kick to either side would produce a serious hole straight through the drywall.

Even in late spring, the basement air was humid and stale, circulated only with a cheap oscillating corner fan turned on high. The tired, off-white paint on the walls bore witness to generations of children's finger prints, New York City street grime and the residue from the physical exertions of the thousands of students who have passed through this *dojang*... this very tough and no-nonsense *dojang* that has remarkably

144

produced hundreds of junior- and senior-level state and national champions. Everything in this place reeked of struggle, persistence and excellence and was therefore the perfect place for her first test.

Grandmaster Kim casually leaned up against the half-wall that separated the practice area from the three-chair reception area by the entryway and signaled for the start of the first round with sharp and clipped orders to bow and then fight.

Immediately, the boy Tony launched into a series of double kicks, each targeting first the upper thigh and then the lower hip. In a match with electronic chest guards, none of those kicks would score and he might even be warned or penalized for aiming so low. But in a playground scrimmage with no referee and very few rules (all of which remain unstated and rarely invoked), learning how to deal with foul play was part of establishing one's bona fides and proving one's substance and mettle as a martial artist.

Daria's strategy was to bring the fight into a clinch in order to neutralize the pounding she was taking on the legs. However, in the clinch Tony transitioned his low kicks into a series of barely concealed illegal knee strikes in order to further punish Daria's legs and hips. Since complaining about a couple of knees to the thighs would result in never being able to play ball again in these parts, I kept silent and waited to see if Daria could figure this mess out herself. She quickly decided that eating knee strikes from close range and not being able to counter with a takedown (which she also correctly sensed would be way out of bounds) was a no-win situation and pushed free from Tony and started circling to her left.

Despite her movement, she ate another set of double kicks to the legs and then another before she clinched again. But this time as she clinched, she cupped Tony's right shoulder in her left hand and delivered a downward reverse punch to the area where the collarbone connects with the sternum, right under the throat. As he gasped and tried to retreat backwards, Daria grabbed a fistful of his Barça jersey (illegal in a tournament, but not necessarily here in the basement) to

145

prevent him from escaping and punched downward again into the same spot. Her third and fourth punches found the open hand he held up to shield his injured collarbone, but her fifth and sixth punches landed cleanly again as Tony reflexively but stupidly pulled away his now-injured hand. Twisting, squirming, and yanking, Tony was eventually able to pull his jersey free from Daria's grasp. He quickly retreated and Daria smartly decided not to press an embarrassed fighter whose damaged pride made him more dangerous and unpredictable. Instead, she waited with her fists held high, advertising her intended counter if he flew in with double kicks again. The round ended with both fighters hurt and indignant.

After about a minute break, during which Grandmaster Kim smirked and Tony slumped against the wall to lick his wounds, Chang was summoned to face Daria. I said nothing to her during the rest period except to tell her not to sit, so her strategy against the unknown Chang was a complete surprise to me.

Like his *dojang*-mate, Chang was also hyper-aggressive and charged the instant Grandmaster Kim yelled *shijak*. But starting a millisecond before him was Daria, who stood her ground and whipped a jumping spin hook kick into the space where Chang's head would be in about 10 milliseconds time. She was off by a few milliseconds, hitting with the bottom of her calf instead of her foot, and her kick was also off by about an inch, hitting Chang on the neck instead of higher up on the jaw, but the results were undeniably spot on. Chang's body buckled like a crash-test dummy upon impact and remained motionless on the ground for a second as Grandmaster Kim's eyes bulged in disbelief. Finally, he sent the third boy over to check on the unconscious Chang, and within a few seconds of the boy's anxious pleading and shaking, Chang's eyes opened. A minute later, with one arm draped over the shoulder of the third boy, Chang drunk-walked over to Grandmaster Kim and collapsed into one of the waiting-area chairs. While they tended to him, I walked over to Daria and asked about her legs.

"I'm okay, but I can feel the charley-horses already," she said in a whisper that I could barely hear over the noise of the fan. "I don't know if I can go the whole hour on these legs though."

I nodded, now understanding why she took such a wild homerun swing against Chang. I reached over to her gym bag and pulled out the chest guard she brought. It was a brand new, stiff and shell-like Adidas chest guard that was at least a couple of sizes too small for her. A lot of times sport competitors will try and get away with the smallest chest guard allowable in order to minimize the legal scoring area, but that was obviously not the right strategy today. Nonetheless, it was better than nothing. I motioned for her to turn around and I loosely tied the chest guard on her, leaving as much give as possible to allow the child-size chest guard to hang low enough to almost reach her hips.

As I tied, I told her the third boy was probably out to make her pay for the knockout and for Tony's collarbone and fingers. Since her legs and hips were stiffening, she had to rely on strength and positioning more than movement and agility. I directed her to fight like a boulder and to step in and block hard with her chest guard against any kick she could not evade. She was to aggressively push and shove against the boy and make him hit the ground as often as she could.

"Eat his attacks, but do it at the right time and at the right angles to minimize the damage to yourself. You want to off-balance him enough to shove him backwards or, better yet, straight into the ground. The more times he lands only half-kicks at full strength and the more times he ends up on his ass after picking up his legs, the better. Eventually you'll wear him out, and he'll start making bigger and bigger mistakes that you can then exploit. Play defense until you can play offense."

She nodded and maybe even smiled a bit as she popped her mouthpiece back in and headed to the center of the mat to wait for the third boy. Grandmaster Kim said nothing about her added equipment and promptly sent his third fighter out to face her.

For the next half hour against the third boy, who was very skilled, very fast, very aggressive and very much so out for blood, Daria barely threw a handful of kicks. Instead, she played Sumo while the boy tried to play Olympic Taekwondo. Most times when he threw a kick Daria would step right into and then beyond the sweet spot, looking to shove him over with a body slam or an illegal forearm while his leg was still up in the air. I counted 56 times he landed on mat. If their fight was scored under standard competition rules, Daria would be either disqualified or losing 100-0 because of all the hits she took and all the pushing penalties she would accrue. But since this was just a Sunday morning practice bout between the students of two of Taekwondo's old guard, it was only the fight that mattered.

As I predicted, the hard checks and the falls eventually wore the boy out and caused him to lose his form and precision. Daria herself was beaten up but also ironically somewhat rested. As the boy faded, she started to pick her spots and advance her attacks, and the two were fairly evenly matched for the remainder of the fight.

Grandmaster Kim obviously saw through the gamesmanship but said nothing as his last remaining student continued to lose steam. At exactly the one-hour mark he ordered the two to stop and brusquely indicated to me that the lesson was over. Daria came over to bow her thanks to Grandmaster Kim and to her opponents and was met with limp handshakes and a wall of silence. I expressed my gratitude again in Korean and was answered with a grunt.

Clearly, we had overstayed our welcome and in a matter of minutes, Daria had her gear shoved back into her gym bag and Tony was unceremoniously unlocking the front door to usher us back out onto the streets.

Emerging from the basement storefront, it took both of us more than a few beats to readjust our realities to the busy commercial New York City street. Would any of these passersby ever believe that this girl just beat up three junior national contenders?

148

We walked a few blocks in silence before I realized she was still wearing her sweat-soaked t-shirt and Taekwondo pants. I asked her why.

"The cockroaches in the bathroom were HUGE!" she shrieked, suddenly releasing all the pent-up tension and anxiety of the last hour. She reflexively hugged herself around the shoulders and threw a small tantrum in the middle of the sidewalk as images of the bugs danced behind her closed eyes.

I couldn't help it and burst out laughing like a mad person over the ridiculousness of this girl. But she kept her eyes closed and continued to stomp her feet like a petulant five-year-old, so I moved in to shield her puerile form from the no-nonsense pedestrians on the Flushing sidewalk. Gently folding my arm around her shoulders, I slowly guided us back toward the parking lot.

Olympians in the Bronx

Thank goodness for my mom's masseuse. By Monday afternoon my legs were almost fully recovered and strong enough to make it through another week of plyometric workouts and competition team sparring sessions. But the bruising from the leg kicks and then the painful deep tissue massage left my hips and outer thighs a nasty blackish purple and green for days.

In unspoken complicity over what happened Sunday, *Sabumnim* spent the week tutoring me on clinching strategies and techniques on how to neutralize low double kicks. He also centered all of the advanced classes and competition classes around simultaneous counters, especially the jumping spin hook kick.

Over lunch on Thursday, he finally broached the topic of the visit to Grandmaster Kim's *dojang* in his usual oblique and subtle way. "How was it?" he asked as a non sequitur, knowing that I had been waiting for the question all week long.

Since the long drive home from Grandmaster Kim's *dojang* I had been trying to process the lesson and the whole Flushing experience. By Thursday I had come to a couple of preliminary conclusions and a reaffirmation.

"It was different than any sparring match here at the *dojang*," I carefully replied. "It was also different than any tournament I've ever been to. Not just because all the rules could be bent, but because for the first time I felt like I could really do this. I can really fight... I mean, not that I'm all that good or anything, or that I'm a world beater… Just that I'm comfortable with it… Sir…."

I blushed at the confession, which sounded like a boast, but really was not. "It felt good. And I realized how much I love Taekwondo all over again."

In response, *Sabumnim* flashed his right knife-hand toward me and made a sudden motion with his body, projecting the full force of his internal energy as if to strike me. I quickly brought my arms up to block, but wasted enough time holding my breath, flinching and thinking rational thoughts of disbelief to know that I would be dead if he wished it so. Of course, nothing happened and after a few super-sonic heartbeats I uncoiled from my defensive posture and watched *Sabumnim* pop another piece of *kimbap* into his mouth. He chewed, swallowed and sipped from his tea before grumbling, "Is that so…."

*   *   *

The following Sunday brought rain and an unseasonable chill. Thinking that something warm would be perfect for breakfast, but also sensing that oatmeal would disappoint, I did a Yelp search for rice porridge. Crawling through the narrow, winding streets of Manhattan's Chinatown I found one of the small hole-in-the-wall places recommended by the users. I illegally parked in the commercial vehicle zone out front and ran in to place my order.

I was the only non-Asian person in the 200-squarefoot storefront and quickly realized that I couldn't read or even guess at a single item on the menu. With a crush of customers and no visible system of ordering, I picked out an elderly woman from the crowd and followed her progress toward the counter. Right after she ordered, it was my turn, and I pointed to the old lady and said, "Same. Same." Give me the same thing as this grandma. The middle-aged woman behind the counter understood and named some incomprehensible price, to which I handed over a $20 and got some change back in return.

Five minutes later I was back in my car with a mysteriously heavy bag of food. I arrived in front of *Sabum* Dae Sung's apartment right at nine o'clock and I found him already waiting outside under a large golf umbrella. After he settled into the passenger seat, I handed over the food and told him that I didn't mind if he ate in the car. So, during our 30-minute drive into the heart of the Bronx he pulled out one box of dim sum after another and offered me a bite of everything before devouring the rest himself. He presented me with one shrimp dumpling on a fork, one pork dumpling, a small folded section of rice noodle, half of a deep-fried potato-y but not quite potato croquette, half of a barbeque pork bun, one stewed chicken's foot (which I declined as, um, too slippery while driving), one savory bite of sticky rice with large boiled peanuts and finally, half of a flaky egg custard tart.

After that last bite I wondered out loud, "There wasn't any rice porridge? But that place is supposed to be famous for their rice porridge."

"You ordered rice porridge too?" he asked incredulously. "That's a lot of food, Miss Piggy."

"Uh...," I started and confessed to how I actually ordered. "I just assumed since this place popped up pretty high on Yelp for rice porridge that everyone would be ordering it..."

Before I had the chance to finish my explanation, he was already clutching his midsection and convulsing with silent, hiccupping laughs while leaning his head against the window to try and contain himself.

"That grandma probably bought enough food for her whole family..." he gasped in between his bouts of laughter. "And I was just about to complain to you about the lack of chopsticks and hot chili oil! But there's no way they would even think of including chopsticks and hot chili oil for a *gweilo*."

"What's that?"

"That would be you. It's a pretty derogatory word that means foreigner."

Does he know Chinese too? As if he read my mind, he casually continued, "Don't worry. I'm *gweilo* too, but they don't realize it until I have to open my mouth."

His laughter trailed off a bit as he pointed out a parking spot on a dilapidated street and said, "We're early. Let's take a little walk and find a bodega to get a Coke so I can wash down the five pounds of food you just fed me."

We bought the Coke and a couple of Gatorades at a nameless bodega run by an Indian guy working behind two layers of bullet-proof plexiglass. From there we walked through the blighted streets of the rundown neighborhood until *Sabum* Dae Sung stopped in front of the strangest-looking *dojang* I have ever seen.

The little two-story red brick building looked residential with a tall chain-linked fence and a locked gate separating it and its tiny front yard from the public. Not only that, but the chain-linked fence was purposely cut at the top to expose spikey, unwelcoming ends that served as a fortifying decorative touch just short of barbed wire. In contrast to the fence however was a candy-striped awning and a large front window mural decorated with cartoon kids dressed in white and blue *doboks*, smiling and advertising: "Day Care! Martial Arts – Karate – White Crane Kung Fu – Taekwondo – Jujitsu – Aikido For All Ages! After School Pickup!" There was also a luridly bright neon sign behind a smaller window on the other side that flashed "Open" in staticky three-second intervals.

Pausing at the gate, *Sabum* Dae Sung pulled out his phone and dialed someone inside. He spoke in native-sounding Spanish to probably let them know we were here. Less than a minute later, a tall Hispanic guy appeared in the doorway with two bare-chested boys at his side and a matronly woman cradling a baby standing guard behind him. He broke out in a smile in greeting *Sabum* Dae Sung and rushed to unlock the gate for us.

The two hugged and spoke quickly and excitedly like long-lost friends as I followed silently behind them into the house. As far as I could tell, to call the converted residence a *dojang* or day care seemed to stretch the legal constructs of municipal zoning and licensing.

Right off the entryway, we passed an untidy, open kitchen opposite a darkened bedroom filled with a colorful mess of toys, picture books, Legos, crayons and tiny furniture. The next room over was a dark and windowless closet with three child-sized cots occupying every square inch of the space. Beyond that, the living area was matted like a traditional *dojang* but was also clearly the domain of two large pit bull mixes who were panting heavily in the humidity and pacing back and forth behind a plastic childproofing barrier that looked inadequate for keeping children out, let alone for keeping the dogs confined. Nearing the opposite end of the house, we passed the largest and messiest room on the floor where piles and piles of stuff spilled from two sets of bunk beds onto the floor and into every corner that I could see.

Our procession continued down a narrow, unfinished wooden staircase and into a grey cinderblock basement. There, a handful of short teenage boys and a tall and strong-looking young woman were warming up and stretching to the beat of Dr. Dre streaming from a cellphone into a set of cheap wireless speakers with the volume reverberating on high. As we entered, *Sabum* Dae Sung's friend went over to lower the volume by half and called his students over to meet me and *Sabum* Dae Sung. Six sets of wary and contemptuous eyes drilled holes through me as they perfunctorily nodded their acknowledgement at the stranger in their midst. A sudden and unexpected adrenaline dump semi-paralyzed my nervous system and I was unable to muster anything more confident than a lame smile and a hopefully not too goody-two-shoes bow in return.

Sabum Dae Sung chuckled at my discomfort and unhelpfully goaded, "Kemena fights 63 kilos and represented Puerto Rico at the Olympics in 2016. I know her brother

Ángel from my competition days. He went to the 2008 Beijing Olympics and the 2012 London Olympics in my weight class."

My brain froze for a second while I tried to process the talent level in the tiny basement *dojang*, but *Sabum* Dae Sung was quick to snap me out of my stupor by giving me a tiny shove toward the bathroom that apparently doubled as a changing room. "They're starting class soon," he said. "Get changed and join them."

Class turned out to be a non-stop series of kicking and conditioning drills done in two lanes up and down the tiny basement. Most of the basement floor was padded in red puzzle mats and the space was distinctly separated into two 30-foot-long lanes with a large square concrete post inconveniently planted in the middle. The students worked hard and screamed and yelled their *kiaps* loud over the hip hop playlist, which thumped uninterrupted throughout the class. One lane was for pad drills with Ángel and the other was for lunges, squats, broad jumps, ducks walks and a whole array of leg killers that made sure no one rested for even a second.

I was not used to the constant *kiaps* or the mind-numbingly loud music, but the yelling and the beats quickly put me in a workout trance and I fell into a rhythm with everyone else. There was no clock on the wall like you would see at most *dojangs* so I had no idea how much time passed between me feeling strong and energetic to me having to dig deep in order to fake every kick and *kiap*. By the time Ángel called for a water break I was light-headed and barely able to keep up my kicking charades.

Sabum Dae Sung approached with a yellow Gatorade and held out it out to me after twisting off the cap.

"Thanks," I said through a raspy *kiap*-aggravated parchedness.

"Maybe I should have warned you that Ángel and his group work pretty hard," he said somewhat smugly. "Still, not bad. That was almost two hours of non-stop practice. You have another hour of drills though and then some sparring."

My legs wobbled a bit at the prospect of only being halfway done. But worse than that, I looked over to see Kemena and one of the boys laughing and dancing from across the room as if the last two hours had been a cake walk for them.

"Oh god, I'm screwed," I thought while trying to project a 'is that all you've got, I could do this for hours' attitude. Staring straight back at me with wolf-like intensity, I could feel Kemena calling my bluff as she continued to sway ferally in time with the music.

Unsurprisingly, Ángel paired me with his sister for the sparring drills. She wordlessly took her place opposite me, and with territorial pheromones oozing rancor and dominance from her every pore, she proceeded to try and pound me into submission. I was used to more friendly sparring drills where partners help each other out in order to practice timing, distance, combinations and angles. But after letting her nail me once, I realized this was going to be a pissing contest of epic proportions.

Because the drill was scripted, we traded back and forth, hitting each other with all our might. Every time my foot bounced off her chest protector, she flashed me a malicious shark-toothed smile with her garishly-decorated mouthpiece. And every time she buried her foot inches deep into my chest protector, I felt my lungs deflate and the forcibly-expelled air catch in that emotionally weepy part of my lower throat. Time and again I had to gulp that involuntary whimper back down with my bile and regather my courage before resetting to start all over again. Just when I felt myself starting to crumble a little with muted sobs of frustration simmering just below my fake bravado, the sadistic partner drills ended and we were granted another water break.

"Welcome to the big boys' club," *Sabum* Dae Sung teased as he brought me the rest of the Gatorade.

As I sipped and pondered how much more of this I wanted to take, he arched his long torso comically sideways to look me in my eyes. "We can stop if this is too much," he said, not without empathy.

He unbent his torso and I looked up at him as he continued in all seriousness, "She is world class. But the difference isn't a matter of talent, size or even training. The difference is in attitude and desire. She is the queen of this *dojang* and an Olympian, and just on account of pride alone she will feel the need to rip you a new one. Also, you're a threat. You must know how girls are when they sense pretty young things parading around their menfolk." He added that last superfluous bit with a hint of wicked mockery before stuffing my helmet onto my head and pushing me back toward the mat before I could chicken out.

Thank god the boys fought each other first. By the time I stepped up to face Kemena, I had regained my resolve and a familiar wave of excitement and nervous energy electrified me from deep within my core and radiated into my limbs. My legs were somewhat rested, and after seeing the mediocre level of the boys' matches, I felt confident that I could take on the fighters from this *dojang*.

Unfortunately, that buoyant wave of conviction was short-lived. Within the first 30 seconds of standing opposite Kemena I was retreating and in full survival mode as the Olympian, who fights two weight classes above mine, attacked with maximum speed, power and venom. All I could do was play defense and actively guard my head against a quick knockout. She hit me everywhere, trying to drive her foot straight through my flesh and bones every time she made contact. Miraculously I lasted through another 90 seconds of retreating and punishment, as I shamelessly cheated with the walls and the concrete post in order to buy myself defense and time.

"She's in your head," *Sabum* Dae Sung said urgently as he dragged me by the elbow into a corner. "All those games she played this morning has gotten to you. You have to fight her in the middle of ring. Start with one hit and then work on another hit. She's not superhuman, she can be hit. No more

157

running away! In order to get better, you have to learn how to beat better."

I was unconvinced. But despite my misgivings, I followed *Sabum* Dae Sung's instructions and resolved to stand my ground even if it meant taking a beating or getting knocked out. We fought for another five rounds, with me gamely hanging on and emptying my entire arsenal to try and figure out how to neutralize her superior attacks. She continued to overwhelm me and took pleasure in pummeling me with her best shots, but surprisingly, I could also slowly sense her frustration rise as she failed to knock me out or make me quit.

As I started to land more shots of my own, I also began to notice other small cracks in her armor. A well-timed lead-leg counter to her throat briefly reddened the corners of her eyes. A wildly aggressive skipping side kick caught her strong enough to produce a little gasp. A flurry of non-stop attacks when I imprudently fought like a madwoman in the middle of the third round caused her to hyperventilate and cantankerously yell for ice with her water during the break. And finally, when the last round was over, she ripped off her helmet and bent over exhausted, with her hands pressed heavily into her knees, no longer dancing and looking slightly less invincible than before. There was also much less vitriol in her eyes and demeanor when we finally shook hands and half-bowed our gratitude at the end.

Later, I let *Sabum* Dae Sung drive while I tucked myself into the passenger seat and zoned out in a wounded daze. I don't know how long he was speaking before I finally tuned in to hear him say, "… fighting hungry and fighting to validate your very existence. When I first got to know him it was his grandmother, parents and eight kids in that house. His father worked three jobs in the Bronx, his mother travelled an hour and a half each way to nanny a kid in Park Slope and he and his grandmother helped keep house and raise his siblings. His father taught him Taekwondo and trained the whole family. I think Ángel was put in charge of the *dojang* and the day care when he was just a kid himself; he never really got past the seventh grade. But somehow, he made himself into a powerhouse Taekwondo player and is now pulling his sister and his brothers up to that same level. These days he's retired and has a wife and three kids living under that roof too."

"Holy shit," I murmured.

"Yeah, anytime you think you're working hard, or life's unfair or you're fighting long odds, just think...," he said with his voice trailing off.

"Yeah..."

*　　*　　*

The following Thursday when *Sabumnim* finally broached the topic of our most recent Sunday excursion I took the chance to amend my previous assessment.

"I have a long way to go," I admitted.

"Hmmm, everyone has a long way to go," he echoed without censure.

Finishing School

Each week, I took her to a different *dojang* where the instructor was either friendly with my father or friendly with me. We visited Ángel and Kemena a second time in June, and Daria's improvement was astounding (although I obviously had to begrudge her that kind of over-the-top praise).

In between, we paid our respects to Grandmaster Shim out on Long Island where she put in a decent performance against his son who was a Junior National Team member at 48 kilos; Grandmaster Pak in Morristown, not far from my father's *dojang*, who attracted many of the best fighters in the Northeast region; Sifu Liu in the Red Hook area of Brooklyn where his students matched up against her using San Da, which is like a Chinese version of Taekwondo, Karate and Muay Thai all combined into one vicious martial art; several members of the Columbia University Taekwondo team who were still hanging around the campus; and Master Martinez in Worchester, Massuchuetts, another one of my contemporaries who now owned his own *dojang* and aspired to train future champions.

My father took me on a similar training circuit when I was 16 years old, explaining that the experience was a finishing school of sorts. The barnstorming fights against different competitors on their home turfs in hostile or at least less-than-friendly environments were meant to round out and polish my Taekwondo education. Unlike a sanctioned tournament where all the competitors were subject to similar conditions, 'asking for a lesson' from unfamiliar opponents, each using different styles in the disorienting surrounds of their home *dojangs,* was a test intended to 'grow hair on your balls,' according to my father.

At the time, I loved visiting different *dojangs* and fighting aggressive new guys. A lot of my opponents trained with no concept of competition fighting and had never stepped foot into a ring. They countered my Olympic aspirations with only the purity of a martial spirit cultivated for maximum open-handed combat efficiency and probably pushed me harder and further than any official tournament ever did.

During that summer the only thing I really objected to was the feeling of being a debutante on display for the sake of my father's ego within his Taekwondo network. After visiting a *dojang* there was always the inevitable *soju*-soaked meal during which my father would fake-humble disparage me (and my brothers) in front of his friends, as was the traditional way among old Korean men. "My good for nothing son can maybe win a few fights here in America, but would never be able to rise above a high school B-level team in Korea." "You can't really push these creampuff kids hard anymore, which means you end up with a bunch of sissy-ass boys." To ad nauseum.

There were also nights when the other kids and I were designated attendants and subserviently bowed and scraped our way through the evening pouring drinks and refilling *bansang* (appetizers) for the grandmasters, who found plenty of ways to demean us and remind us that we were still just powerless little boys. And then there was one evening in a private room at a posh Korean restaurant where two of Grandmaster Pak's top students and I were ordered to drop our pants so the grandmasters could compare the maturity of our manhoods.

I am sure it was all in the name of some form of shibboleth required to join their club, but added to everything else, that socially tumultuous Taekwondo cotillion season completely turned me off of my father's Taekwondo universe. Despite the excitement of the fights, I could not wait to escape the strictures and subculture that ultimately colored my perception of Taekwondo practice.

Now, when I return to these worn-out *dojangs* and present my adult self to these rough-hewn old men still trapped in their incongruous lives of pining for a kind of nearly extinct martial authenticity, while still being financially obligated to soullessly pander to helicopter parents who demanded monthly belt promotions for their little sweet 'ums, I feel boundless relief if not downright superiority over my escape from their fate. Having been granted the gifts of time and distance, I am now able to disregard all the social and political nonsense of that bygone time and rediscover the life-affirming beauty of the fight itself. And watching Daria battle against the new generation of fighters produced under that old guard rekindled some vestige of my father's legacy deep within me – a legacy that I now sensed to be inexorably stamped into my core and essence.

The last exam of my finishing school experience was thrust upon me without me ever suspecting it as such. My father had made arrangements for us to visit his old friend Grandmaster Oh in Los Angeles, but when we arrived at the airport, he held out only one set of tickets. 'Obey Grandmaster Oh, don't embarrass me, and don't get yourself killed,' was what I remember him telling me at the gate.

Among my father's friends, I always played the game of who fits where. Did they know each other from the military, or more precisely the Flying Tigers? Did their affiliations extend back to their Taekwondo days in Korea? Or were they new acquaintances who forged a different kind of relationship in the Korean Taekwondo circles of America? Despite having no evidence to back my convictions, with Grandmaster Oh I had no doubt that their brotherhood sprung from their shared combat services with the Flying Tigers.

During my two-week apprenticeship with Grandmaster Oh I spent the days working alongside him and his son at his upscale *dojang* in Santa Monica near the beach; and the nights were spent prowling the seedier bars and hangouts of Koreatown and its adjacent neighborhood of South Central. I learned how to properly curse in Korean and Spanish, roll

162

cigarettes and handle my liquor. I was also introduced to the world of casual sex and casual street violence. My first afternoon in his *dojang* was spent practicing with a 3.5-inch Benchmade spring-loaded combat knife, and after passing Grandmaster Oh's test on the basic deployment and use of the knife I was instructed to carry it everywhere we went, but only to use it if my Taekwondo was not enough.

I thought the knife was overkill, but it turned out that Grandmaster Oh was a genius at picking bar fights and street fights with young men of questionable legal or citizenship status in the parts of town that the LAPD seemingly never patrolled and where the locals rarely bothered to file a report for anything short of homicide. He would purposely stick out like a sore thumb and behave like an obnoxious wannabe tough guy, drinking loudly and cursing drunkenly until some poor sap took him for a soft target and tried to land a cheap shot. At that point, he expected either his son or me to jump in and take care of the mess while he sat back and assessed our performances.

From his son Andrew I learned how to block haymakers and reverse them into half-nelsons. I also learned how to move my head and deflect like a boxer before stepping in and transitioning to slashing elbow strikes. Andrew also taught me the art of dealing with multiple attackers in small spaces and how to neutralize knives without having to deploy my own (throwing chairs, bottles or pint glasses at center mass before disarming was the key). By the second week, I was thrust into these fights solo and handled myself well enough to emerge with only a shallow knife wound on my left forearm, which still remains today as a reminder of my education. At the end of my visit, Grandmaster Oh shook my hand like a man and told me I was welcome back any time. And a few years later, I chose UCLA for college and spent another four years at his finishing school.

Now it was Daria's turn at a final indoctrination, and I had a feeling as to what my father wanted. On the last Sunday in June, less than two weeks before the U.S. National

Championships, I instructed her to show up at my friend's *dojang* in the South Broad Street neighborhood of Newark, New Jersey. I warned her that it was a rough part of town and suggested that she use public transportation instead of risk getting her fancy BMW burglarized or car-jacked. I also told her I would meet her out front, but if I was running late that she should go in and introduce herself to Master Ahmed El Sawalhy.

With my buddy Ahmed (80kg Olympian at the 2004 Athens Olympics representing Egypt), I asked him to let his students rough her up a little bit and to push her to the edge. I told him it was a test and that I would not be showing up until it was over. I explained that my presence would always hold her back from ever discovering the true range and depth of her own confidence and that in situations of adversity she needed to learn how to stand up for herself. Having been forced during his own career to conquer similar demons, my friend understood and agreed to be complicit.

That Sunday I drove in on my new but used Kawasaki Ninja racing bike that was painted a beautiful matte black and bore only a few scratches and one small ding from the negligence of its previous owner. It was a gift to myself for acing the Boards, and I now reveled in the physical power and delight of the bike as I sped down the Interstate toward Newark. I arrived a little before noon and secured my bike behind a diner three blocks from Ahmed's *dojang*. With time to kill, I settled into a booth at the diner and had a rubbery Taylor ham and egg sandwich with a nasty cup of watery, burnt coffee for the worst brunch ever. My first clinical rotation assignment for the next semester was emergency medicine so I pulled out a corresponding set of flash cards and started to familiarize myself with the subject. An hour later, after declining several refill attempts on the coffee, I gathered my things and headed for Elite Combat Systems.

As I walked into my friend's *dojang* I immediately sensed the hurt in her demeanor that was as unconcealed and barefaced as the split lip and the small mouse blossoming

164

under one eye. Ignoring her silent recriminations, I went straight to confer with Ahmed in his office. He gave me a summary of their morning practice and reassured me that she fought with a lot heart against his best junior male fighters. As I thanked him, he reached over to shake my hand and clap me on the back while emphasizing that she was welcome back anytime.

When I returned to collect her, she remained testy and petulant even as I nudged her through the door. On the walk back to the diner I tried to lighten her mood by conveying Ahmed's unvarnished praise of her abilities and her fighting spirit. "It takes a brave soul to walk into an unknown *dojang* and face those challenges alone," I started. "I'm sure my father has fed you his standard line of how he doesn't believe that when the student is ready the teacher appears. But what he might not have told you is his belief that when the student is truly ready, the teacher disappears. Lao Tzu, I think."

I was going to elaborate, but as we approached the diner alleyway a group of three young men were in the process of picking up my locked bike and carrying it away. What the fuck?! I chased after the bastards and caught up to them before they cleared the alleyway. Sensing my approach, they dropped the bike on its side and turned with the intention of fighting me for their prize. The guy closest to me rushed forward with a classic haymaker. Seeing no weapon in his hands, I dropped my level and used a shoulder to tackle him in his midsection. I drove him backward as far back as I could, straight toward the second guy before reaching down with both hands and pulling his legs out from under him while piling driving his weight straight into his friend.

As I dealt with those two, Daria hurled her gym bag into the face of the third guy who was concentrating on his buddies and not the girl who he probably ignored as inconsequential. As he flinched and brought his hands up to deflect the bag, she flew forward to catch his left arm and wrenched it behind his back for a hammer lock. Before he could muscle his way out of the lock, she redirected her

165

momentum in a tight counter-clockwise circle and used her right hand at the base of his neck to pound his face into the alleyway wall. It only took two good knocks on the coarse stucco wall before the guy slumped to the ground.

Meanwhile, I had grabbed the leg of the first guy and dislocated his knee with a knee bar, but that move gave his buddy a chance to scramble out from under him. His buddy was now standing over me and gauging how best to maul me with his steel-toed Timberlands when Daria snapped a side kick into the transverse lateral part of his knee, forcing it sideways in a direction nature never intended.

I quickly stood up, righted the bike and pointed its nose toward the street before retrieving an extra helmet from the trunk for Daria. She shouldered her gym bag like a backpack and fastened the helmet before stiffening like a board.

"Climb up behind me and grab tight around my waist," I yelled. "We have to get out of here."

She still could not move, and stood there motionless and expressionless.

"Come on!" I revved the bike hard and made a motion to grab her. Thankfully the roar of the engine snapped her out of her indecisiveness. As she climbed on and leaned forward to secure herself to me, a small crowd of teens started to gather at the entrance of the alley. I revved the bike again and moved forward with just enough speed to convince the onlookers to scatter as we approached. Once we hit the road, I opened the throttle and raced out of the neighborhood, not letting up until we reached the Interstate. She held me in a death grip the entire time.

I decided to detour to my father's *dojang* to get her cleaned up and settled down before driving her home. She was still catatonically silent as we entered the dark and empty *dojang*, and I was about to suggest that she take a shower while I brewed some tea when I looked over to see her weepy, lustful eyes begging for an embrace and maybe more.

It's a pretty well-known fact that experiencing and surviving stressful combat situations can trigger some serious

PTSD-related heightened emotions afterwards. There must be some primeval survival code imprinted in our DNA that made it natural for us to immediately want to reaffirm our life forces through intimate contact after coming down from the euphoria of escaping from danger or death.

My own emotions started to stir at the thought of her excitement and the look in her eyes. But I took a large measured step backwards as she leaned forward. A long time ago, I had desperately sought comfort and release in the arms of plenty of anonymous women after bar fights and street fights under Grandmaster Oh's tutelage to know that that was not what I wanted for her or myself.

She started tearing and trembling at my rejection but I left her there shaken and confused while I headed to my father's office to make tea.

Demons

Before *Sabum* Dae Sung disappeared from my life again that Sunday he made tea. Before he made tea, I longed desperately to throw myself at him and cling to him body, mind and flesh, as if my life depended upon it. I had never desired anything more, and if it wasn't for his rejection and the sobering setting of the *dojang*, I might have been bold enough to force a different outcome. Instead, I shriveled and briefly became a lost soul.

He made tea and then lectured into the ether about my morning matches at Master Sawalhy's *dojang*, about the skirmish with the bike thieves, about the differences between street fighting and sport fighting, about the next steps I needed to take to improve my game, about the Flying Tigers, about some Master Oh who I didn't know, about a lot of things I didn't care about and failed to comprehend. He droned on and on about Taekwondo while I stared mutely into my insipid barley tea, hating his obfuscations of the real underlying tension between us and yet wishing he would never stop babbling.

Eventually he lapsed into a silence that neither of us could break. We left the *dojang* as the sun was setting and he drove me home on his bike. And despite the fact that he cruised slowly and carefully along the winding residential streets, I held on tighter than before and never wanted to let him go. When we arrived, I reluctantly dismounted and was about to invite him inside when he held out his hand for his helmet and wished me luck.

"Graduation day, champ," he said, treating me like a little sister/golden retriever mix. "You're going to do great."

And then he was gone, coasting back down the street without even a backward wave.

I texted him a few times later that evening. It started with innocuous one-liners like "Thanks" and "Do you think I'm ready for Nationals?" and "Will you please be my coach at Nationals?" But then it quickly devolved into the long-winded and solipsistic. "I need you at Nationals and the Trials. Only you can bring the best out of me and help me realize my potential. My dreams depend on you!" When his replies were not forthcoming, I unwittingly careened into a personal wilderness. "Is this it? Are you abandoning me? Is this goodbye forever? Don't you care about what happens to me and my dreams?"

Twenty-seven unanswered text messages and an anxious, sleepless night later I was calling him the next morning and leaving voicemails like, "Um, hi. Sorry to keep bothering, but this is really important. Nationals are so close and I was wondering if you can tell me what I should be working on. Any last-minute advice? Call me...."

I spent the week in a daze, barely able to go through the motions at the *dojang* and constantly checking my phone for any signs of communication from *Sabum* Dae Sung. *Sabumnim* never inquired about the weekend but lightened my training and teaching responsibilities considerably. Unfortunately, that meant I had even more time to obsess about *Sabum* Dae Sung and his sudden absence from my life. Consumed by the disillusions and attendant anxieties that now haunted my mind and sabotaged my normal sense of self, I started questioning the value of my Taekwondo practice without *Sabum* Dae Sung by my side. It was like my motivation for excellence and achievement relied solely on *Sabum* Dae Sung's presence to witness it. I suddenly couldn't imagine a time when it wasn't so.

I even went as far as daydreaming about crashing and burning at Nationals just to make him feel guilty for his abandonment; and then of course, he would recognize the wantonness of his selfishness and return to be with me through the Trials, the Worlds, the Olympics and then possibly forever.

Also, in a surprising fit of irrepressible jealousy that further blindsided my rational mind, I found myself neurotically cyber-stalking his beautiful girlfriend one night. All I knew was that her name was Naomi and she attended Columbia Medical School, but that was plenty enough to mire my lesser self in a sleepless night of mining the Googlesphere for anything I could find on her. It wasn't that hard, and I immediately hit upon several news articles about a prestigious research grant she received last year. From those sources, I learned that she was a second-generation Korean-American from a family of doctors and professors. Not only was she a medical student, but she was also pursuing a Ph.D. in biomedical physics and nuclear medicine at Columbia. Goddamn her! The anguish was excruciating and soul-crippling. There were no publicly-posted photos of her with *Sabum* Dae Sung that I could find, but in my mind, I had already spliced together a couples shot and could not scrub it from my increasingly bitter psyche.

When Sunday arrived again, I made an early start and followed my increasingly warped instincts across the Hudson River, down to the Lower East Side and then back up toward Washington Heights. I parked myself outside *Sabum* Dae Sung's apartment with a Gaspe Nova smoked salmon and bagel platter from Russ & Daughters. I even pre-ordered a caviar and blini supplement online; and now the fish, schmears, bagels, sliced tomatoes, capers, onions, pickles, rye bread, Siberian Baerii caviar and buckwheat blinis were all spread across my backseat in a feast fit for six to eight, according to the menu description and the bagel count. Excited, I then sat back and waited. I knew we were not on for our usual nine o'clock meeting time, but I figured he would eventually come out of or head back to his apartment. I even rehearsed in my mind how to graciously deal with his girlfriend when I invited him into my car for brunch.

It turned out to be one of those rare perfect summer days in New York City where the temperature rose above 80 degrees but the stultifying humidity was kept at bay by some munificent low-pressure system. It seemed like everyone had ventured outside to relish the mild weather and Sunday release like only tightly-wound and environmentally-hardened New Yorkers could. But several hours into my curbside vigil there was still no sign of *Sabum* Dae Sung or his girlfriend. I continued to wait past the normal brunching hours, imagining a stylish mid-afternoon start for urbanites, and kept the car idling and the air conditioning blasting in order to preserve the food. By late afternoon, the usual Merino leather scent of my car was being overwhelmed by the fish market odors of the slowly decomposing food, and I had to open the windows with the air conditioning still on full blast to recirculate and dilute the air. I had not eaten all day and now twisted around to face the back seat in order to make myself an unadorned lox and cream cheese sandwich, all the while carefully rearranging the lox pile and smoothing over the surface of the cream cheese to cosmetically make it appear like neither had been touched. I then continued to wait.

Was it surprising that the demons that had tortured me all week long did not resurface until the Sabbath ended with the late setting of the post-solstitial sun? I actually gave the universe until way past twilight before I finally succumbed to my frustrations and cleared the now fetid food from my car and into the trash bins outside *Sabum* Dae Sung's apartment. I then fled the scene of my humiliation and punished my BMW by gunning it and weaving it through stop and start traffic across the George Washington Bridge and along the narrow routes and country roads of North Bergen County. I had no destination in mind and no purpose in hand, except to speed, tailgate and then viciously pass anything in my way. I drove faster than my mind could race, and found some respite in the total concentration needed to play this stupid, dangerous game. My fuel light finally came on somewhere in Parsippany, but I pushed the car and my nerves another 25 miles toward Western Pennsylvania before I was able to back myself off the ledge.

After I refueled and downed a gas station soda after not drinking anything all day, I numbly wound my way back home in a comatose state of autopilot. This time, seemingly interminable tears of exhaustion and desolation served to quiet my mind and temporarily confound my thought demons.

Nationals and Team Trials

I finally came to a heavily-rationalized truce with myself on the eve of the Nationals. I concluded that the way to get *Sabum* Dae Sung back into my life was not through crashing and burning at Nationals and hoping that he would come to my rescue, but by achieving and winning beyond his greatest expectations of me. Then, maybe he will take notice. Or at the very least *Sabumnim* might once again force him back into being my coach.

Unfortunately, when the time came, the U.S. Nationals turned out to be anti-climactic and really not even worth the mention. The top two fighters in my weight class were already members of Team USA and skipped the Nationals in order to focus their preparations on defending their spots at the Team Trials. As a result, I dominated the other lesser-accomplished state champions with the same authority I was now used to displaying at regional tournaments. It was too easy. As I stood atop the center podium at Nationals, the cameras caught me dispassionately examining the useless hunk of shiny metal that meant nothing to me and probably even less to a six-time national champion like *Sabum* Dae Sung.

I knew I had to make the National Team to merit his attention.

The Team Trials were just a couple of weeks after the Nationals, and *Sabumnim* and I spent that time specifically preparing for each of eight invited athletes in my weight class. I amassed all the videos and YouTube clips I could find of them and we methodically watched, took notes, and created match scenarios and game plans for each fighter. In particular we focused on Gracie Figueroa, the reigning queen at 49 kilograms and a fixture on the National Team for the past three years. There was plenty of footage of both her domestic and international fights and *Sabumnim* helped me work through it all, pinpointing her tendencies, highlighting her vulnerabilities, figuring out the rhythm of her footwork and timing, and building match strategies that would match my strengths with her perceived weaknesses. For the first week after Nationals, I worked out lightly and spent most of my time meditating in *Sabumnim*'s office while he taught class. I would close my eyes, steady my breathing and then imagine my ideal fights with all eight of elite athletes in my division. I devoted the most time to Gracie, and practiced like this for hours each day.

The Team Trials were held at the Olympic Training Center in Colorado Springs and *Sabumnim* persuaded my parents to take me a week early so I could acclimate to the higher altitude. Although I was one of the nation's elite athletes invited to the fight-off for a spot on the National Team, I did not have workout privileges at the Olympic Training Center. Instead, *Sabumnim* arranged private sessions for me at a local *dojang*, and his friend Grandmaster Rhee personally held pads for me and put me through the workouts prescribed by *Sabumnim*. In addition to ensuring that my endurance could withstand the thin mountain air, Grandmaster Rhee put me through round after round after round of simulated sparring matches where he played Gracie and I drilled the essence of my game plan until it felt less like an abstraction and more like a cracked wartime code that would be my secret advantage. By the end of the week, I felt like I had been sparring Gracie my entire life and could always get the better of her. And despite the irrationalities that still plagued my mind and the continued unsteady sway of my emotions, when I fought and focused on Taekwondo, I felt nothing but confidence.

In order to keep the *dojang* open for as long as possible, *Sabumnim* did not arrive until the morning of the fight-offs. He took the first flight out from La Guardia at five in the morning and arrived in time to meet us in the lobby of the National Training Center around seven. Once he arrived, he had a few words with my parents and then signed me in and led me to an auxiliary gymnasium that would be the holding area for all the fighters. There, over 100 athletes crowded into an area matted with eight practice rings. Each competitor was accompanied by at least one coach and some even brought a retinue of sparring partners, trainers and masseuses. Although some of the athletes were already warming-up or burning off excess energy by sparring in the rings or drilling with their coaches, most everyone else milled around the large projection screen that dominated one wall of the gymnasium, waiting for the official brackets and fight order to be posted. After what seemed like an interminable wait through coaches' meetings, referees' meeting, an athletes' meeting, a health and safety (read: drug testing) meeting and introductory words from the suits at USA Taekwondo, the brackets were finally posted. In my division, I drew the third seed behind Gracie and the National B Team member, which meant that I was positioned at the opposite end of the bracket from Gracie and would only get a chance to face her in the finals, if it came to that. Now that my path through the Team Trials was set, I became increasingly excited and could not wait for the competition start.

Thinking that I should change immediately and start warming up, I was headed for the locker room when *Sabumnim* took me by the elbow and directed me to a far corner of the gymnasium, away from the matted practice area and the just-posted brackets. He pointed to a spot on the floor and indicated that I was to sit. He then lowered himself into a crossed-legged position 90 degrees from the spot where he pointed and waited while I dumped my gear against the wall and slumped to the ground next to him. Thinking only about warming-up and preparing to fight, I eased my legs into a hurdlers' stretch and was forcing my chin to the knee of my extended leg when he started to speak.

"Why are you here today?"

175

"What do you mean, Sir?" I reflexively asked, genuinely surprised by the question, but still focused on my stretching. "I'm here to win. I'm here to make the National Team." …and to win *Sabum* Dae Sung back into my life, I added silently and emphatically to myself.

"And then what?" he gently continued. "What is your plan afterwards?"

"You know!" I exclaimed. "The Worlds next year and then the Olympics in 2020." And then happily ever after with *Sabum* Dae Sung, I joyfully intoned inwardly.

"Hmmm…. And then what?"

"What do you mean 'and then what?'" I was now confused. What kind of pep talk is this?

"There is the possibility that some or none of what you plan will ever happen," he continued. "And then what? Or let me go back to the original question. Why are you here today?"

Wasn't he supposed to be encouraging me and spurring me onto victory? Why was he introducing negative thoughts into my head right now?! I was already extremely on edge and increasingly agitated when I let uncharacteristically snapped back, "Well, why are you here today?"

"Ah," he said, calmly indulging my impatience. "That's an important question too."

Then he smiled before gently answering, "I'm here to see you try and fulfill your potential."

"Right," I said, sensing positivity in his response. "My National Team potential. My Olympic potential." My potential for love and happiness.

"No, not exactly."

He slowly shook his head.

"National Team status and becoming an Olympian… those are results, not potential. Results can be influenced by fate and any number of things beyond your control. Your potential is your path and your spirit and your practice. It is the 'do' part of your Taekwondo training. Realizing your potential should be the reason why you are here today…

because is the only thing you can control. The results will be what they will be."

He paused. And then when he got no response from me, he added, "That is how you shine."

*   *   *

I was only able to contemplate what *Sabumnim* said for the brief 50 or so steps it took for me to reach the locker rooms because once I crossed that threshold a torrent of anxieties and expectations and the feelings of desperation wrought from staking a lifetime's worth of work on three short rounds of competition was magnified by the tension emanating from all the other assembled competitors wrestling with the same thoughts. I couldn't help but immediately identify and assimilate with this tribe of aspirants like myself, as our half-naked locker room tough-girl postures and the stilted attempts at comradery or psychological warfare (depending on your personality, I guess) all worked to compound the enormity of the moment. I casually sought out Gracie through the crowd, and gave an involuntary shudder when I saw how long and chiseled her body actually was. From across the room, it looked like she had at least two inches and several pounds of lean muscle on me. Damn. I quickly looked away and tried to refocus.

National Team. Worlds. Olympics. *Sabum* Dae Sung. Making my parents proud. Being a champion for my *dojang*. That is why I'm here.

The Best Laid Plans

My first match was against an awkwardly tall and very bony Junior Olympic Champion who *Sabumnim* had scouted as the least-nuanced and least-adaptable fighter in the whole field. He had pointed out that she was probably used to dominating Junior-level competition with her length and size. And from the footage we studied, it seemed like she had not yet developed any other dimension to her game. Nevertheless, *Sabumnim* cautioned that her legs were tailored-made for Taekwondo and I had to be careful not to give her too many opportunities to take shots at my head. Our game plan was to let her initiate most of the action and then play defense by blocking and adjusting the angles and distance in order to counter-attack. The ideal fight was to methodically impose a thousand paper cuts by picking my spots and striking with a simple round kick or back kick to the bottom of her chest protector. I was to avoid the clinch where her high crescent kicks would be difficult to block, and I was to avoid too many extended exchanges where I might leave my head exposed and in her strike zone for too long.

I was mildly surprised that the fight unfolded just as *Sabumnim* predicted. She aggressively pursued the high-value head shots while I darted in and out of her range with quick but unspectacular counters. As the scoreboard started slowly compounding in my favor, her attacks became more aggressive but also wilder and more predictable and easier to defend. By the third round I felt like I understood her timing and style better than she even did, and right before the end of the match

I was able to time a perfect back kick counter that knocked her to the ground for good. I caught her right where the chest protector met the hip bone and she fell to the mat and stayed down through the one-minute medical timeout.

Unfortunately, I also paid a terrible price. I stood right where she fell, ostensibly waiting for a restart, but really, I knew the moment my foot drove into her hip bone that I myself might not be able to walk off the mat, let alone finish the fight if she was able to stand back up. The bottom of my foot felt like I had just tried to break through seven boards, but missed and caught the corner. I subtly shifted my weight all over the base of my foot, trying to assess the damage and trying to prevent the fascia from cramping. Looking back, I wonder if she could have willed herself back onto her feet to finish the fight if she knew how incapacitated I was. Most likely, but no one will ever know.

When the technical knockout and medical forfeit were declared official, I painfully hobbled, using my good leg and just the smallest bit of the big toe of my injured foot to inch my way back to the middle of the ring in order to bow out. My opponent, who was now standing, and her coach were stupefied by the extent of my injury. I think so was *Sabumnim*, because he ran onto the mat after I was declared the victor and cradled me out of the competition area.

"Is it the heel or the middle of the foot?" he asked with me in his arms.

"Heel I think, like I tried to break through too many boards and missed."

"Hmmm…" was all he said as he eventually deposited me near the same quiet corner where we started the day. An event doctor had followed us into the holding area and was now asking if we needed his assistance. My thoughts drifted briefly to *Sabum* Dae Sung, but *Sabumnim* asked the doctor if he had access to a portable X-Ray machine. A couple of phone calls later and *Sabumnim* and the doctor were taking turns carrying me across the Olympic Training Center campus

179

toward the main medical facilities where a surprisingly quick X-Ray was taken.

"Nothing is broken," the doctor started, "But judging by the amount of pain you're in you might have torn the fascia and given yourself a serious bone bruise. Only an MRI can confirm that. Under normal circumstances, I would recommend two to four weeks of rest and crutches or a walking boot if you have to be on your feet. But…"

"Can you just tape me up and make it so I can get through the next two fights?" I pleaded, much like he must have expected. "I have to keep going."

Thankfully the doctor nodded his assent and got to work. In addition to taping my heel and midfoot, he also handed me a paper cup containing painkillers. Just before I was about to take them, *Sabumnim* asked, "She has a drug test at the end of the day, can she be taking these?"

The doctor just laughed and said if oral painkillers were a banned substance then everyone on the campus and elite athletes the world over would be testing positive. "I used to give Toradol or Ketorolac injections, but that is in the grey area now. But if you really need it after your next fight though…"

Both *Sabumnim* and I were a little shocked, but I downed the pills before he could object again. The doctor then handed me another packet and told me to take a second dose if I make it to the finals.

Once I was taped, I hopped off the exam table and onto my good foot before taking a few fully-weighted steps and forcing myself to ignore the pain. As I gingerly bounced on my toes and tried pivoting on the ball of my injured foot, I heard *Sabumnim* negotiating with the doctor for a set of crutches.

"No way," I said. "I can manage."

"Use them anyway," he smiled. "It's the least you can do for someone who just carried you all this way."

I adamantly refused, and *Sabumnim* let me have my way, patiently trailing after me with the crutches in hand while I slowly tried to relearn how to walk with a mummified right foot.

"It isn't that I don't think you can't handle the pain," he said, once we were outside. "And it isn't for the sake of your foot."

I looked at him.

"There are so many elements to a fight, not the least of which is strategy."

"I can't use the crutches as a weapon on the mat," I said with a borderline snarky undertone toward my teacher who I usually would not dare question. I was just frustrated and struggling hard not to let despair overwhelm me.

"Hmmm…" he brushed off my flippancy. "No one yet knows the nature of your injury. But if your next opponent were to hear of or even see you return from the infirmary on crutches, might that not cause her to reevaluate? If you can get her to underestimate your current capabilities…. It might not work, but some strategy is better than no strategy."

I stopped my stride and nodded my understanding.

"Okay," he said. "Now let's have a seat on that bench."

This time I obeyed without asking why. As I sat, he knelt and slid off my left sandal and proceeded to tape my left heel and midfoot in exactly the same way the doctor had ministered to my injured right foot. When he finished, he pointed to the crutches and said, "Now use the crutches like you have an injured left foot. Let's see if they remember or even saw the injury."

With that, he walked back toward the main gymnasium with me fake-hobbling on my good foot in his wake.

The Result

*S*abumnim and I went over our revised strategies for the National B Team opponent I would face next in the semi-final round. Like he predicted, my hobbling back into the gymnasium on crutches created quite an undercurrent of whispers and speculation among all the competitors. Next was to figure out how my opponent might adjust her tactics to my injury.

"It can be one of three alternatives," he said. "First, maybe she gets aggressive and immediately attacks to test your mobility and tries to force you to your supposedly weakened left side. If they assume it's an ankle injury or a broken bone, that could be their tactic. In that case, you must be prepared for a small retreating step and then an immediate counter-attack. We've studied her timing. She's fast, but it can be done, especially if you know when she's coming."

I nodded.

"But, there's also the possibility that her coach will urge caution because you have both feet taped in the same way. What I've done is hardly original. People have been trying to disguise and fake injuries forever. If that's the case, she might be instructed to hold back in the first five to ten seconds and dance around with feints to try and get you to show the extent of your mobility and injury. But even if she plays conservatively like that, in the back of her mind she will be thinking a little too much about how to identify your injury. That little bit of uncertainty and extra half-second she uses to try and glean and process information might be enough hesitation for you to exploit. You might only have a small window here, but it's possible she could be caught flat-footed by an aggressive and unusual attack. I think maybe a skipping side kick to the throat area?"

I nodded again, surprised at the level of detail in his thinking.

"And the third alternative would be her smartest option and the one I would recommend if I was her coach. Really, she should just stick with her original game plan and not change anything based on your injury. If your injury really did present an opportunity for her, she should be skilled enough to flow into it and exploit it if and when she feels the opening. If that is the case, you have to stick with what we practiced. You have to trust in your preparation and in your body. We can then adjust during the match."

I nodded, but was hoping against hope for one of the first two scenarios. The bottom of my foot was so tender and painful that I was not sure I could fight my regular fight and make it through three rounds.

As instructed, I limped onto the mat favoring my perfectly-fine left side while putting an enormous amount of strain on my painful right foot. We bowed in and right after the referee shouted *Shijak!* for the start, I continued the ruse by taking a defensive step backward and assuming an awkward right-foot forward fighting stance. The hope was that she had studied all of my previous fights and was now taking a split second to subconsciously process the extraneous fact that I had never started a match in such a way.

Sabumnim had told me to try and sense a flat-footedness in her processing before attacking, but I instead chose the riverboat gambling route and immediately flew at her with a skipping side kick to the throat before she even took her first breath, let alone first step or first bounce of the match. I exploded off my left leg and buried my right heel into the side of her neck right below the jawline. She was so caught off guard that her hands never even came up to try and block the attack. Instead, they hung uselessly by her sides as she landed like a felled tree onto the mat. I had guessed right. The poor girl hesitated and didn't see the unorthodox and extremely aggressive opening move coming, and the match was over in four seconds.

I was forced to stay in the ring and on my feet until the medical staff arrived to huddle over her still-fallen form and eventually carry her off on a stretcher as a precautionary measure. And then, after my hand was finally raised in the empty ring, *Sabumnim* violated all protocol and crossed onto the mat in order to carry me off in his arms.

*   *   *

Thank goodness there was a three-hour break before the finals in the evening, during which time another doctor worked on my heel before rewrapping it and ordering me to keep it propped on a heating pad as I rested and recovered. As he continued his rounds among the other athletes, I was able to catch a fitful 20-minute nap in a corner of the auxiliary gym; and after I woke, he returned to answer my prayers with an offer of a painkilling injection. Despite *Sabumnim's* muted grumblings, I eagerly consented. And even as the needle pinched into the sole of my foot to dispense the medical opiate, I could feel an immediate flood of relief and a renewed sense of strength and optimism rushing through my entire self. A couple of seconds later, as the doctor started to rewrap my foot, I smiled the full depth of my revitalized confidence into *Sabumnim's* still-disapproving eyes.

The finals were scheduled by ascending weight classes and my fight-off was to be the second of the evening. The winners of all the final fights would secure their places on the National Team and be invited to the Pan-American Games and various international Grand Prix events where they can start accumulating standing points toward World and Olympic qualification. The losers would continue to toil in obscurity and only occasionally be sent to represent Team USA at lower-tier international events that offer fewer, if any, World or

Olympic qualifying points. At stake that night wasn't just a National Team spot for this year, but also a much clearer path toward the Olympics in two years. In other words, everything was on the line.

Like he always does, *Sabumnim* prepared me by having me close my eyes and meditate on the fight. I once again let our game plan flow through my body from start to finish and when I opened my eyes, he tapped me on the forehead and lightly pounded me on the chest guard and said that all matches were won with my mind and my heart.

"Show me what is in your mind and your heart today," was all he said before he escorted me to the ring.

The match unfolded much like how *Sabumnim* anticipated weeks ago during our film study. We spent the first two rounds feeling each other out and probing each other's weaknesses. The lead drifted back and forth with neither of us able to open more than a two- or three-point gap on the other.

Before the start of the third round *Sabumnim* crouched in front of the chair in my corner, and with my legs propped on his thigh he massaged out the lactic acid and applied enough cold spray to my heel to numb out any residual pain.

"I think at some point she will try and end it," he said while he worked on my legs. "Be aware. She's not going to settle for a close fight, which at this point could tilt either way. The National Team spot has been hers for three years and she will try and decisively take what she thinks belongs to her. But you can use that against her. Be more patient than her and don't get drawn into trading blow for blow. Maybe even slow play your attacks and feed her aggression. Eventually, she'll go for the knockout counter. Keep your eyes open. You know how to counter her counter."

He smiled, as if he could already see into the future. Then he gave me a playful tap across my helmet, a light-hearted gesture that surprisingly calmed me and reinforced my confidence in his strategy. I bowed my gratitude to him and stepped back into the ring.

The score went back and forth again for nearly the entire round. We were very evenly matched and at this rate it seemed like the fighter who scored last would emerge the victor. So, with 30 seconds left in the contest, I decided to take fate into my own hands and try *Sabumnim's* tactic. I made an intentionally clumsy feint and then baited her with a simple off the line round kick at about 80 percent of my regular speed. From our video study of Gracie, I knew that her favorite counterattack in this situation was a spinning hook kick to the head, and with me making an inelegant step followed by a slow attack I was hoping to draw that out of her.

And it played out exactly as we imagined. She seized upon my weak attack and timed a perfect spin hook kick to my head. But because I had anticipated it, I was able to then launch a spin hook kick of my own a split second after she initiated hers... the perfect counter to her counter. The execution of my kick changed the angle of my head just enough to make her miss. And because she missed, her head was left exposed for a brief millisecond, during which time my toes swiped across her cheek and nose for a five-point score. She was momentarily stunned right after the hit, and I felt myself leaping backwards out of her range and launching my fist in an uppercut through the air, celebrating even before the buzzer rang a few seconds later.

I won! With an amazing highlight reel head shot no less! I was on the National Team! I won! I won! I won!

Except the scoreboard didn't register anything. In fact, the scoreboard flashed that Gracie had beaten me by one point, 13-12. The referee looked confused. There was commotion at the scoring table as all the match officials started toward the head judge. Gracie stood rooted in her spot and threw her hands up toward her coach. The crowd started rumbling with speculation as to what happened, and I slumped to my knees in the center of the ring and held my head in disbelief as I frantically searched out *Sabumnim* for help.

In a daze, I saw him approaching the ring with a blue challenge block in his hands. He explained something to the referee while miming the head shot with his hand, and the referee nodded as he accepted the challenge block and approached the replay official at the scoring table.

Okay, okay, I thought. They were going to get it squared away with the replay. Thank goodness for replay challenges. I got up off the mat and sagged, emotionally drained, into *Sabumnim's* arms. He steadied me and then barked at me to get a hold of myself, which I somehow did.

"It's okay," I told myself. I know what happened. Head shots were usually automatically scored by the electronic head gear, but since my kick only hit her face and not her helmet, a separate judge was responsible for scoring it. It must have been a human error! The judge must have missed it from his angle, but the replay cameras will rectify that. I sighed in relief and let the celebratory emotions well up inside of me again.

"Calm down," *Sabumnim* warned.

But I couldn't. I knew my foot hit, and I knew I had won. It was just a matter of time before the video review confirmed it. I looked across the mat and the grimace etched across Gracie's lips and the worried look on her coach's face seemed to confirm it as well. I was secretly jubilant again.

Several long minutes passed while the referee, replay judge and head judge watched the exchange over and over again. Finally, the referee walked back to the center of the ring, held up the blue challenge block and waved his hand back and forth to signal that the challenge was denied. At first, no one understood his official charades, but then when his hand flew toward Gracie's corner, declaring her the victor, all my senses except for anger and despair abandoned me.

"WHAT THE FUCK?!?!" I shouted in the center of the ring.

WHAT THE FUCK?!?! I lost it and rushed the scoring table.

"WHAT THE FUCK?!?!" I screamed at the judges who stared back stone-faced at me.

187

"WHAT THE FUCK?!?!" "WHAT THE FUCK?!?!" I went berserk and upended the scoring table with all its computers and video equipment and water bottles and bullshit official pieces of paper.

"What the fuck…." I whimpered to myself as *Sabumnim* restrained me with a full nelson and dragged me out of the competition area.

Sitting

Sabumnim sat me on the floor in the same corner of the auxiliary gymnasium where our day started in what seemed to be forever ago. He silently untied my chest protector, took off my helmet and then draped a hoodie over my shoulders as I held my head in my lap and cried slobbering tears mixed with incoherent and now blubbering curses.

When my angry words lost meaning, even to my ears, I vented further by pounding the floor with both fists and then throwing all my equipment and belongings as far as I could. *Sabumnim* seemed to ignore the tantrum and acknowledged my behavior only briefly when he stood to retrieve the hoodie I had flung away and replaced it on my shoulders. Then I cried some more.

Eventually everything ran dry and I was left with a violent case of post-tears hiccups that forced me to find relief in the fetal position. I closed my eyes and surrendered to the spasms until *Sabumnim* knelt beside me with a bottle of water and a gentle hand guiding me back in the sitting position. I drank and my breathing calmed as he rhythmically ran his hand up and down my back.

I must have fallen asleep, because when I opened my eyes again, I could barely lift my torso from off of my crossed legs. My back and my hips ached terribly. I lifted my head slightly to see *Sabumnim* sitting cross-legged at a 90-degree angle to my left. His back was straight and his eyes were closed. I slowly unfolded my torso and started to push myself into a standing position when his hand reached out to stop me.

"Sit," he said softly.

My mouth was too dry to verbalize a dissent, so I conceded. I remained seated and took inventory of myself. My head was throbbing from behind my left eye, all the way back into my neck. My hair was a mess and I badly needed a shower. My knees hurt, my back hurt and my feet were asleep.

"I'm hungry," I said.

At this *Sabumnim* smiled and said he could fix that. He pulled out his cellphone and called someone about food. After that, we sat in silence until a young man delivered a paper bag containing two peanut butter and strawberry jam sandwiches on white bread and two red Gatorades. I tore through the plastic wrap and stuffed big bites of the sandwich into my mouth, briefly asphyxiating myself with the peanut butter but able to wash it all down with the Gatorade. *Sabumnim* only ate half of his sandwich and offered me the other half. After we ate, I stuck my elbows into my knees and propped my cheeks onto my elbows and pouted. "I won you know."

"You won," he acknowledged.

Then I started crying again, unsure of how to further plead my case or explain myself. "But I won," was all that I could manage as I let my head slip back into my lap. This time I was able to stop the tears cold, as my self-pity met with a wall of angry, violent fire from somewhere deep within me. I was about to rage again when I felt *Sabumnim's* hand on my head.

"These obsessions and the negative emotions that come with them will ultimately limit your potential," he started.

I looked up, confused.

"This path of competition where you exhaust all of your energy and spirit for the sake of beating someone for a brief moment in time will leave you empty when the season of contests is over," he continued somewhat severely.

"And even after you have given everything to these competitions, the inability to live with the results and accept anything less than victory in this world of games will slowly, over time, fill your heart with bitterness."

190

Then his tone softened. "I don't want that for you, Daria. Chasing glory and recognition through these victories… that is not what Taekwondo is about. You are losing sight of the 'do' in Taekwondo."

I felt my eyes harden as I reflexively narrowed my mind and rebelled against his challenge to my competitive spirit and personal sense of values. He noticed my defiance but continued, "And this extreme resentment and anger you are experiencing over one instance of injustice is slowly distorting your thoughts and instincts with hate. You destroyed a lot of things today with that anger, and if you insist on continuing down that road you will eventually lose the ability and the fortitude and the support that's necessary to rebuild and move forward."

I remained silent, but my shoulders sagged a bit at that assessment.

"Most people think that heaven and hell are only matters of the religious afterlife. But from my experience, I see people unintentionally creating and slipping into their own personal hell all the time. And once they allow themselves to descend into this hell, living becomes impossible."

He looked at me, and though I expected disappointment in his eyes, I saw the depths of his sadness and helplessness instead.

Residual tears had continued to slide down my face as he spoke. "What should I do?" I asked.

"You have to let it go," he replied in barely a whisper. "You competed well, let it go. You kicked her in the face, but the judges didn't see it that way, let it go. You came in second place, let it go. You may have impressed some people and some people will never be impressed by you, let it go."

Overwhelmed, I closed my eyes. I tried to digest his words, but the logic got mixed up with the anger that still constricted the pathways of my heart. The effort exhausted me and I drifted off again.

191

I was even more tired when I finally re-opened my eyes. What time was it? *Sabumnim* was still sitting beside me with his eyes closed.

"Hmmm?" he asked.

"How do I let it go? I am so pissed! Pissed! And, hopelessly sad…."

"Use your heart."

"But my heart is so angry and about to explode with madness."

"Then use someone else's heart. Just because it's someone else's heart doesn't mean that it's any less of a heart. Use your parents' hearts. What do you see?"

I closed my eyes, and instantly my own worthless heart broke at the thought of what my parents must be going through right now. What have I done? This time I cried tears of a different sadness. When I could cry no longer, I squeezed myself into a tight little ball and involuntarily moaned at the thought of how much they would sacrifice of themselves to try and make my suffering disappear. Reflecting on the depths of their love eventually confounded the worse demons seething within me, and through that grace, I finally felt myself starting to let go.

As I relaxed, *Sabumnim* exhaled beside me and slowly declined his head.

The Zoo

I opened my eyes in my parents' hotel room bed late the next morning. The curtains had been parted and I laid there for several minutes trying to comprehend the indigo depths of the lake and the seemingly endless expanse of the Cheyenne Mountains in front of me. The view from my room had been of a manicured interior garden, so this panorama took some getting used to.

Eventually I rolled over and acknowledged the rapid soft-touch clacking on my mom's laptop. She sat cross-legged on the sofa in a pants suit looking simultaneously like a professionally-dressed college student and an overly-casual corporate executive. CNN played on mute next to her and a continental breakfast was spread out on the coffee table.

"Morning, Mom," I whispered hoarsely.

Her attention lifted and she smiled. "Good morning, D." Then she held up one finger towards me and returned to her electronic thoughts.

It took two and a half languid log rolls for me to find the edge of the bed, and even as I luxuriated in the movement, I couldn't help but notice that I was still in my *dobok* from yesterday. *Dobok*. Yesterday. I really needed a toothbrush and a shower. And coffee. Everything ached, but my head hurt the most.

I padded gingerly toward the breakfast spread, taking care not to put too much weight on my tender right heel. As I lifted the heavy silver-plated coffee urn and poured into a golden-striped demitasse, I exulted in the possibility of an exquisite brew and found myself wondering whether my dad had a chance to experience the same. Then, with my mom's attention still buried in her laptop, I sat on the floor next to her and started to eat like a person who had never tasted pancakes or croissants or berries or butter or jam. At first, I nibbled, unsure, but then I feasted and savored like I was breaking a long hard fast. The carnal pleasure of the coffee and the repast eventually restored a certain sense of physical well-being, but it also rebooted my brain and allowed all the negative emotions associated yesterday's injustices and humiliations to start stampeding their way back into my consciousness. Gradually, my throat started to constrict and my vision began to narrow.

Sabumnim might have cured me of my anger last night, but the despair was still raw and festering. As the feelings of loss and hopelessness overwhelmed me once again, I suddenly stopped chewing and swallowing and started hyperventilating and crying dry tears with my mouth still full and a wedge of pancake still trapped between my fingertips. I don't remember when my mom joined me on the floor or how long she had to hold me until my mind went numb again. She eventually gave up on her work and drew a bath for her somnambulant child and shampooed my hair while I blearily whined and blubbered, mostly to myself. Afterwards she wrapped me in a robe and sent me back to bed.

It wasn't until I awoke a second time that I wondered about my dad and *Sabumnim*.

"Your teacher carried you back here after midnight," my mom told me. "And then he had to deal with your extremely upset father."

"Where is Dad? What happened last night?"

"We filmed the entire fight, and from what we and everyone around us could tell, you clearly kicked the poor girl in the face and should have won. Your father was infuriated with the refereeing and stormed the judges table right after you caused your little scene. Long after your teacher led you away, your father was still cursing and yelling and physically threatening everyone who looked like an official. They

194

eventually had to call security to escort him out of the building."

My mom sighed. "Then he spent the rest of the evening obsessing about who to call and how to exert his influence to avenge his little girl. You know how aggressive your father can get. He wanted his federal connections to open investigations into the Olympic Committee and Team USA. And he also called his buddies at Treasury to ask about full tax audits of USA Taekwondo and every executive and director associated with it. Let's just say he was on the warpath and in a very vengeful mood."

I was now fully awake and stunned. "Did he really call Arnie at the FBI? And he knows people at the IRS?"

My mom nodded. "But when your teacher finally brought you back, your father changed course and re-directed all his anger towards him. You slept through it all, but I thought for sure your father was going to throw a punch."

"And?" I could hardly breathe.

"Just as your father was getting really loud, really rude and really out of control, your teacher leaned in and whispered something to him and then took him by the arm and led him out of the room."

"What did he say? What happened after that?"

"I don't know, but I'm guessing there must have been quite a bit of Scotch involved. They didn't come back until dawn when your not-so-sober father rushed in for a quick shower before he and Master Ahn left for the airport... you do remember that we were supposed to be on a seven o'clock shuttle back to Newark today, right?"

"Oh... crap."

"When he was getting ready to leave your father did say, 'He's right, you know. We can't let this experience embitter her and wreck her spirit. It's done. It's over. We have to let it go and help her move on.'

"Then he actually took a minute and laughed and said something like, 'You're not going to believe this, but Master Ahn thinks it's more important that D reads Chekov than wins at these tournaments.' Your father said he thought Taekwondo people lived for the Olympics, but apparently Master Ahn thinks that all this suffering over a scoreboard is just self-inflicted misery and measuring success this way is self-delusional."

My mom paused and then flashed me a version of the amused and indulgent look she usually gives my father when he goes off on a tangent. She continued, "Your father then launched into a speech about Aristotelian ethics and Confucian virtues and also peppered in a little Mencius and Plato in a kind of incoherent East meets West jumble about the ultimate purpose of humanity."

She laughed. "No kidding. I think he and your teacher must have had a few drinks and then stayed up all night philosophizing about the meaning of life and your place in it."

She then gently added, "I'm sure they fell down that existential rabbit hole while trying to figure out how to protect you and prevent you from getting mired in this destructive rut you seem to be digging for yourself. You've been pretty high-strung for quite a few weeks now, and yesterday felt like a tipping point, a troubling one…"

With that subtle reproach, a mind-wrenching amount of guilt started to creep in to add to my despair.

"Uhhh…." I started meekly. "I'm sorry about all the trouble I caused you and dad and *Sabumnim*. You had to miss work today to take care of me, huh? After spending a whole week out here because of me… and worrying about me all these years and supporting me and letting me chase after all this and then watching me fall apart yesterday. I'm so sorry, Mom."

I buried my head deep into her chest and held onto to her like I used to squeeze my raggedly stuffed rabbit in infantile times of distress and contrition and confusion and overall wretchedness. My mom stood there, stroking my hair and absorbing my tears and granting my succor. When I finally let go, she slowly removed me to arms-length and the profundity of her look bore straight through to my heart and let me know that she accepted second-place Daria and devastated Daria and love-stricken Daria and the slobbering-mess of a half-grown child Daria and dreamer Daria and selfishly lost in her own world Daria. I relaxed. Powerless against this kind of love, the life-constricting knot of misery that had spread across my chest slowly unclenched and my mind started to clear.

"Mom." I returned thoughts of eternal gratitude.

Two beats later she disrupted the peace she had created by breaking from my embrace and incongruously suggesting, "Let's play hooky and go to the zoo. It's only a few blocks away, and they have brown bears."

I actually laughed at her ridiculousness. We do visit a lot of zoos when we travel, mostly because my mom loves bears and sea otters. I always try and remind her of the Calvin and Hobbes comic strip where Hobbes the animate stuffed tiger declares to his little boy owner Calvin that visiting zoos for entertainment is just like visiting prisons for fun, but that irony held no sway over my mom's fascination with caged wildlife. "Then let's go to Alaska and see them in the wild," she always counters.

In that moment, it was like she could hear the Calvin and Hobbes dialogue running through my head and she cut me off before I could get started, "The Cheyenne Zoo has more grizzlies than the Bronx Zoo. Bigger too. I looked it up."

All I could do was smile. And she took that as a sign of life.

A Minor Case of Heat Stroke

My funk continued throughout the summer. *Sabum* Dae Sung never returned to *dojang* or acknowledged any of my texts or achievements. And *Sabumnim* continued to insist that I sit and think or unthink until I could completely let go of my anger and anguish, so I spent a lot of long and hot afternoon hours sitting cross-legged in an empty *dojang* trying to find my equilibrium and trying to find my 'heart.'

I avoided all sparring practice and instead taught myself a 540-degree spin hook kick from a series of YouTube videos and worked on trying to break three successively higher-held boards (knee high, midsection and head high) with each half rotation of the kick. The kids were very impressed with my efforts, and I was able to rediscover a little joy and amusement in my practice.

I also accompanied my mom to the Bronx Zoo three times in four weeks to see the debut of a baby gorilla, baby penguins and baby sea lions. My dad resurrected his lectures about college, and we compromised with three more Rutgers extension classes: Introduction to Macroeconomics, Plato's Republic and Level 3 Korean.

The summer dragged on until mid-August when I was officially named to Team USA as a B Team member and assigned to compete in Taoyuan, Chinese Taipei at a World Taekwondo Grand Prix event near the end of September. Gracie, the A Team member, was assigned to the more prestigious events in Rome, Moscow and Manchester, England, but I was still unexpectedly excited about my first opportunity to compete internationally. For the first time since the Team Trials, I felt a tiny spark that rekindled a little of my Olympic motivations.

The Taoyuan Grand Prix event was to be preceded by a mandatory two-week national training camp in Colorado Springs where my bona fides were to be tested again and sharpened by the best coaches and players in the nation. I knew I would get a chance to compete against Gracie there, and the thought of a rematch, even behind closed doors at a training camp, sent my mind and emotions racing. Even as *Sabumnim* continued his daily admonishments on equanimity and seeking balance and perspective, I found myself daydreaming more and more about crushing Gracie and maybe reversing our standings on the national team.

In preparation for the training camp and the Grand Prix, I started studying film again on everyone in my weight class and on my off days I traveled to the Bronx for day-long training sessions with Ángel and Kemena. Kemena was getting ready to compete for Puerto Rico at the Pan-Am Games, and I volunteered to be her sparring partner. In return, she and her brother schooled me on the nuances of the international Taekwondo game and the particularities of each nation's players.

They shared stories of their experiences on travel, international drug testing, last minute weight cuts in a foreign country and the added stresses that come with representing a nation and traveling with a team comprised of teammates you might not like and coaches, executives and officials who don't always have your best interests in mind. Despite their logistical horror stories and despite the fact that I was relegated to a backwaters Grand Prix event with other international bench-warmers, on the eve of the national training camp I was nearly bursting with excitement at the opportunity. For the first time since the Team Trials, I could envision my Taekwondo destiny again.

*   *   *

Five days before I was to leave for Colorado Springs again and a week before the academic year was to start, signaling a seasonal renewal for Taekwondo schools when kids return to the *dojang* after their summer breaks, I was slogging through another humid and oppressive afternoon as *Sabumnim's* assistant instructor. *Sabumnim* was as frugal with the air conditioning as he was with central heating, so the *dojang* air was sticky, stultifying and very unpleasant. I was daydreaming a bit while trying to teach an uninterested six-year-old how to do a front kick, and at the opposite end of the *dojang Sabumnim* was teaching a new pattern to three teenagers.

It happened faster than I was able to process, but at some point, while demonstrating the pattern *Sabumnim* took an uncharacteristically clumsy step and fell to the mat face first. By the time I reached him he was conscious, but unable to form coherent words or move enough to sit up.

Then in a cartoonishly muddled string of events, one of the parents called 9-1-1 and tended to *Sabumnim* while the six-year-old wailed and I hugged the shaken teenager who had reached *Sabumnim* first and thought he had died. No wonder eye-witness accounts of traumatic events are notoriously unreliable. I could barely remember how the kids got home, when I changed out of my *dobok* or how I thought to gather *Sabumnim's* clothes, wallet and cellphone. I even somehow conceived to press *Sabumnim's* thumb to his iPhone in order to unlock his contacts to search for his sons. Unwittingly, I called and left voice messages for his sons in their birth order, leaving *Sabum* Dae Sung for last. Why? What did I say? I don't really remember. When the sons did not answer, I went blindly searching for his daughters-in-law. I don't even know their names! Then the ambulance arrived.

An hour later I was waiting alone in the emergency room at Hackensack University Medical Center when a nurse came over to tell me that *Sabumnim* was awake and wanted to speak with me. I walked with her expecting the worse and

200

found him lying prone on the hospital bed without the energy to prop himself up or to ask for an adjustment.

I looked down at his enfeebled and diminished form and had no words and lacked the requisite life experiences to project anything but the genuine sadness and apprehension that was churning inside of me. Treating me like the distraught child I must have seemed, *Sabumnim* smiled with some effort and tried his best to reassure me, "Don't worry, Daria. It's not a heart attack or a stroke. I'm okay; maybe just too hot or too old or a little of both. I just need to rest a little. Thank you for being such a good kid. Please go home. Tae Suk is coming soon. I'm okay. Thank you…. Thank you…."

"Okay, Sir," I said, not at all relieved as his voice slowly went dry and trailed off with the effort. "I'll call my mom to pick me up, but in the meantime, I'll wait here with you until the nurse kicks me out." I looked over to see the nurse nodding her assent before I pulled a vinyl upholstered chair up to his bedside and watched as *Sabumnim* slowly succumbed to fatigue.

My mom showed up before Tae Suk or even a doctor did and squeezed me tight before interrogating me. After listening to the minimal details I could provide, she insisted that we stay until his family arrived. Then, being the nosy and forthright sort, she circled around to find *Sabumnim*'s bedside chart and flipped it open to confirm what he told me. "His EKG is normal and they've ordered a bunch of blood tests and a CT scan for later. Right now, they suspect heat stroke and are pumping him with saline and fluids"

She then replaced the chart and settled into my chair, forcing me to go search for another one in the hallway. As I dragged a second chair beside her, she pulled out a king-sized Snickers bar and offered me half, along with a large bottle of water.

"I know you're training, but there aren't too many good options in the machine out front and you probably need a little sugar in your system right now." We munched in silence and alternated between playing on our phones and watching

Jeopardy and then Wheel of Fortune on mute before Tae Suk finally showed up.

After we politely excused ourselves from *Sabumnim's* bedside and after we picked up my car from the *dojang* and stopped for Thai takeout before heading home, and as I zoned out on my couch and stared vacantly at my phone, I couldn't help but wonder why *Sabum* Dae Sung never bothered to call me back. I eventually drifted off to sleep, unsettled by that more than anything else.

Crossroads

The full impact of the situation didn't hit until two days later in a semi-private room at the same hospital where *Sabumnim* arranged a meeting with his sons and me and my parents. As if his extended stay in the hospital for something as seemingly innocuous as the original diagnosis of heat stroke didn't already raise alarm bells, the fact that he insisted that my parents accompany me to his bedside truly filled me with dread. When we arrived, I was initially relieved to see that *Sabumnim's* eyes and demeanor had regained quite a bit of his former vitality and command. But he was still dressed in an institutional gown and sat only half-way up, aided in large part by the mechanical support of his hospital bed. And the clouded, wary looks on the faces of *Sabum* Dae Sung and his brothers also belied *Sabumnim's* countenance of strength and spoke of a different reality.

I bowed my greetings to *Sabumnim* and repeated the same toward his family while my mom boldly strode to his bedside and took one of his hands in both of hers. My dad stood off to one side but somberly nodded in response to *Sabumnim's* gaze when it rose to meet his. "Thank you for coming to see a sick, old man today," he started while sandwiching my mom's hands between his to thank her for the warmth. "Non-Hodgkin's lymphoma they say. It's some kind of cancer. The radiation started today and the first round of chemo is this afternoon."

I saw my mom squeeze him tighter in sadness and sympathy, and *Sabumnim* patted her hands once in acknowledgement before lifting his eyes to mine and continuing, "I'm very sorry Daria for the favor I have to ask, but I need you to keep the *dojang* alive while I go through this treatment. Unfortunately, that means skipping the national camp and your first international meet…."

Before he could finish his thought and before I had a chance to process the gravity of the request, *Sabum* Dae Sung and Tae Suk simultaneously flew in with their vociferous objections.

"I told you, just fucking close the damn *dojang*! You're too old and too sick to continue anyway. You don't need the money! I make more than enough to fucking support you and give you whatever you need in retirement." Those were Tae Suk's vehement words for the sake of the English-speakers in the room. He followed that up with an even angrier sounding string of invectives in Korean to which his brothers viscerally responded as if they had heard a collective war cry.

Then *Sabum* Dae Sung picked up where his brother left off but took another tactic and aimed his hostile words as much toward me as toward his father. "You want this poor girl to give up on going to the Grand Prix as part of the national team in order to keep that little backwater *dojang* going? It's just like you to ask for such a selfish sacrifice. Don't you see, Daria? He's now trying to use you just like he always used us. He doesn't see you as a person or a student, it's always just about him and his *dojang* and his pride and his Taekwondo. Are you really going to give up on your dreams to perpetuate all that bullshit?"

My dad took a protective step forward to physically shield me from the wrath-filled intensity of their attacks while I stood dumbstruck and struggled to comprehend the situation. Not surprisingly, the commotion attracted all sorts of attention from the hospital staff stationed just outside the open door, and a couple of very stern and persuasive nurses immediately banished all of us from the room. Only my mom managed to stay a split second longer and bid *Sabumnim* a proper goodbye.

Outside in the waiting area *Sabum* Dae Sung seemed to regain his composure a little and explained the situation more clearly for me and my family. "It's either Stage I or Stage II and statistically speaking his five-year survival prospects are pretty good. But in order to get to remission he has a full course of radiation and then probably four courses of pretty serious chemo that will be one week on and three weeks off. If that doesn't work, they'll change the dosage and try another four courses of chemo. He's definitely not going to be well enough to run that *dojang* for the rest of this year and maybe into next year. Don't you see? The only reasonable choice is to close it."

He then turned to me and continued, "If you put your life on hold to keep that *dojang* open for him, who knows how long you'll be sacrificing your dreams. For your own sake, you have to understand that you're only this age, this skilled and this sharpened once in your lifetime. If you don't start on the international circuit now, you're not getting to the Olympics in just two short years. There's no way!" His attitude was intractable, but his logic was irrefutable.

My dad nodded and thanked him, but swiftly cut him off as irritation started to creep back into *Sabum* Dae Sung's approach and demeanor. "Go take care of your father, son. Please tell him we will be in touch."

With that my mom and dad protectively secured me from either side and guided me toward the exit.

Milk Sugar Love

Ilost a day, consumed by the wayward tides of my emotions and fears, which destroyed all semblance of higher reasoning and zombified my existence into a pajama-wearing state of anxiety and incessant Googling of non-Hodgkin's lymphoma. Besides *Sabumnim's* health, I also worried about my future and pondered my obligations to my teacher and the *dojang*. What *Sabum* Dae Sung said made a lot of sense but his advice left me feeling little a hollow. On the other hand, the thought of missing the national training camp and not competing at the Grand Prix after all these years of hard work was almost unfathomable. I vacillated between feeling empty and feeling the pain of a heretofore inconceivable sacrifice.

On the day before I was scheduled to fly to Colorado Springs for the training camp my mom found me curled up on my couch at noon eating extra crunchy peanut butter from a jar and watching some lady cook from her sprawling cattle ranch on the Food Network. My mom invited herself in carrying an insulated freezer bag that contained a pint each of mint chocolate chip and Earl Grey ice cream from Milk Sugar Love… my favorite. I watched as she retrieved two spoons from the kitchenette and then nudged a spot open on the couch beside me.

I half-heartedly protested, "I'm training, Mom. No ice cream…."

She laid my spoon down on the coffee table and popped open the mint chocolate chip, scraping the lid clean before starting on the pint.

"Let's go to Hawaii," she said. "Or the Bahamas, if you think a short trip would be better."

She then pulled me close and took a bite of ice cream with her spooning arm locked around me.

"Aren't you supposed to be at work, Mom?" I asked.

"My group just successfully launched the generic little blue pill after crushing it for 20 years with the original," my mom said with both a hint of humor and pride. "I think I've earned a little R&R. Plus, I was in this morning and everyone's already gone for the long weekend. I did a little paperwork and thought about maybe going shopping or getting my nails done. But then it hit me... What if I could convince you and Dad to take a quick trip to Hawaii?"

I snorted. "Good luck with that. Dad hasn't slept in days trying to close his deal on some company in Japan. And Hawaii isn't really a quick trip from New Jersey, you know. Plus, I can't go away now..."

She smiled and continued to lick her spoon. "It's on the way to both Taiwan and Japan. You can compete, your father can work and I'll be on a beach in Maui."

She then playfully spooned a small mouthful and fed it to me airplane-style while my head remained reclined in the crook of her arm. It was delicious. We then took turns eating from the pint, but my glazed-over eyes never left the chicken spaghetti casserole that the ranch woman was assembling, and my mom eventually lapsed into a shared television coma beside me.

During a commercial break I finally broke the lazy summer afternoon, ice cream-eating and television-watching spell by grousing, "I like the show, but it really bothers me that she never scrapes a can or a pot or anything clean. There's always like two bites of everything leftover. On the cutting board too. She always leaves small piles of unused ingredients. I bet those little scraps of onions and tomato and chicken all

207

end up in the garbage and it kills me! She should really take a lesson from the Italian grandma on PBS. Lidia rinses out all her cans and pours it into whatever she's making. And all her prepped ingredients actually go into the dish! She never wastes anything! God, I hate stupid, careless people!"

Before verbalizing that pet peeve, I had no idea how bothered I was.

My mom then hugged me closer until I couldn't hold it in any longer.

"What about the Olympics?" I whimpered over and over again until I was a hiccupping mess, unburdening all of my pent-up fears that sounded so selfish and counter to my true sensibilities that I had purposefully been suppressing them until now, when I finally surrendered to the non-judgmental confessional offered by my mom's embrace.

"I... want... sooo... bad... to go to... the Grand Prix... and the... training... camp. It's the first... step... toward 2020." My mom listened and then sagely produced a stack of brown recycled-paper napkins from the ice cream place just as I made a move to wipe my tears and snot with the inside of my t-shirt.

"I want... to help... the *dojang*... and teaching the kids... means so much... to me... but the Olympics!" I wailed at the universe, not really expecting karmic equity or enlightenment. And after crying for *Sabumnim* for days, I finally broke down and wept for myself.

As I created a small mountain of sodden brown paper crumples and snuggled deeper into my mom's lap in order to stifle my tears, she opened the now-melty pint of Earl Grey and absorbed my sobbing into her repose. The chicken spaghetti casserole episode ended and a Tex-Mex episode started without even a commercial pause. Such was the strategy of time-sucking marathons; and my mom continued to watch as I trembled in her lap.

She finally spoke just as my sobs mellowed into lethargy and my conscious grief and misery melted into the indifference of midday torpor. "Jeez, I see what you mean and it's driving me crazy too. Look at all that shredded cheese she spilled onto the counter and all the bits of onion and jalapeño dice that are still clinging to the bowls. And talk about not rinsing out a bottle! She left at least an inch of enchilada sauce in there and tossed it in the trash!"

I looked up to see my mom truly disapproving of the wastefulness, but also smiling as she casually poked fun at my previous rant. All cried out and in need of something to soothe my residual sadness, I reached up with my hand and waited as she maneuvered a spoonful of Earl Grey into my grasp.

"Can I try it with some peanut butter?" I asked as I floated the empty spoon upward for a refill.

She handed over my custom spoonful and started stroking my hair as I licked up the genius creation. "You have an amazingly generous and thoughtful old soul D," she said wistfully. "That will serve you well in the face of the inevitable uncertainties and heartbreaks of life. Regardless of what you decide, just know that the people who love you will always continue to love and support you. That includes your teacher too."

She then changed the channel and continued feeding me ice cream and stroking my hair until I slipped into a soulless slumber.

A Long Ride Home

I told her she was an idiot when I saw her a few weeks later. Not only did she sacrifice her spot at the national training camp, but that missed training camp also resulted in a forfeit of her place on Team USA. She was right back at square zero. She was once again a nobody with no national ranking, relegated to fighting other nobodies at inconsequential local tournaments. Not only that, she was also currently sacrificing her training to take on the fulltime care of both my father and the *dojang*. And not that she needed it, but I doubt that my father compensated her a dime for either. What an altruistic moron.

After Tae Suk's wife balked at driving an hour each way to shuttle her father-in-law to his chemo sessions and other various appointments, Tae Suk hired an adult nanny of sorts for our father. That admittedly tactless and bureaucratic infantilization of the grandmaster occasioned another round of explosive, angry and hurtful accusations between father and sons, the result of which was our father telling us that Daria would take care of his appointments from now on. In his words, he did not need the help of a hired stranger.

As far as I could tell, Daria now spent her mornings in waiting rooms at the hospital and her afternoons and evenings teaching at the *dojang*. My father had insisted on being at the *dojang* every day, regardless of his nausea, fatigue, pain and withering physical stature, and spent most of his days resting quietly in the office before Daria dropped him back home in the evenings. I learned more about this situation in early

October when my surgery rotation finally ended and my days normalized with an internal medicine rotation that only required me to work 12-hour shifts. On the first day I was released at a reasonable hour I hopped on my Kawasaki and gunned it straight to the *dojang*.

I arrived to see adult students leaving the *dojang* and Daria working on some sort of pattern with an unknown older instructor dressed in a plain white uniform and a tattered greyish belt. She stopped mid-movement to bow towards me but the instructor only glanced obliquely in my direction by way of the mirrors fronting the practice area before bidding her to continue with the lesson. I ignored them both and headed straight for my father's office.

This was his second round of chemo after a three-week break and I expected him to be lying down. Instead, I found him sitting upright in a full lotus position and meditating while facing the far wall. I watched his stillness for several minutes and then resignedly withdrew from the sanctum of his office and returned to the practice area. By this time, the last students of the day had left and only Daria and this unknown instructor remained on the mat. With nothing else to do, I watched while they worked.

"Hold. Ground your stance. Exhale from here…" he said before slamming a hand into her lower belly while she held the move. Then he kicked her inner thigh and slammed another open palm into the side of her ribs and when she wobbled, he said, "Foundation too weak. Where is your breathing? Try again."

They repeated the same seven steps for the next half hour, with the instructor slamming his open hand into her shoulders, arms, core and legs, testing for something she was meant to feel but that I could not see. After that came the hand strikes, which he first made her perform to his sternum. It was a straight punch, fingertip thrust and a lateral back fist combination. Not only was she unable to hurt him with any of her strikes, but eventually her fingers and wrist surrendered against the more hardened target.

As she shook out her hands to relieve the strain on her ligaments and sinew, he directed her to a new contraption hanging from the brick wall in the weight area. It looked like a leather, sand-filled pouch about the size of a small seat cushion lying flush against the wall. He showed her the same sequence of punch, thrust and back fist in a demonstration that lightly shook the building and then gestured for her to try the same. With her first attempt at a punch, she recoiled instantly upon contact and grabbed at her wrist and fingers while crouching away from the bag in agony. The instructor laughed and then showed her the sequence again in slow motion before telling her to practice on her own as he walked toward me and the office.

"Dae Sung?" he asked as he neared where I stood. "I am Morikawa, your father's friend."

I half-bowed reflexively in greeting. "Are you here to see my father?"

"I am here to lend him whatever strength and support I can."

As if anticipating his cue, my father came out of his office and bowed in the old man's direction before looking past him to check on Daria who was intently trying to pound away at the unyielding sandbag. "No idea how to use her hands," he mumbled with a slight smile before turning his attention to me. "Morikawa *Sensei* has brought some medicine. Come join us."

As I entered the office, Morikawa slipped away to change out of his uniform and my father directed me to microwave some food and open the bottle of *sake* sitting on his desk. I recognized the red Pyrex containers and pried them open to find mountains of Daria's mom's pot roast inside. I heated that up along with a large container of rice and brought everything, along with a Tupperware full of salad and *kimchi,* to the coffee table. I poured for Morikawa and myself but looked disapprovingly at my father when he nudged his cup forward.

"Are you kidding me?" I almost yelled. "Absolutely not during chemo!" I sanctimoniously withheld the bottle.

"This is how the young generation speaks to their elders," my father said impassively as Morikawa somehow disappeared the bottle from my grasp and poured a few drops into the cup my father now held up to him with both hands. "Thank you, my friend."

The two toasted and drank without giving me a second glance and started in on the pot roast.

"Hmmm, delicious. This is Korean food?" Morikawa asked.

"The girl's mother has been preparing meals for me during the weeks when I am particularly worn out. The first time I ate her pot roast I knew it was a close relative of *galbijjim*. It was such an exciting discovery that I couldn't help but humbly suggest adding a few spoonfuls of *gochujang* and some garlic paste and ginger, and now we have a half-American, half-Korean dish."

He smiled. "Bless her patience and tolerance for an old man meddling with her recipes."

Morikawa nodded appreciatively, drained his *sake* and poured again for himself but not for my father.

"The other things she makes are very American though. Nowadays, I eat lasagna, meatloaf, chicken salad, and lots of meatballs. But Daria is a good kid and always brings me *kimchi* to make it taste more familiar to my tongue," my father continued, laughing heartily at his good fortune.

"Is that why you asked me to teach her *Sanchin*?"

"Neh, such understanding is vital for a complete martial artist, no?" my father answered rhetorically in between negligible nibbles of food that he was having difficulty forcing down. "*Sanchin kata* and breathing and the *shime* and the hand conditioning... they exist in traditional Taekwondo but somehow got lost on the way to creating this strange sport that we call Olympic Taekwondo. Now it seems like we only try to jump and spin and kick to the head for points, and we have forgotten how to use our hands and our internal energy."

As their conversation veered toward *Sanchin*, which I gathered was the pattern Daria was practicing and *shime*, which

213

apparently was the basis for the strikes Morikawa used to test her posture and strength and breathing, I began to wonder what else I might have missed when I rebelled against my father and his friends during my teenage years.

I was now half-pretending not to listen as my father continued with a reference to the body conditioning of western boxing, and the discussion continued along that vein. "Not only do they harden their bodies with blows from medicine balls and other hard objects, but they also practice taking hits to the face and head. That's important too, no? Getting struck in the face area emphasizes the need for a strong neck and teaches you how to properly take a hit without getting knocked out. That's not even to mention learning how to continue fighting with facial injuries and developing the emotional temperament required to take such punishing hits. When you go to the face, it becomes much more personal than just a body shot...."

"Don't tell me you want that pretty girl to get hit in the face!" Morikawa exclaimed, cutting my father off with his objection.

"It might be necessary for her education; I might have to find her a boxing teacher," my father mused before finding his way back on topic. "But, yes, please Morikawa *Sensei*, please teach her breathing and *Sanchin* and how to use her hands first."

"For you *Kwangjangnim*, yes."

My father reached for the *sake* bottle and poured for Morikawa and then toasted him with barely a drop of drink from his own cup to wet his lips. That was how it went until Morikawa turned to me and asked for tea. I instinctively bristled at his request, recalling with mild indignation my teenage years of serving and fetching for my father's friends.

"Please," my father said, sensing my truculence. "He is my guest."

I got up and steeped a pot of *boricha* and brought that, along with two mugs, back to the table and set everything in front of Morikawa without pouring. He acknowledged me

214

with barely a grunt and turned to decant a small amount of tea into my father's rice bowl, which had barely been touched.

"Let it soak," he gruffly ordered my father. "Then drink down the rice even if you have no appetite. You cannot fight this without energy."

My father sighed and dutifully stirred the now watery rice with his chopsticks before choking down a mouthful. Morikawa nodded and then added another measure of hot tea and waited.

To mask my embarrassment, I gathered up the dirty dishes and headed toward the bathroom sink to make myself more useful. As I exited the office, I noticed Daria still resolutely struggling with the punching pad, and I momentarily experienced a disorienting wave of vertigo in my father's alternate universe.

When I returned, Morikawa had polished off the *sake* and my father had finished his rice. Both looked contented.

"Would you like a ride home; or will the girl take you?" Morikawa asked as he rose to take his leave.

"Ah, I was hoping Dae Sung would offer me a ride on his motorcycle," my father answered unexpectedly.

"Yes, of course. Well, until tomorrow." They bowed and Morikawa left.

"How did you know I bought a motorcycle?" I asked.

"Daria," he answered. "Please wash these last few things and let's go home."

Ten minutes later we were headed out the door, and Daria was back on the mat reviewing the first seven steps of *Sanchin*.

"Breathing and tensing at the right time is important. With every move, be aware of where your breath is coming from. Morikawa *Sensei* will be back tomorrow for another lesson." Those were my father's parting instructions, and I saw Daria hold her bow of acknowledgement until after we closed and locked the front door.

When we got to my bike, I stowed my bag and pulled out the spare helmet while my father slowly circled the 650cc racing machine and ran his hand over the matte black finish.

"Ever been on a bike?" I asked.

"My commanding officer rode a 1963 BMW R60 and sent me all around Seoul running errands for him on that bike. I loved it as if it were my own. But no way could I ever afford something like that in Korea at the time," my father answered, surprising me once again.

I straddled the bike and waited for my father to slowly and gingerly do the same behind me. I then guided his shockingly thin arms around my waist and suffered my second vertiginous moment of the evening when he leaned forward and hugged me tight. I took a deep breath and gunned the engine to emotionally neutralize the tears now rolling down my face. I drove carefully and smoothly, having no choice but to let my unfettered tears flow into the cool breeze of the early fall evening, taking the long way home and wishing the ride would never end.

Leading a Horse to Water

My universe expanded with a number of new teachers during the fall and into the winter months. I met several of *Sabumnim's* martial arts brothers and was surprised to learn that many of them had never shared their knowledge or taught their craft to anyone before. Instead, they were retired engineers, pharmacists, businessmen, academics and even one chicken farmer.

They heard of *Sabumnim's* illness from each other and visited the *dojang* one after another to offer support and companionship. When they came by themselves, they brought wine and liquor. When they came with their wives or children, the *dojang* overflowed with casseroles, stews and other Korean comfort foods. During that time, my duties expanded beyond teaching to include pouring drinks and refilling rice and soup bowls on almost a nightly basis. It was all a little awkward because even after three semesters of Korean I was still having trouble piecing together basic conversations and often sat uncomfortably in their presence wondering what was so funny or tragic or merited such long discussions. But *Sabumnim* insisted that I remain at the table and learn from the interactions that I could barely understand. "Listen with your heart," he said. "Not all knowledge and sentiments are conveyed with words."

With most of those visits I was also invariably gifted with a unique opportunity for a private lesson at *Sabumnim's* behest. "She is still young and a little clumsy and slow to learn. And her form is heavily influenced by sport Taekwondo. But if you could please teach her something to make her a more competent martial artist...," *Sabumnim* would beseech of his friends. As a result, I benefitted from various grandmasters watching and correcting my patterns; a former Korean national judo champion drilling me in his favorite throw every day for over a month; a Russian-Korean sambo teacher adding to my knowledge of how to transition from stand-up to ground work; and a Grandmaster Oh from Los Angeles gifting me with a heavy, serrated spring-loaded knife (quite possibly illegal, I think) and teaching me the basics of how to carry, deploy and strike.

The friends and visitors came and went, but with two of the instructors *Sabumnim* went to even greater lengths to request that they accept me as a student. The first was Morikawa *Sensei*, who was a retired professor of metallurgy at Stevens Institute of Technology and an expert in an older Okinawan karate style that emphasized body hardening and internal breath control, two elements of training that *Sabumnim* said was difficult to learn through modern Taekwondo.

The second was Chen *Sifu*, who ran a dry goods store in the Sunset Park neighborhood of Brooklyn. The unassuming man was always draped in ill-fitting khakis and a plain grey sweatshirt and looked to be 20 years younger than *Sabumnim*, but in fact turned out to be more than 10 years older and *Sabumnim's* teacher. The first time he took me to see Chen *Sifu* he actually greeted the dry goods store owner with a kneeling bow. I was so stunned by the gesture that it took a hard tug on my arm from *Sabumnim* for me to realize that I should be doing the same. That day, and every Sunday thereafter, I was allowed to join in *Sabumnim's* private lesson, but Chen *Sifu* has thus far completely ignored my existence.

"Don't worry about it," *Sabumnim* told me after one very cold Sunday afternoon spent shivering in a full lotus position on the floor of the uninsulated storage room behind Chen *Sifu's* storefront. "I visited his shop every Sunday for almost eight years before he finally granted me a lesson."

"Eight years...?" I gasped to myself.

"At first, I didn't even know if he was the teacher I was looking for. I had only heard rumors from older Korean and Chinese martial artists about Chen *Sifu's* training, but no one knew for sure. Then one Sunday I was at the counter paying for an aluminum pot and a pack of dishtowels when he finally smiled at me, and I knew. He invited me into the back room for tea, and all he said was 'when the timing is right, enlightenment is possible.' That afternoon I ended up making the tea and serving it to him. That was about 27 years ago."

I was flabbergasted. "Who is he?"

"Chen *Sifu* is a 30th generation monk trained in Mahayana Buddhism at a monastery in Dengfeng, China," *Sabumnim* answered obliquely. I had no idea what any of that meant or why any of that was relevant.

He continued, "During the Cultural Revolution, his family helped him escape to San Francisco and then New York City. At the time the Communist Party was starting to incarcerate and re-educate many of the country's religious and cultural leaders, forcing them into labor camps and beating them and sometimes even executing them if they refused to renounce their beliefs and their training. In order to protect himself and preserve what he was taught, Chen *Sifu* left everything behind and came here."

"He doesn't look like a monk," was all that I could think of to say.

"What does a monk look like?" *Sabumnim* asked. "And why does it matter if he is or is not a monk? Actually, Chen *Sifu* is just an immigrant shopkeeper with no temple, no robes and no students except for me, as far as I can tell."

I was confused. "What are you trying to learn from him?"

"Now that's a better question," he smiled. "I was in my mid-30s when I realized there was a limit to my Taekwondo practice. I had trained in martial arts my entire young life and then honed my skills and really learned how to fight when the Korean army sent me to Vietnam. During the war there is no type of martial combat that I wasn't exposed to. We were a lightly-armed unit that operated without the benefit of air raids or chemicals and most of our fighting was done intimately, from close range. Vietnam sharpened my combat skills to the point where I wondered whether I still had human limitations….as a martial artist.

"And then I came to America and opened up a little *dojang* that struggled to attract students and survive. Obviously, I had to change my philosophies and practice in order to adapt my Taekwondo to suburban New Jersey in order not go out of business. But somewhere along the way I might have gotten a little lost or a little bored. I was unsure about my future teaching this watered-down version of Taekwondo, but I also sensed that there had to be something more to Taekwondo than just using my hands and feet as weapons to destroy my opponents. My martial arts could not just be about fighting; nor could it be just about money and making a living. But I couldn't figure out what I was looking for.

"Initially I went searching for a teacher of Tai Chi or *chi gong* or some other internal martial art, thinking that maybe I needed a counterbalance to the brutal physicality of the fighting art I learned. That was when I first started hearing outrageous stories about Chen *Sifu*. In both Chinatown and Koreatown, he was legendary for his healing abilities and his seemingly superhuman feats of strength and stamina and, um… how to you call it, virility? Vitality? So, I went looking for him and wanted to learn the secrets of his internal energy or *neigong*.

"But then a very strange thing happened. After I found him and then after eight years of asking for lessons and then a few more years of meditating in his back room, I realized that what he was teaching me was far more than just his martial art. In fact, I eventually came to understand that by the time he finally accepted me as a student, I was already seeking something beyond any sort of martial art."

"Huh?" I asked, now even more confused.

He smiled, "The Chinese call it *chan*."

"What exactly is that?" I pressed. "Is that what I'm supposed to learn too?"

My teacher slowly shook his head in a way that neither answered my question nor denied my supposition. "I was looking for peace and understanding. And I found it while pursuing *chan*."

He then glanced sideways into my incredulous eyes and smiled again. "Please don't think I'm being difficult or withholding information or leading you down a dead-end path. I really don't know how to explain it with words or actions. But I do have a feeling about you and what you might need in the future. Please be patient and continue to study with Chen *Sifu*."

"But it doesn't even seem like he wants to teach me."

At that *Sabumnim* laughed. "If that was the case, he would have already asked you to make a purchase or leave."

When the Student Is Ready...

As the end of the year approached, *Sabum* Dae Sung started showing up at the *dojang* more often. He said he had been assigned to a psych rotation at the hospital and instead of working 16-hour days like during his surgery rotation or 12-hour days like his last rotation, he now had normal 8-hour days and an occasional day off. When he was around, he spent a lot of time with *Sabumnim* in the office, but if *Sabumnim* needed to rest or was busy with visitors, *Sabum* Dae Sung seemed to take pleasure in whiling his time away by playing devil's advocate with me.

"So you haven't competed since the summer, huh?" he started one evening during the 15-minute break I had between classes. "Your dreams of the Olympics were really that pathetic? That weak? That disposable?"

"Unreal," he scoffed.

My insides churned as I suffered a cortisol dump that suddenly leadened my body. I inhaled deeply to remind myself to stay in the present and not wallow in the past six months, but nonetheless, I was partially relieved to be able to unburden myself with an honest answer. "It's killing me."

"Well then, instead of keeping sharp and working with Ángel and Kemena why are you wasting your time meditating and learning some old karate form? What good is that going to do? That's not going to get you to 2020."

I shrugged. "I don't know. I just really don't know right now."

"Well, I do know," he said. "My brothers and I went through exactly the same thing you're going through now. He's forcing you to go where he wants you to go. He's leading you down his path and not really giving a flip about what you want. It's always been about his worldview and his Taekwondo, and you just end up being a sacrificial pawn."

I sighed as he gave voice to some of my own deepest fears. I looked away from him and had to consciously beat back my doubts for the thousandth time. Thank goodness there were already enough students assembled on the mat for me to start an early warm-up. When my heart rate returned to normal, I halfheartedly excused myself and stepped back onto the mat to teach.

*   *   *

Sabumnim underwent his last course of chemo right before Christmas. By that time, he was feeling stronger and was able to teach more classes. He even started practicing again. Everyone was optimistic about his remission, and selfishly by extension I was optimistic about being able to get back on track to realizing my international competition dreams.

My replacement on Team USA had bombed in Taoyuan, and Gracie also struggled at her Grand Prixes, failing to get out of the Round of 16 in any of her three tries. Neither of them had accumulated any qualifying points for either the World Championships next year or the Olympics in 2020, so theoretically I was still on equal footing. On top of that, a couple of Team USA officials reached out during this time and encouraged me to compete at the US Open in February and other lower-tier international open tournaments in the spring as an unofficial member of Team USA. I was told that they could not provide me with the support or resources of the national team, but they did send me a package of Team USA gear and a note reassuring me that the Olympic Committee would keep track of my progress and factor everything into consideration for future national team selections. It was all very ambiguous and offered only a tiny sliver of hope, but still, I was unexpectedly elated.

My parents had the financial resources to send me to these international events, but I hadn't fully understood the value of going to these unsanctioned tournaments by myself or even realized that I was still on the national team radar. But now, I cautiously allowed myself to start dreaming about the Olympics again and made plans by researching the requirements and logistics of the international open tournaments the national team coaches had suggested. After emailing back and forth with Team USA coaches and officials, I eventually circled the US Open, the Dutch Open and the Canadian Open on my 2019 calendar and started to arrange my training objectives and travel plans around those events. With those goals in mind and with *Sabumnim's* recovery headed in the right direction, I could finally see a way forward.

On a quiet Friday afternoon right before the start of the winter holiday break at the *dojang* I excitedly approached *Sabumnim* in his office with my training plan and a proposal for a reduced teaching load in the new year. He patiently listened to what I had to say and nodded in acknowledgement of my rekindled ambitions, but offered nothing more. "I think we should have lunch and talk," was all he said. Then he slowly pushed himself up from behind his desk and left the office to ask one of the senior black belts to teach the afternoon classes in my stead.

"Don't we have lunch and talk almost every day?" I wondered.

But this lunch was different. First, he asked me to change out of my *dobok* and wait while he made a couple of phone calls. And then we left the *dojang* right in the middle of class. The students were confused, as was I, but no one thought to question *Sabumnim*. Since I had driven him in this morning, we took my car and I followed his directions across the George Washington Bridge and down the Henry Hudson into Midtown Manhattan. I parked in an outrageously priced garage on Park Avenue in the 30s, and we walked two short blocks to a restaurant located in a townhouse in the middle of a quiet residential street.

"I'm going to see Dae Sung right after this and I have a few errands in the city, so I hope you don't mind me dragging you way out here," he said as we approached a centuries-old townhouse halfway down the block. Without expecting an answer, he pointed toward an unmarked entrance and proceeded down the four stone steps in front of me. Just as we reached the massive, charcoal-darkened wooden front door it slowly inched open and a maître d' dressed in a rough-hewn indigo fold-over top and matching pants bowed us across the threshold.

As I breathlessly adjusted to the otherworldly atmosphere beyond the entrance *Sabumnim* quietly explained, "I come here when I need to think and when I want to speak plainly."

Once we entered beyond the small courtyard garden and left our shoes and coats with an attendant in the vestibule, it felt like time and space had somehow been reimagined to convey us to a rural farm-house retreat from a bygone era. The rustic austerity of the interior was as magnificent and comforting as it was oddly nostalgic, as if our past selves had chanced to meet and interact as neighbors or friends or even family in just such a setting.

We were seated on thin cushions that rested upon natural woven grass mats and in front of us was an open charcoal brazier that emitted a powerful warmth but no flames. Our waiter, who comported himself like a lord of this manor proudly welcoming distinguished guests into his homestead, presented us each with a uniquely hand-calligraphed menu that bore descriptions of the meal in both black-inked drawings and a flowing, undecipherable script. After we were warmed with tea and hand towels, we were then served a simple but unforgettable lunch.

We started with lightly-grilled mountain vegetables, none of which I had ever seen before. That was followed by two varieties of homemade silken tofu; a faintly green edamame tofu and a slightly pink tomato tofu. The flavors then intensified with a side dish of sticky fermented beans mixed with avocado and a raw quail egg, and a shared platter of various root vegetables pickled in fermented rice bran. All the while, our waiter carefully gutted and speared small silvery freshwater fish onto thin green bamboo rods and slowly roasted them over the far edges of the charcoal pile. A dark and rich mushroom and vegetable broth was also prepared in front of us and simmered in an iron pot suspended from a rod that hung directly over the brazier. When we finished the vegetables and tofu, a clay pot was unearthed from beneath the pile of charcoal to reveal a steaming treasure trove of truffled wild rice, which was served as the main dish alongside the soup and roasted fish. The first serving was the most tender, fragrant rice I could imagine. And the second serving was the crispy, crunchy bits of slightly scorched rice scraped from the walls and bottom of the clay pot and immersed in a shallow bowl of herbal tea, which served to soften the rice and add an unearthly depth of flavor. *Sabumnim* and I enjoyed everything in reverential silence until our green tea was finally switched to a barley mix, signaling the end of our meal.

"I come here to imagine a country life," *Sabumnim* said with just a hint of irony, as he sipped his tea. "Something quieter and more elemental. Maybe something that resonates better with my nature."

I nodded, and he smiled. "Thank you for indulging me. Now to answer your questions…"

Then, while still cupping the barley tea in both hands as if in prayer or perhaps as a sign of contrition, *Sabumnim* said, "The timing is almost right. You are so close, but this cancer in my body is forcing me to give you a final little push. I was hoping that maybe in five or six years, after you make an attempt at the Olympics and after you finish your college degree, that you would intuitively gravitate toward searching out a new level to your practice. As of now, you are almost ready to work with Morikawa *Sensei* and almost ready to hear what he has to say. What he teaches you can grasp, if you are open it to. But if I were to be honest with you and with myself, you might be more than a decade away from understanding the value of Chen *Sifu's* lessons. But time is sometimes short, and I decided to take the chance."

He then paused, as if to think or perhaps to reconsider the extent to which I was able to follow. Not knowing how to react, I held my breath and intuitively nodded. Then he continued, "I'm not sure how much Dae Sung has shared with you.... he has a lot of misgivings and doubts about the Taekwondo life he was born into. He has this idea of me as a sword maker who forges iron into weapons, creating them in either my own selfish likeness or in service of my own self-important needs. And he is not entirely incorrect. Providence has connected my sons and my students to me in this lifetime, and I have always felt a profound responsibility to give them the best of what I have. Dae Sung thinks that I am motivated by vanity when I temper my students and their spirits to pass on my art. He thinks that ultimately my ego damages the final product and causes it to be blemished and brittle and a little insecure...."

Sabumnim sighed. "But honestly there is no vanity. It is all done with sincerity. Unfortunately, though, despite my best efforts otherwise, my own shortcomings are oftentimes reflected and magnified in my sons and my students. But that doesn't mean that the swords are imperfect. Instead, what he doesn't understand yet is that all I see is beauty, each one with a soul and a polish and a path untold. And once it leaves my hands, each one will strengthen and evolve according to its own unique life's passage. That, I look forward to, and do not try to control."

He paused again and this time his slow exhale became a slightly more temporal and sardonic smile. "This last round of chemo is done, and regardless of whether there is remission, I have to start the next phase of my life. I haven't told my sons or anyone else yet, but with what time I have left there are brothers I must find and final promises I have to fulfill. Even if there is remission, I know my remaining passage is short."

What is he trying to say? My initial confusion suddenly morphed into fears of loss and abandonment as my imagination amplified his words and jumped wildly to conclusions that I could not accept. But just as I felt my throat constrict and the corners of my eyes begin to squeeze back tears, I looked up across the table and was able to recompose myself under a long and patient gaze of boundless equanimity. *Sabumnim* waited in silence until I was able to let go of my anxieties.

When I was ready, he continued. "Daria, I have long wished to leave my Taekwondo legacy and *dojang* to you. And over these past few months I've been trying to ease your path forward by introducing other mentors and teachers into your world. I would trust any of these martial artists and gentlemen with my life, and I have asked that they continue to look after you and give you any guidance or assistance you might need. But ultimately you have to decide who and what will shape your future.

"Although I had planned on a longer and more gradual transition, I am offering my *dojang* to you now. Please don't feel compelled to accept it for my sake or anyone else's sake. Choose only for yourself, because this is not an easy path. A *dojang* is only a valuable place when it has the proper spirit and intention giving it life and nurturing its purpose. If you don't feel that is your true calling then you cannot take on this responsibility. It would be too much."

Too much? This already *is* too much. When a stable universe suddenly disappears into a black hole, it is decidedly *way* too much. My thoughts briefly short-circuited as I pondered the possibility that advanced physics might be easier to comprehend than this life-altering moment.

The overwrought tension and emotions in my eyes and posture must have encouraged *Sabumnim* to then add, "Daria, you have already honored me with your loyalty and diligence and devotion as a student. Now my only wish for you is your happiness."

I don't think I so much as heard those words as I later maybe remembered those sentiments. In the moment, the only thing that registered was my occluded sense of reasoning and overall state of panic.

What? I wanted to demand. What do you mean?! Why are you doing this to me?!

You can't do this! I silently implored. Why are you leaving? What am I to do?

This is not fair! I whined from deep within my marrow.

Eventually my eyes looked up to find his, and I said nothing.

He was waiting for me. "Look here and here for your answers," he hinted gently with a familiar gesture toward my heart and my mind.

I was confused but obediently looked inward, expecting instant wisdom and clarity. Instead, I saw nothing except for the figure of *Sabumnim* asking for the check and then paying in cash before getting up and excusing himself. Are we leaving? But I haven't figured anything out yet! What's the right answer?

I got up to follow him out, but he waved me back. "Dessert is coming and then *hojicha*. I want you to take some time and think. This is a good place for it, and sweets are supposed to stimulate the brain. Don't be sad; I'll see you tomorrow."

As he retreated back into the vestibule and then disappeared into the congested concrete reality of Midtown Manhattan, I remained rooted beside the still-warm brazier. Right as he left, our waiter surreptitiously appeared with a wooden box from which he gently scooped out two freshly-made mochi, each resting on a sturdy dark green leaf, and set them to toast on a small iron griddle placed over the coals. I slumped back onto the floor cushion and watched the mochi slowly puff and then brown. If not for the mesmerizing prospect of the sweets, I might have been tempted to curl up by the charcoal warmth and whimper the disquietudes of a lost child.

· · ·

After the mochi finished toasting, the waiter returned with a pair of long chopsticks and retrieved the now caramelized and gooey treats from the grill and placed them on a rough-hewn ceramic dish. He then used that and a few other minimal gestures to lure me outdoors behind the townhouse where a fleece blanket and a pot of *hojicha* were already awaiting me on the wooden decking that framed a small but meticulously-tended garden. I wrapped myself in the blanket before accepting the sweets.

Perhaps this was *Sabumnim's* intention all along. I sat cross-legged directly on the wooden deck and slowly enjoyed the warm glutinous rice and red bean dessert along with the earthy, pungent tea and my mind was blissfully emptied. In the weak late afternoon winter light, the stark and hibernating garden seemed to absorb everything into its calculated state of repose. All the city noise, all the artificial illuminations, all my thoughts and all of human pretense were silenced. I sat and ate my mochi.

When I finally opened my eyes anew, I felt nothing but gratitude.

*   *   *

Later that night I walked into my parents' study and asked to join in on their nightcap. My mom mocked-raised an eyebrow but my dad wordlessly poured a good measure of Scotch into a finely-cut crystal tumbler.

"It's a Balvenie 25," he said as he handed me the glass and turned the bottle so I could see the label. "Here. Hold it up so you can see the color. Now, slowly breathe in 25 years of patience and craftsmanship, and then take just a drop on your lips and tell me what you taste."

"Oh!" Taking more than just a sip, I was struck by the drink's intensity and not sure how to react to the burn of aged barley and peat until the spirit's contrails mellowed into an exotic mix of honey and spice on my palette. "Whoa."

He laughed. "You should always drink your whiskeys like that, but tonight I have to water it down for you. You have an early morning tomorrow, right?" He then added a large ice cube and a couple ounces of water to my glass. I noticed that he and my mom drank theirs neat with a glass of ice water on the side.

"What's on your mind, D?"

I told them about the past four months at the *dojang* and tried to explain how the intersection of my dreams and doubts and duties were all clashing in my mind. I finished with a summary of what *Sabumnim* said and offered over lunch today, complete with all his convoluted analogies, and then waited for my mom and dad's assessment.

My mom spoke first and nonchalantly said, "So, our little adolescent eagle is being shoved out of the nest."

My dad lingered over a slow sip of his drink before harmonizing, "I see a gangly bird who tumbled down a cliff and is now sitting dazed in a pile of her own dander."

"Very poetic guys," I snarked in the flippant tone of a typical teenager but then quickly re-composed myself. "Right after *Sabumnim* left today I felt so confused and sad, like I was losing a huge part of my life. I just couldn't imagine Taekwondo without him. I couldn't imagine the *dojang* without him. I couldn't imagine my life without him. And I couldn't imagine trying to compete without him. I was thinking about how much he's done for me and what a big part of my life he's been; and I feel nothing but gratitude towards him. But now what?

"After lunch, I walked around Manhattan for a long time until it got too cold. Then I got my car and randomly drove around hoping that an answer would just come to me. I went all the way up to Bear Mountain and then back down the Palisades, and I stopped to stare at the Hudson for a little bit. I finally thought I was giving up and coming home a little while ago, but for some reason I ended up back at the *dojang* way after it closed.

"And that's when the answer came to me. I knew, just pulling in the parking lot. And I really knew the second I opened the door and smelled the smell of the *dojang*. I understood that nothing has ever captured my imagination as much as Taekwondo has. I love the sport; I love the art; I love the people; I love teaching and everything about the *dojang*. Inside it was dark and a little cold, but it felt like home. Just standing in the middle of mat I could feel him there too. And then I realized that I could always find him there, and that I could always find him any time I wanted.

"Have you guys ever known anything with that much certainty before? It's so weird. But I knew that that was where I belonged the most.

"I'm going to accept *Sabumnim's* offer and take over the *dojang*."

My parents silently looked at each other before my dad sighed and walked behind his desk. He knelt and unlocked the bottom drawer and pulled out a leather portfolio, which he handed over to me.

"I'll summarize, but read through the documents carefully for yourself. Master Ahn has already sold his *dojang* to me for $1. The agreement my lawyer drafted is that I would hold the school in trust for you and help you manage the business until three conditions are met, after which I can turn everything over to you. First, you must graduate from college. Second, you must demonstrate that you can successfully operate the business on your own. And third, you must reaffirm on your twenty-sixth birthday that this is what you want. If any of those conditions are not met by your twenty-

232

sixth birthday or if you choose not to take over the business now, then I have the option of either selling or closing the school. If I sell, the proceeds will go to you."

"What?" I said in utter disbelief. "When did this happen? *Sabumnim* already transferred the school to you? I don't get it."

"It happened right after Master Ahn left the hospital in September. But, D, we have been mulling over this eventuality ever since you scared us years ago by insisting on dropping out of high school and pursuing this... this dream of yours. By we, I mean us and Master Ahn. And it's been almost a six-year journey so far. His cancer only pushed the timeline forward.

"Have you ever given any thought to how difficult this process has been on your parents and your teacher? In fact, in our initial distress your mother and I came down much harder on your poor teacher than we ever did on you. You, I wanted to lock in a dungeon with a private tutor but him, I wanted to shoot.

"Don't worry, I've already told him that to his face... several times."

"Daaaaad!!!" I was appalled.

"Did you think we would just let you drop out of high school and spend all your time at the Taekwondo school without thoroughly vetting the teacher who would be responsible for your formative education?" he continued with a heavy touch of probably well-deserved paternal exasperation.

My mom continued as my dad turned away and found an excuse to touch up everyone's drinks in order to divert his mind from the anguish that I had apparently caused everyone not that long ago. "I would say that Master Ahn put up with a lot when you decided to make Taekwondo and the Olympics your dream. From the beginning, your father insisted that we meet with him every Friday morning at the Chit Chat Diner for breakfast and a full-on interrogation session."

"I like their omelets."

"Honey! Your father insisted on detailed weekly reports of all your training, all the classes you taught, and all the people you interacted with at the *dojang*... especially the boys," my mom said and laughed in a way that made me unsure whether she was spilling the beans for my benefit or teasing my dad for her amusement. "By the way, your father also held Master Ahn personally responsible for any grade below an A that you got, not to mention every black eye, broken bone and tiny little boo-boo you ever suffered. There was a lot of yelling and angry, hurtful words from your beloved but cantankerous father during those first couple of years. Your poor teacher must have somehow considered you worth the effort, because he endured a litany of abuse from your father with absolute grace and humility."

"Hey now, you made me play the bad guy," my dad huffed in his own defense. "I was just giving voice to what we both thought."

I took a big sip of my drink. It didn't matter. My head was already spinning. "Weekly meetings? I can't believe.... Is that why *Sabumnim* made Chul Ho tutor me in math for four years? And that one time I got a C in Physics, I'm pretty sure I ran a marathon in the parking lot as punishment! Wait! Does this also have anything to do with the two classes at Rutgers I have to take every semester now?"

"Well, it turns out that your teacher has far stronger persuasive powers over our uniquely wayward daughter than we have," my dad softly grumbled with an undertone of wounded pride.

"Okay, okay," my mom interjected. "That's enough for one night. D, take everything your father just gave you and read it over and think it over. And if your mind is made up, I'm going to invite Master Ahn over for dinner. This discussion doesn't make sense without him present."

She then got up and planted a kiss on my head before giving me a tiny shove in my dad's direction. After saying goodnight, I took the papers and left their study feeling disoriented but oddly more secure in my decision than before.

... the Teacher Disappears

Even though I was more nervous about Sunday dinner than I was for the finals at nationals or the team trials, it turned out to be great. We started with caviar, pickled herring and smoked salmon blinis paired with shots of ice-cold vodka; my dad's Sunday favorite. My mom subtly offered me a diluted pour, but I opted for water with *Sabumnim* sitting straight across from me. The three of them drank like old friends, and my parents shared a slightly bemused glance between themselves when *Sabumnim* insisted that I do all the pouring as the most junior person at the table.

After they finished the bottle, my dad opened and decanted a 2005 Silver Oak Cabernet while my mom excused herself and headed to the back patio. "Clear the plates and bring out the tray of side dishes I left on the counter," she said, and I got up to make myself useful.

On the tray was an assortment of pickled vegetables, a warm spinach and sesame salad, a mélange of marinated mushrooms, a stir fry of some light-colored squash in a sea of tiny dried fish, cubes of tofu topped with soy sauce, ginger and scallions, a dish of raw garlic and spicy-looking green peppers, fermented soy bean paste, and six different types of *kimchi*. I recognized the regular *kimchi*, but there was also radish *kimchi*, spring onion *kimchi*, some bulbous root vegetable *kimchi*... my mom must have cleaned out the *kimchi* aisle at HMart for this. As I brought out the tray, I saw my mom and dad settle and adjust a large ceramic grill filled with gnarly, black charcoal embers onto the table. Whoa! That was definitely a first for my mom's beloved antique table.

While my dad and *Sabumnim* stoked and tended to the embers and arranged and rearranged all the side dishes to fit around the grill, I followed my mom back into the kitchen and filled four rice bowls while she brought out a huge platter of marinated *galbi* steak. Reseated, we all marveled at the spread and delighted at the novelty of indoor barbequing on a cold wintry night. As my dad poured the wine and *Sabumnim* grilled the meats, a wave of premature nostalgia washed over my mind's eye, as if I was already reliving one of the happiest moments of my life. I looked over at my mom and knew she could read my thoughts. We ate slowly, like an ancient tribe, fortifying old alliances and ensuring future harmony through fire and communal meat and drink.

Sabumnim ate with more appetite and gusto than I've seen in months. At one point, he was gushing over my mom's *galbi*. "I am Korean and this is the best *galbi* I have ever had! You marinated this yourself?"

My mom smiled in her usual warm and self-assured way, made slightly more beguiling by the amount of vodka and wine influencing her speech. "All the recipes I Googled required grated Asian pear, which is something New Jersey apparently doesn't import in December. But I thought it must be the calpain enzyme in the pears that those recipes were after, so I experimented with other natural tenderizers. Actinidin from kiwis, papain from papayas, protease from apples, the acid from oranges. Guess what worked?"

My dad chuckled half-charmed and half-amused at my mom's nerdiness, while *Sabumnim* belly-laughed and said, "I should have known that a doctor of chemistry would be an outstanding cook! You marinated and grilled up meat with all those fruits?!"

"To get it right for tonight... of course. By the way, it was the bromelain from pineapple! Which in hindsight should have been obvious, given how widely it's used in Latin

American and Southeast Asian grilling." This time we all laughed at my geeky, earnest and lovely mom.

And so it went, until we finished the entire feast and cleared the way for dessert. My mom brought out tiny ramekins of my favorite Earl Grey and vanilla bean panna cotta and a plate of crispy butter cookies. My dad re-set the table with fluted glassware and popped open a 2002 Gaston Chiquet. When all four glasses were filled, he quietly lifted his toward *Sabumnim* and said, "Thank you for helping us raise our daughter. Your boundless caring, strict guidance and inspiration have set her on a path we can truly be proud of."

After my dad's toast, I looked shyly around the table and followed his example. "Thank you, dad. Thank you, mom. Thank you, *Sabumnim* for the life you have all given me." I then bowed my eyes quickly downward into my panna cotta just in case I or anyone else might have been thinking of crying.

After dinner, my dad set me to the task of cleaning the dishes and making coffee while he and mom and *Sabumnim* disappeared into his study. I joined them a little later with a large Chemex and four of my dad's most favorite Haviland & Parlon cups. He admired my selection of porcelainware and inhaled deeply from the Chemex before pouring for everyone. "Finally, Daria chooses the Gesha," he said, mostly to himself.

"Is it very cold there?" my mom asked, continuing their conversation while motioning for me to join her on the chaise. *Sabumnim* occupied a club chair in front of the desk and my dad had pulled his chair from behind the desk to sit facing everyone.

"The temple is remote and the altitude is quite high, so most likely it is not so warm."

"But why not retire somewhere more comfortable and convenient?" my dad asked.

Sabumnim sighed into his coffee and answered with a whisper of preternatural sensitivity, "I am ready to find comfort in this last evolution of my Taekwondo practice."

Then looking mostly in my direction as he explained, "From the time I was young and decided to follow my destiny in Taekwondo, I sought to master this fighting art by training to become stronger, more skilled and more technically superior in order to become a perfect martial weapon. I learned how to kill during the war and continued to fight viciously afterwards in the peace in order to pursue this violent refinement.

"It was only after years of training and fighting that I finally realized that Taekwondo was not a means or a weapon. The years revealed to me that my abilities in Taekwondo gave me a standing through which I could communicate and shape the actions and thinking of the people around me. By more fully understanding my humanity I finally learned how to teach and how to lead and how to live. And when that happened, there was a profound calmness in my heart.

"Now, with the help of Chen *Sifu* and after a lifetime of experience and self-education, I believe that there is another step I have to take. I have to learn how to conquer myself and return to the natural state. There, true peace is possible in the absence of ego, wants, desires and the many other habitualized human instincts that prevent us from fully experiencing harmony."

He inhaled deeply from his coffee and admired the hints of lavender and vanilla before sipping and concluding, "So, it doesn't matter if it's a little cold where I'm going."

Then he reached into his pocket and handed me an envelope and my father a slip of paper before taking both of my mom's hands into his and said, "Thank you for a magical evening. I will always hold tonight in my heart."

I opened the envelope and held out a six-figure cashier's check towards my dad.

"What is this?" my dad asked, immediately making a move to stuff the check back toward *Sabumnim*.

Sabumnim laughed and handed the check back to me. "Six years of back pay for helping me at the *dojang*. Sorry it comes out to slightly less than minimum wage."

"No, no, no, no, no, no," my dad insisted. "She can't take that."

"I know, I know," *Sabumnim* answered in my direction. "But please accept it anyway. Running a *dojang* is not so easy.

And when times are bad, I want you to have a little cushion. That way, you won't have to ask your dad for a loan." *Sabumnim* smiled at me and then winked at my dad.

"And that is the village and the temple where I will be," he continued, pointing to the slip of paper in my dad's hand.

"Can we visit?" my mom asked.

"Of course," *Sabumnim* answered. "Please bring a bottle of something good. And if you cannot find me or if I am resting, have a drink and enjoy the view from the mountain top. If you leave me a cup, my spirit will know that my cherished friends came to see me."

Sabumnim departed after a round of hugs and lightly flowing tears. It was well after midnight when I walked him to his car.

After spending most of my life under his tutelage, I had no words for this moment and chose to bow my profound love and gratitude. He smiled and returned the gesture tenfold before disappearing into the moonless night.

Where to Find Him

When he gathered the family to tell us the news of his retreat to an obscure Buddhist temple in rural South Korea, the enduring disconnect between father and sons was further strained to almost the point of futility. In fact, Tae Suk and his wife had recently made a down payment on a retirement community condo near their home and had planned to unveil their largess as an early Christmas present. Eui Song, in a lifelong allegiance to his best friend and older brother, was proud of his own commitment to pay the mortgage on my father's retirement relocation. And, I, as the distant third son, had been deemed irrelevant in the financial discussions concerning my father's future. Regardless, all three of us felt viscerally betrayed by my father's announcement and were united in our accusations of his lunacy, imprudence, and ultimately, his selfishness.

"We made all these arrangements to take care of you in your old age," Tae Suk said in a way that implied he had already ascended to assume leadership of the extended Ahn clan in light of our father's infirmity. "It's our duty to look after our aged father, so why are you rejecting us, your family, to pursue some wildly impractical lifestyle half way around the world?"

That initial skirmish occurred in early December, but we all thought a favorable peace could be had once my father realized the extent of his sons' caring and thoughtfulness. Unfortunately, a second battle was waged shortly thereafter.

"You're giving the *dojang* to some girl?" Tae Suk exclaimed, again taking the lead among the three brothers.

"Shouldn't it stay in the family? What about the next generation? Haven't you given any thought to my sons?"

In his hasty default to indignation over everything my father said and did these days, Tae Suk must have forgotten that his eldest son wore another Taekwondo master's name on his *dobok* and had in fact never stepped foot into his grandfather's *dojang*. And not only did none of us want the *dojang*, but it was also highly unlikely that Tae Suk or his wife would ever allow any their own children to assume the business. We sat around uncomfortably swallowing Tae Suk's tripe, but made no attempt to offer my father a truce by acknowledging reality. My father calmly bore Tae Suk's anger without any attempts to deflect the verbal assaults on his person or character and merely reiterated, "It's already been done."

The war dragged on and infected the usually fraught holiday season with even more anxiety and discord. Another blow up occurred after tests revealed that my father's cancer was not in remission and that at least another four rounds of chemotherapy was necessary. This precipitated a flood of daily group emails that now weighed the benefits of assisted living facilities against the merits of a part-time visiting nurse at the retirement condo. Tae Suk's and Eui Song's emails now came with attached spreadsheets amortizing the cost of such care, taking into account expected life expectancy as a variable, along with the quality of care, the escalating cost of care as an inverse function of health and the projected income from the liquidation of our father's assets (including, in one string of emails with Eui Song's lawyer friend, the likelihood of success in a litigation to reclaim ownership of the *dojang*). My father was copied on all the correspondences but never replied.

Finally, the generalissimo grandmaster deescalated the war in his own way with a pronouncement two days before Christmas, on a Sunday afternoon at Tae Suk's home, with the grandchildren running around and Tae Suk's wife preparing a roast turkey in place of the *galbijjim* my father had always made for the holidays.

241

"I leave for Korea on the 25th," our father said plainly during a Giants versus Colts football game playing on mute in the family room.

"What?!" Tae Suk convulsed. "After all we are doing for you?! Have you not been paying attention to any of the arrangements we've made for you?"

My father remained silent, but reached for the gift he brought and pulled out a 25-year-old Macallan. He sent me to find glassware while he unsealed the bottle. When I returned, I took the bottle from him and started to pour. When I got to the fourth tumbler Tae Suk jumped up and said, "Hey! He can't have any. Can you drink with cancer? No! Right, Dae Sung?" I looked at my angry brothers and then at my expressionless father and poured anyway.

Once served, we reflexively held our glasses up for a toast, but having nothing festive or positive to say, retracted them awkwardly into our laps and then onto our lips. Thankfully the divine quality of the whiskey momentarily redeemed us our calloused souls.

"My sons...," my father started.

But my brothers interrupted in turn, "No way are you leaving!" And then, "That's insane! You're old and sick and you want to go away to die on some cold mountain far away from your family?!" Followed by, "And to deprive the kids of their grandfather?!"

More whiskey was poured, but the drink was increasing laced with acridness as my brothers protested and then accused and then threatened, all the way up until the Giants lost and early Christmas dinner was served. After a few polite bites of turkey and stuffing, and with my brothers still fuming and the kids running out of patience at the formal dining room setting, my father croaked out an exhausted request, "I need to lie down. This is too much for an old man. Dae Sung, please take me home."

At that we were silenced and relieved, and the tension finally broke. The children escaped to their video games and Tae Suk's wife tended to dessert while we bundled my father in

242

two layers of mountaineering fleece and Tae Suk's ski jacket and gloves and helped him climb up behind me on my bike. He had arrived in a cab, but was now adamant that he left on my motorcycle.

It was a bracingly cold evening and I rode slowly, trying to reconcile all the feelings that were currently being squeezed to the surface by my father riding behind me. Half an hour into our 45-minute drive, I slowed and turned into the parking lot of a poorly-lit taqueria that stood like a shanty in an otherwise middle-class neighborhood not far from where I once attended high school. My father dismounted wordlessly and followed me inside the empty but warm establishment. He took a seat and remained stoic as I used the restroom and then ordered.

Not a word passed between us even as our *champurrados* arrived, but my father immediately enveloped the warmth between his stiff and frozen hands and inhaled deeply of the foreign spices. The grandmaster has a weakness for chocolate, and I enjoyed him enjoying his first sip of the rich and ancient restorative. After the *champurrados*, I asked for a special dispensation of hand-ground pour-over coffee, knowing from years of patronage that the *Señora* kept a legitimate stash of beans for herself in the back. A good while later, with my father warmed and my own head cleared, we got back on the bike and savored the simple adventure of tempered horsepower on empty streets and eventually wound our way home.

*   *   *

All through the night the emails pinged about elder care and the level of diminished mental capacity required for guardianship and even veered into the realm of civil commitment. However, by Monday morning reality pushed the brothers another step toward capitulation. There was a long-planned winter holiday to Disney World for Tae Suk's family, and Eui Song was summoned to Austin, Texas where one of his firm's largest clients received a Securities and Exchange Commission notice of an investigation regarding questionable accounting practices. I had a 12-hour shift in the maternity ward but was released early and fought rush hour traffic to get in a final word with my father. I arrived at his home a little after 6 o'clock and found the house empty, not just of my father, but of everything.

The *dojang* was on winter holiday, but I instinctively headed there anyway. I was so unexpectedly happy to find him there that I almost shouted out my relief at his presence on the otherwise empty mat. It was only years of habit that slowed me at the entrance and prompted me to remove my shoes and bow before rushing into the *dojang* proper. I strode toward the mat and started to speak all my questions and concerns about his future but I froze as he jumped toward me with a flying knife-hand strike, followed by an axe kick. He briefly made eye contact, but then quickly refocused as he exhaled into a closed stance with a heaven hand before launching into a series of jumping, retreating reverse-turning kicks that shockingly belied his age and illness. After another long sequence of complicated steps and hand techniques, a simple reverse punch sprung from nowhere and everywhere in his body and suddenly the pattern was complete. He looked at me and acknowledged my presence but said nothing and continued with his practice.

For the first time since I was little, I watched my father with awe and admiration. The patterns were familiar but long since lost to me. Instead, it was his elemental power and immutable martial spirit that evoked the artless dreams of courage and bravery from a more innocent time, long before I learned of fighting and winning and pride. His practice was an expression of both the kinetic and the potential in one person and his movement seemed like the essence of his joy and his life. I watched and felt my heart wander to places I didn't know still existed.

When he started *Moon Moo* something compelled me to take my place behind him and copy the best I could. He completed the pattern with me several steps behind and waited for me to finish before repeating the entire pattern again; this time slower so my memory could catch up. He continued to repeat *Moon Moo* at a deliberate pace until finally it was my rhythm leading his, and then he took a step back to observe. It was at least an hour later before I could flow without thought and recapture the feeling of unbounded gravity in my movement. When I finished, he nodded and moved onto the next pattern, with me continuing to trail behind him.

Another hour or so passed before he finally stopped and addressed me with words. "I'm going to shower. Just give me 15 minutes and we'll talk."

A little while later we were seated at the low coffee table in his office. I brewed tea and my father produced a Tupperware container containing two sandwiches, each cut into four squares. There was an egg salad sandwich and a ham and cucumber sandwich, both on white bread and both flavored with mayonnaise and yellow mustard.

"No *kimbap*?" I asked, inexplicably forlorn.

"Too many ingredients and too much preparation required for *kimbap*," my father answered through a healthy mouthful of egg salad. "Easier to make sandwiches in an empty kitchen."

"What happened to the house?"

"I sold it," he answered while chewing. "Closed this morning. Goodwill came right afterwards and took everything."

"Everything?"

"I have been packing for weeks. I left some boxes of childhood things in the corner over there. If you and your brothers want to look through it, just let Daria know."

"And your car?"

"Twenty-seven hundred dollars. Same price as a Macallan 25." At this he smiled.

"Are you going to be okay? How are you going to get your chemo?"

"There are hospitals and smart doctors in Korea. I am still a Korean citizen and I have been paying my national insurance premiums, so medical care is no problem. I will keep fighting."

"What if we need you? How can we reach you if you're so far away?"

"You boys are good at email," he said, rather wryly, I thought.

He then seemed to reconsider his flippancy and put his sandwich down. Changing his expression and tone to something similar to what he once used to teach us boys proper manners, the virtues of Confucianism, the meaning of bravery and valor and his philosophies on humanity he said, "If you really need me, I hope the best of me is already a part of you. Come to the *dojang* and watch the children practice; go sprint up that hill and rediscover how to push the boundaries of your physical and mental fortitude; close your eyes and feel the grace and power of Taekwondo practice flowing through your body; and I will be there." He placed his open palm on my chest and then with both hands pulled my head close and gently touched his forehead to mine.

And yet, I still whimpered, "But what if you need us...?"

With a look of unfathomable sadness and detachment, he blinked once and lowered his gaze to tell me that he had moved beyond that. My breath was inexorably caught between a choke and a sob, and he gave me several long silent moments to try and reconcile the dissonance between our everlasting bond and his unilateral farewell.

While I suppressed my little boy cries of abandonment my father got up and retrieved a bottle of Highland 12, meant probably to further consolidate our past and to obscure our futures. After he poured, he sat and asked about my clinical rotations and my residency and specialty choices. He was especially animated when he asked for details about my *jiujitsu* practice. We also talked about motorcycles and Master Oh's obsession with knives, and he made me write down his *galbijjim* recipe, another way I could find him, he said. We ran out of whiskey around midnight, and he got up again with a sigh. This time he came back with three large Moleskin notebooks.

"Give these to Daria after you finish reading them," he said without sitting back down.

"Why don't you just leave them here for her?"

"I was going to, but now I would like you to read them first."

I took the Moleskins and opened the top one to flip through dense pages of notes and illustrations inked with my father's fountain pen and composed in his deliberate hand. As I skimmed in wonder, my father cleaned up the dishware and left me in his office. I lost track of time and finally closed the first book right before dawn. I got up to search for my father in the pitch-black *dojang* and found him sitting in a full lotus, meditating on the practice mat. Not wanting to disturb him, I laid down beside him and stretched the contented stretch of peace and whiskey and happiness before curling up and falling into a deep and easy sleep.

*   *   *

When I awoke, the *dojang* heat was on and I was hugging a big balled-up pile of my winter jacket and my father's *dobok* top. And my father was gone.

Afterward

I showed up on cold Monday morning in the new year and found her polishing the mirrors. The lights were off, the heat was off and the *dojang* smelled of Windex mixed with the indescribable, but intimately familiar, essence of Ahn's Taekwondo distilled through almost 50 years of practice and tens of thousands of aspiring martial artists. I returned both her formal bow and her homecoming smile.

"I'll wait until you finish," I said as I headed to my father's office to drop off my bag and coat. Almost everything was just as my father had left it a few weeks ago, except for the row of smaller uniforms that now hung from the drying rack and a pour-over coffee set up that took over some shelf space next to the hot water dispenser and tea pot. I sat in a chair opposite my father's desk and waited.

When she entered a little while later, she hesitated and looked visibility conflicted as to how to situate herself in her own office. I laughed and waved her toward my father's chair behind the desk and insisted even as her sense of propriety struggled against the honor. She sat uneasily in the large faux-leather chair molded to my father's form and I refrained from making a joke about her being the new *Kwangjangnim*. Instead, I pulled out a beautiful pastry box from Dominique Ansel Bakery and revealed two lemon passion fruit cronuts that I waited 30 minutes in line for this morning. I watched her smile first with her eyes and then with her entire being at the unexpected treat. After she filled a Chemex with freshly brewed coffee and poured dainty portions into two stunningly blue cobalt demitasses, we sat opposite each other at my father's desk and enjoyed our breakfast.

I asked about her holiday, and she told me about an amazing trip to Hawaii with her parents even though her workaholic father commuted between Hawaii and Tokyo all throughout in order to close a deal before the end of the fiscal year. After an excited rehashing of pig roasts, hikes up to volcanic mountains and general lazing about in paradise, she paused and considered and then expectantly whispered in confessional tone, "My dad also made a trip to Busan from Tokyo and rented a car to go see *Sabumnim*."

"He did?!" I was shocked. "Why?!"

"I think they're friends," she said somewhat shyly, as if still trying to decide whether to fully trust me. "When I kept asking for details, all my dad would say is that he went up a mountain to have a cup of tea and watch the sun set with an old friend.

"When I asked what they talked about, he said, love."

"Love?" I echoed incredulously before telling her that I also went to go see the old man over New Year's and that we definitely did not talk about love.

Instead, I told her about taking my father to meet his new doctors who started him on a different course of chemotherapy last week. I also described staying over at the temple with my father, where every morning before dawn in below-freezing temperatures we would scrub the wooden decking and the stone lanterns and the large boulders in the garden with wash rags before heading to the meditation halls for an hour and a half of seated meditation followed by a half hour of walking meditation. I told her of our two daily meals in the morning and at noon that unvaryingly consisted of unpolished rice, a bowl of vegetable soup and a couple bites of pickles. Then there was the communal gardening and cleaning and washing and sewing that filled the hours between the morning and evening meditations. After that, everyone was in bed on an empty stomach an hour after the sun set.

"The whole place is silent," I continued, in an admittedly gossipy unburdening of my disbelief. "And freezing! I never once got warm during my six days there. The water is freezing, the bedding is freezing, and the meals do nothing to warm you up. But the strange thing is that my father looked healthier and happier than ever. In his spare time, he reads and writes and practices patterns and teaches basic Taekwondo to the villagers."

I had rambled on for a bit before noticing that she had been silent and seemingly unfazed by my father's new lifestyle. I stopped my dialogue and tried to induce a reaction with my silence.

"Hmmm," was all she said from behind the desk.

And then it dawned on me. "Oh my God, you are exactly like him! I bet in 50 years you will end up washing rocks and practicing *Moon Moo* in the snow at the ends of the earth!" I was suddenly more certain of that than anything my instincts have ever tried to tell me. That realization reminded me to pull out my father's three Moleskin notebooks and hand them over to her.

"My father asked me to give these to you."

She opened one of the notebooks and before she finished skimming the first page, tears started to stream down her face. While she reached for a Kleenex from behind her, I flipped open the last notebook and found the heading 'Daily Training Suggestions and Strategies for the 2020 Olympics', which I showed to her as she turned around.

She slowly flipped through that section until her tears made reading impossible.

"Go put on your sneakers," I said gently as I slipped the notebooks from her hands. "Time to train. The grandmaster made me promise to watch over you."

Acknowledgements

This project was born during the COVID pandemic at a time when New York City was on lock-down and my *dojang* was shuttered indefinitely. Writing this novel and thinking through my philosophy on traditional martial arts and its value in our modern society helped to keep the idea of my *dojang* alive.

Like many small businesses that depend on personal and community interactions, the practical business of my *dojang* and idealistic dreams of teaching and perpetuating the practice of traditional martial arts almost did not make it through the pandemic. The fact that my *dojang* is still open today is in large part a testament to my students. Thank you for continuing your practice by insisting on private lessons. Thank you for kicking and punching through all sorts of winter weather at St. Vartan's Park and various other outdoor plazas, playgrounds and public spaces throughout the city. Your support and your enthusiasm for Taekwondo have kept the dream of our *dojang* alive.

I would also like to thank my family and friends for everything they have done for me. But in particular, I would like to thank my little sister Sybil for cheering me up with the best care packages in the world and for casually doing little loving things like keeping my Amazon gift balance abundantly replenished through all the darkest months. And although it is too late, I would like to express my eternal gratitude to my grandmother Wendy, who loved me like the sun.

Even after
All this time

The Sun never says
To the earth,
"You owe me."

Look what happens
With a love like that.
It lights the whole sky.

Hafiz

www.ingramcontent.com/pod-product-compliance
Lightning Source LLC
Chambersburg PA
CBHW051426170626
46809CB00006B/2344